Full Figured 11:

Carl Weber Presents

Full Figured 11:

Carl Weber Presents

Treasure Hernandez

and Katt

www.urbanbooks.net

Urban Books, LLC
300 Farmingdale Road, NY-Route 109
Farmingdale, NY 11735

ISBN 13: 978-1-62286-689-2
ISBN 10: 1-62286-689-4

First Mass Market Printing April 2018
First Trade Paperback Printing June 2017
Printed in the United States of America

10 9 8 7 6 5 4 3 2 1

Distributed by Kensington Publishing Corp.
Submit orders to:
Customer Service
400 Hahn Road
Westminster, MD 21157-4627
Phone: 1-800-733-3000
Fax: 1-800-659-243

Full Figured 11:

Carl Weber Presents

by

Treasure Hernandez

and Katt

"Lights, Camera, Action!"

Treasure Hernandez

Prologue

The shoot was over, and Janiyah was happy that she had completed another successful session. She was proud to be a full-figured model, and proud that she was able to put big girls in a position to compete with skinny women in the modeling industry. As she sat in a chair, unwinding from the shoot, she looked at the photographer. He was going through the pictures and putting everything together.

He noticed Janiyah watching him. "Janiyah, you want to see the pics?"

She didn't waste any time. She jumped up and walked to where the photographer was standing. The photographer scrolled through the viewfinder on the Canon t3i DSLR camera. She was pleased to see various poses of her enjoying life in a black one-piece bathing suit, with and without the summer skirt. She was equally pleased with the way her strappy black Jimmy Choo sandals elongated her legs.

"You think I can use one or two of them for my Web site?" she asked. She didn't want to show all of the pictures before the ad appeared in Ashley Stewart, but she figured she'd tease them on Instagram.

"Janiyah, I wish I could, but you know if Ashley Stewart knew I let you post one of these pictures before it appeared in their catalog, you and I would be in trouble." The photographer saw the look of despair in Janiyah's eyes. "You know I'm telling the truth."

Janiyah did know he was telling the truth, and she didn't want to jeopardize her valuable relationships with all of the clothing designers and retail stores. She was one of the most rec-ognized models who showcased full-figured clothing. People sought her all around the world. She definitely didn't want to lose any of those accounts and the money she earned from them. Janiyah was well aware that she didn't have to work. Her husband Gun was a very successful "businessman." He made a very good living being a major drug supplier in his hometown, and he gave Janiyah anything her heart desired. Although Janiyah appreciated everything he did for her, she considered herself an independent woman and had vowed a long time ago to never depend on a man's income. She let Gun spoil and give her the finer things in life, but she still made sure to make her own money. The pay made it possible for her to treat herself or Gun and be proud that she did it with her own earnings. It also made it possible for her to have money saved for a rainy day. In case Gun was ever locked up or killed, she would be prepared.

Janiyah and Gun were an unlikely pair, coming from such different worlds, but from the first day they met, it was love at first sight. Gun referred to that day as the day the beast met his beauty. Most people assumed she would marry another model or some rich billionaire, but Janiyah was in love.

Janiyah looked at the rest of the pictures, and she was definitely pleased that she was going to have another stunning appearance in the Ashley Stewart catalog. Once the pictures hit the catalog, Janiyah would send out the page numbers to family, friends, and followers so they could look out for her. She couldn't one-hundred percent claim that she was the sole reason some of the clothing designers had sales, but she felt she had some hand in raising interest in the clothes she modeled. Besides, she liked the fact that she proved that big girls can wear whatever anyone else wears.

Janiyah said her good-byes and headed to her dressing room. She opened the door, and the scent of lavender and jasmine incense were still in the air. She took a deep breath, and the aroma calmed her spirit. Janiyah had it good to be able to have a dressing room set up the way she liked. She leaned down, unbuckled her sandals, and slid them off. Then she brought her arm in front of her, stuffed her hand down her shirt, and unsnapped her bra, releasing her breasts into much-needed freedom.

She hopped into a chair. It felt good to be off her feet. Janiyah admired her legs as she lifted them off the ground, wishing that her husband was around to massage her feet. As she closed her eyes, she relaxed and took in a deep breath. Without warning, she felt a hand around her throat, and her chair leaned back. Save for her quick grip on her assailant's arm, she would have fallen out of the chair.

"I see we meet again." The voice of her attacker startled her.

Janiyah looked up and was face to face with a pair menacing eyes. He had on a black ski mask that covered almost his entire face. His eyes were the only thing visible. He was a buff man, probably about twice her size. Janiyah immediately knew she wouldn't stand a chance trying to fight her way from the tight grip he had on her.

He lifted her out of the chair and pushed her back into the corner.

"Scream and I'm gonna push your teeth down your throat," the man threatened.

For her safety, Janiyah complied and kept silent. Her body stiffened. She could feel something poking her. Before she was able to identify what it was, the sound of a belt coming undone caused her alarm. Janiyah looked down to see the man's pants around his ankles, his member pulsating and aiming at her.

The attacker's hand ran up her skirt and pushed the bottom of her bathing suit to the side. He looked her in the eyes as he ran his slender fingers up and down the crevice of her vagina. He teased, pushing part of a finger in at a time. "Damn, that's nice and wet."

"Would you please . . ." Janiyah begged.

"Naw, baby girl. Time to pay up," he insisted as he worked at ripping the bathing suit from Janiyah's body. He used his newly lubricated hand to rub Janiyah's juices on his member. "Dick teasing me all these years . . . you oughta know that shit ain't cool."

Janiyah had no idea what the man was talking about. For starters, she had no idea who the man even was. For him to say she'd been teasing him for years was even more perplexing. She had never been the type to flirt with men, especially since she'd been with Gun. She would never disrespect her husband like that.

With a little force, he ripped the bottom of her bathing suit. Then a finger slipped inside of Janiyah and found her clitoris. He rubbed it softly, moaning as his fingers slid from side to side. "Yeah, I knew it'd feel nice and warm down there."

Janiyah had to think fast. She refused to become a victim of rape, especially after standing all day and working a job she loved. An object rubbed against her breast, and she remembered that it was the pen she had used earlier in the day to sign her contract. As the man was worried about taking proper precautions and sheathing himself with the latex glove, Janiyah worked to figure out how she was going to get the pen out of her cleavage without alarming him.

She glared into his eyes again. The tip of his head was getting closer, and while she squeezed her vaginal muscles to refuse entry, she lifted her right leg up and wrapped it around his legs for support.

"Oh, you like this, don't you? You ready for this big dick?" he questioned.

"Yeah," Janiyah moaned breathlessly. She kept her eyes on her target as he worked to get inside her. Janiyah took her chance and wrapped her left arm around his neck.

"Girl, if you wanted me to pick you up, you should've said something." The man crouched down and lifted Janiyah.

Janiyah used the opportunity to wrap her other leg around his waist, and before the tip of his penis could invade her any further, Janiyah quickly reached for the pen with her right hand and stabbed him in the shoulder area right near his throat.

"Aaaaggghhh!" He screamed and struggled to breathe as Janiyah pulled out the pen and stabbed him again. He grabbed Janiyah by her left arm and threw her like a rag doll across the room.

Janiyah felt her body slam against the wall, shattering the silver-rimmed mirror that hung on it. She felt shards of glass fall onto her as she collapsed to the floor. All she could do was put her head into her chest and shield herself with her arms as pieces of glass landed all around her.

"This ain't over, bitch!" she heard from across the room. On instinct, Janiyah reached for a shard of glass from the broken mirror. She could hear more glass breaking as he came closer to her. As soon as she felt him just a few inches away, Janiyah lunged at the man.

"Die, motherfuckeeeer!" She screamed as she turned around and plunged the broken piece of glass into his chest with all her might. She was completely taken aback when she realized the man she'd stabbed was her photographer and not her assailant. She watched her photographer fall back and struggle to breathe. She scanned the room for the man in the ski mask, but he was gone. It was as if he had vanished into thin air. She felt the entire room begin to spin. She looked down at her bloodied hands and couldn't stop herself from shaking. Just then, a security man ran into the room.

"Oh my God!" he exclaimed when he saw the photographer on the floor, blood spewing from his chest. "What did you do?" he said as he looked up at Janiyah.

"I–I–I don't know," she stammered. "He tried to rape me! He was touching me!" Janiyah began hyperventilating, and a full anxiety attack ensued. The security guard called 911 as he tried to calm Janiyah down and keep an eye on the wounded photographer.

The police finally arrived, and Janiyah was still in a daze. In an unexpected turn of events, the police cuffed her and sent the photographer to the hospital. She protested and told them a man had come into the dressing room and tried to rape her, but they ignored her pleas. As they escorted her from her dressing room to the back of the cop car, Janiyah was so filled with adrenaline she struggled to tell right from left. They took her to the hospital to clean her up from the cuts and the bruises, all the while keeping her in handcuffs.

After the cops took a look at the surveillance cameras, they learned that she was telling the truth about a man in a ski mask. Unfortunately, there wasn't much they could do to track the man down except hold onto to his DNA as evidence, in case they ever had a suspect.

Even under the circumstances, the photographer chose to press charges against Janiyah for stabbing him.

In the back of her mind, Janiyah tried to make sense of everything that had happened, and how she was going to get out of the mess she was in.

Chapter One

Two Years Later

Janiyah lay back in her bunk and opened the letter that had just been handed to her by the CO. She loved getting these letters. It was the only contact with the outside world that she got. Gun wasn't able to visit as often as they both would have liked. Considering his situation, he didn't feel comfortable coming around prisons or any kind of law enforcement. Janiyah could feel her heart almost skip a beat from the excitement of reading Gun's letter.

The time is coming, baby. I'm never gonna stop looking for the motherfucker that tried to rape you. He's gonna pay for all the pain and suffering he put you through. When I find out who it was that did that to you, I will personally get in his ass and royally fuck him up and make sure

I see him take his last breath. But let me not keep writing about that. Don't want your CO trippin'.

At that moment, Janiyah looked around her cell then hopped up to see where the COs were. Surely they had read the letter her husband had written. Since no one had confiscated the letter or pulled her in for questioning, she knew that whichever CO was scanning the letter wasn't on their job today.

Or they just didn't care.

Anyway, you know I'm still gonna hold you down just like you held me down— always putting up with all my shit. We're in this for life, and nothing is ever going to change that. I'm always gonna look out for you.

And I'm going to that support group. You always hear about women looking out for their men on lockup, but guess what? It's a number of dudes holding it down for their females out here, too. I got you, babe. I'm not going anywhere. I told you seven years ago when we got married that I was never gonna leave your side, and I meant that. I promise while you're in there, I'm still gonna be working hard so that when you get out, you have nothing to worry about. I got my soldiers doing overtime to increase sales and get our paper up.

I still can't believe they found you guilty and gave you three years. I mean, it's not like you really stabbed him on purpose. You thought he was somebody else. Anybody woulda made the same mistake. It's a messed-up justice system. Shit just ain't right.

Anyway, stay strong while you're in there. I'ma put more money in your commissary so you can get all that feminine shit y'all be using to stay pretty. I know my bae always likes to look on point. LOL.

Stay on top of your game and fuck them bitches if they come at you crazy. You know they're just jealous. Remember, you was a model before you got in this motherfucker, and you still my number one plus-sized model when you get out.

Love you, baby

Gun Wade

Janiyah loved that Gun had such a deep love for her. He always made her feel like a queen regardless of any situation, whether good or bad. With her being locked up for the last couple of years, most men would have left her already, but Gun had stuck by her through everything. He sent letters every week, and always made sure she had everything she needed.

Jainyah loved her husband, and after seeing how committed and loyal he was to her, she loved him even more for it. A tear fell from Janiyah's eye when she thought of Gun's love and dedication to a sista locked up. Most dudes would have their things inside the first broad walking, but he wasn't that type of man. Their relationship was much deeper than that. Gun loved her, and she loved him back. She missed her husband terribly. Many times, she lay in her bunk reminiscing about the things they used to do together. She missed being able to hold his hand and cuddle up with him in bed, laying her head on his chest. She missed their weekly Monday Netflix and chill ritual.

There were days she found herself wishing to wake up in her own bed and learn that the last two years hadn't really happened. She hoped to God that this had all been a bad dream. With her having one year left, the best thing for her to do was to stay out of trouble and keep herself busy to pass the time. She couldn't wait to get back to her man and the life she was forced to walk away from.

Janiyah reached under her mattress and took out her notepad to begin writing her response to Gun. It was five minutes before she began writing. She had to get her mind in a really good place before she dropped any ink on the sheet. She was running out of paper, and she wouldn't be able to re-up until the following week, so this letter needed to count. She began spilling her thoughts on paper.

Just as she was getting into a groove, the door burst open and a CO she didn't recognize rushed into the room. As she sized up the bullish-looking chick, Janiyah's senses tightened, and she got the feeling that the she-man was nothing but trouble.

"Wade, strip!" she ordered as another CO entered the room and began turning the cell upside down.

Complying, Janiyah removed her tan khakis and shirt quickly. She kept her eyes on the CO who was grilling her, as she quickly shoved her state-issued pants and bloomers to the ground.

"Turn around and assume the position," the CO ordered.

Following orders, Janiyah stepped out of her clothes. She turned around and walked to the wall. All she had on were the state-issued, low-cut Bob Bakers and some white tube socks.

"Well, look at this." One of the COs started messing with her as they patted her down.

Janiyah could feel the latex gloves probing her body. The women were aggressive as they patted her down. One of the COs forcefully pulled her butt cheeks apart. A lubricated finger was forcefully entering her anal cavity, pushing itself in and out of her.

"I think we got us a tight bitch."

Janiyah didn't know who this new CO was, and she didn't care, for that matter. She wasn't going to let some bitch come in and violate her for no reason. As the CO who was sliding another finger inside of her turned her head to say something to the other CO, Janiyah took the opportunity and elbowed the CO in the jaw.

"We got us a fighter." The other CO attempted to cuff Janiyah, but she continued swinging.

Both COs began using street force, kicking and punching Janiyah as she continued to defend herself. Janiyah knew being violated was not supposed to be part of the strip search. She looked at the door, hoping she'd be able to make an escape, but saw another CO guarding the entrance.

A low whistle to the tune of "Love Train" became audible. That's when Janiyah knew these weren't regular COs; these were COs that had been paid off by members of the Set It Off Bitches coming for her ass. The Set It Off Bitches were a group of prison girls that belonged to The Nietas street gang. They had been messing with Janiyah for months, and she knew it was only a matter of time before shit hit the fan with them. She was cool with them at first, but when she refused to cut a rival inmate of theirs, they saw that as a direct violation against them. As Janiyah continued fighting and defending herself, she could hear the electric humming of the taser, but she couldn't tell which of the COs had it.

She felt the hot metal pierce her skin and give her an electric shock. Janiyah's ability to defend herself weakened as the first ten-second shot jolted her system. Immediately, another ten-second shot was issued in rapid succession. By the time the third shot penetrated her skin, Janiyah had fallen to the ground and lost control of her bodily functions.

The last thing she saw was a CO spraying pepper spray in her face while she received another jolt of electricity.

Chapter Two

Water was supposed to heal everything. Clean the body, cleanse the soul. Preachers dipped men in bodies of water to baptize them. Some women submerged in the wetness to give birth or to purify themselves. Lather with soap, rinse off. Water was supposed to be good for you inside and out. Detoxify and purify from inside and out.

"Aw, shit, they really fucked her up." Janiyah heard an inmate in the next stall yelling.

Hot steam enveloped her body and sent vapors in the air. The calming effect had her in an illusion, taking her away from her current situation. She leaned against the tiled wall as she inhaled and exhaled. Janiyah's eyes felt heavy as she followed death's cousin into a temporary sleep. Hearing her name and the fact that she was expelling blood from some orifice on her body forced Janiyah to attempt to lift an eyelid.

Her ears jumped up like they were leaping from a springboard. Her body tried to straighten up from its current leaning position. Janiyah tried to see the water gathering around her feet. She could feel it; she knew she was getting wet.

Janiyah slowly moved her arm across the wall to grasp the handle so she could turn the water off. Her eyes fluttered faster than a hummingbird could flap its wings. She grabbed the handle and exerted all her strength into turning the handle. It felt like it was taking forever for the waterfall to slowly dissipate. The reach for the towel that was hanging on the hook took more effort than normal. When she could finally hold it, Janiyah brought the dampened rag to her face so she could wipe away the excess water.

"This bitch is just lying there taking up a shower stall." Another inmate talked about her like the situation personally inconvenienced her.

"Yeah, don't say nothing to the CO standing at the door until I'm done in here. I don't want this bitch fucking up my shower time," another inmate announced.

The two sets of feet squished in their flip-flops as they went in the opposite direction from where Janiyah was standing. She wondered how long they'd been standing there—or if they were responsible for what had happened to her.

Her mind was spinning. Janiyah felt like she was stuck, looking at a psychedelic pinwheel that was turning fast enough to make her dizzy. She couldn't focus on anything.

Janiyah expelled blood and chunks of food from her mouth. She drooled a thick saliva that ran down her chin and dropped into the drain. She shook her head and looked down. A few drops of blood splattered and turned a light pink once they mixed with the unscented lather she used to wash with. Janiyah struggled to stand, yet she was determined to stand up on her own. She put a hand to her face so she could feel if she had any cuts. She was okay with bruises, but if her face was cut up, her career was as good as dead. Nobody would hire a scarred model.

"I can't be cut up." Janiyah talked to herself. "God, please don't let my face be cut up." Janiyah winced as she gently guided her fingers along her eyes, cheeks, and mouth. Some areas felt soft and tender, so she knew she had swelling, but thankfully, she didn't feel any open wounds.

Trying to remember what happened caused her head to hurt. The migraine she experienced was worse than the electroshocks she felt when she consumed too much gum with phenylalinine in it.

"Yo, model girl."

Janiyah felt a pair of hands escorting her out of the stall. The water traveling under the soles of her feet made it slippery and difficult to walk. Soap and urine nestled between her toes as she felt her body being lifted in the air.

"We gotta get you to medical."

The voice sounded familiar, but she couldn't remember who the lady was or where she knew her from. Janiyah's body was lifted up and tossed over someone's shoulder like a rag doll, which was what Janiyah felt like. She was at the mercy of whoever had her in her grasp. Her face lightly grazed the small of this woman's back. The smell of the generic soap was strong. The harsh chemical scent pierced her nose. She didn't understand why they said the soap was unscented. They should have called it like it was: nasty chemicals scent.

Janiyah tried to open her eyes and see her surroundings, but lifting her eyelids felt like adding fifty extra pounds on a bench press at once. She hadn't had a chance to see her fingers before she was lifted up. She wanted to look at them and make sure they weren't red or brown. Janiyah struggled to lift her hand up to where she could see. She gave up and figured it really didn't matter at that point.

Being carried from the shower only served to make Janiyah even more lightheaded. She wanted to barf but feared that expelling any more fluids from her body would cause whoever was carrying her to drop her. Janiyah feared she'd land on her head, possibly break her neck . . . possibly die.

Despite Janiyah's current situation, she believed she had a life to live, that life outside of the belly of the beast was possible. Janiyah wanted to show everyone that her circumstances hadn't broken her and that she wasn't going to let anything bring her down. She was determined to make it out of there alive and ready to take on the responsibilities she had outside. Janiyah had a booming modeling career to get back to, and despite everything, there were young, plus-sized babies who looked up to her. She knew that was her calling.

"CO!" the woman who had her over her shoulder bellowed. "CO, I need help!"

The woman began to pick up her pace, and Janiyah's head wobbled like a bobblehead. It went faster and faster, and Janiyah's mind continued to play tricks on her as the pinwheel turned. More blood and food chunks tried to force their way from her mouth. Janiyah almost choked trying to hold everything in and swallow it back. The contents burned like scalding hot water from a teapot going down her esophagus and back into her stomach.

"CO!" the woman carrying Janiyah called out.

Janiyah felt another set of hands grasp her from under her arms. A few seconds later, her body was being gently placed on the cold cement. She couldn't hold it any longer, and her mouth betrayed her brain and expelled everything she'd just swallowed. The taste in her mouth was horrendous. If Janiyah wasn't feeling so busted, she might have felt bad for anyone who had the displeasure of being within a few feet of her. But she didn't even have the strength to care.

"Yo, thanks for helping me. You didn't get barfed on, did you?"

"Naw, the little joker missed me by a few inches."

The man, whose voice also sounded familiar, replied, "Rockwell, Phylicia—what happened to Wade?"

Janiyah couldn't focus on who had inquired about her well-being. She was too busy expelling more fluid and chunks and struggling not to pass out.

"Someone stabbed her on her left side!"

Janiyah heard the news as she could feel someone trying to touch an area right above her hip. The shock caused her to moan softly. Janiyah did not have the energy to release the boisterous scream she felt inside.

"Call for medical."

The action around her seemed like a horrible parody of *Grey's Anatomy*. Jibberish filled her ears for a few more minutes, and soon she was unable to hear anything at all. The pinwheels went faster and faster, and she no longer attempted to open her eyes. The darkness of having her eyes closed was easier for her to handle.

Janiyah had been beaten *and* stabbed. All she needed to be was crucified, and she could pay for her own sins.

Chapter Three

"Niyah Wade!" A firm voice penetrated her ears.

Her eyes opened. She hated being distracted from her dreams. This wasn't really a dream as much as it was a memory. Janiyah had just done her first runway for an African designer who flew her out to London. Amere Kikayou was of Kenyan descent, but he'd lived in "the city," as he and others called London, since he was ten. Amere loved big girls and felt like they should be celebrated like the skinny girls were. He found Janiyah after friending her Facebook profile, and it took a lot of convincing to show her that he was the real deal.

Once Amere showed Janiyah his Web site and then asked for Gun's number so he could personally ask her husband for permission, Janiyah was sold. Amere flew both Janiyah and Gun to London, made sure they stayed in good hotels, and had assistants help them navigate one of the largest cities in the world. Amere took photos of the two of them enjoying London's financial district.

Amere's photos of the couple went viral. Janiyah became a household name, and his African-themed designs became a classic; simultaneously showing African pride and uplifting the big girl figure.

"Niyah Wade!" The woman's voice continued, just as sharp. Janiyah recognized her tone, and she knew the woman was upset with her. Only Oz mispronounced Janiyah's government name, and she only did it when she was upset with Janiyah. A good number of the inmates called her Niyah, and most of the COs called her Wade. A few people called her Ja to be funny in their attempt to give her a hood name. She only answered to Janiyah or Wade.

Janiyah turned to face Oz. The disappointment was all over her face. Her rich, chocolate-colored skin reminded Janiyah of DeJ Loaf. Her tapered Mohawk helped her look younger than the forty-nine years of age she knew Oz to be. Below each of her eyes were two teardrop tattoos that stuck out like sore thumbs on her otherwise unblemished face. Her nose was big, and her chin was large and sharp. When she opened her mouth, Janiyah could've sworn she was wearing veneers, because her teeth stayed bright white.

Oz was crouched in the seat next to her bed. Janiyah tried to sit up and found that she had been bandaged tightly, and she couldn't bear the pain to move an inch.

"Just relax, mama. You been through a lot these past few days," Oz commanded.

Her real name was Osmonda Rockwell. Everyone there called her Oz. She wore her name like a term of endearment. She once told Janiyah that ever since she saw the television show on HBO, she knew she was destined to become a real-life character.

Oz was there for life for murdering five on a failed armed robbery attempt. The way Oz told the story, she and her accomplice had staked out this couple for months. They targeted the family because the man of the house had done her accomplice's sister dirty. She didn't like being the side piece to a wife and two children. They broke in the house and didn't anticipate that the man would be ready for them. He was waiting with a gun. As soon as they entered the home, he shot her partner. Oz jumped out of the way in time and was able to get off a fatal shot, which sent the man to his grave. To avoid leaving witnesses, Oz ran upstairs and shot the wife as she was trying to call 911 on her cell phone. She then marched into the children's rooms and killed the two kids like they were characters in a military video game. When she ran back downstairs, she saw her accomplice attempt to get up, and she shot her twice to put her down, treating her like she was a thorough-bred with a broken ankle. Oz killed her to keep her from snitching. Oz was ruthless back in her day, and even though Oz had changed her ways since being locked up, Janiyah was always care-ful around her.

Oz said she stayed in a hotel following the murder. She paid a gigolo to engage her through-out the night. What she hadn't anticipated was that the family had paid for a top-notch security system that had taken a picture of her when she entered the house. With no money and the overwhelming evidence stacked against her, Oz turned herself in. She was twenty-six at the time and had been locked up since.

"I need to sit up," Janiyah replied. She hated when people stood over her, especially if she was laying down. "How did I get here?" Janiyah asked.

"I found you and carried you to a CO. You got stabbed twice," Oz informed Janiyah like she was delivering the six o'clock news.

"Thank you." Janiyah knew Oz was the only inmate on the yard who cared enough for her to do that.

"Yeah, well, you'd better be thankful. I spent two days in the hole for carrying you to the yard."

"I'm sorry. That ain't right. You saved me."

"Whatever. It ain't nothing." Oz shrugged her shoulders. "I took that time to meditate and pray to my God. 'As I walk through the valley of the shadow of death, I shall fear no evil.'" Oz quoted from the Bible. "The hole don't scare me. Anyway, back to you. Of course, no one knows who stabbed you."

"Oh, wow. I didn't see that one coming," Janiyah replied sarcastically.

"You know how it goes, baby girl. People see, but nobody talks around here," Oz said as she took a seat. "I'm glad you're okay, though. You had me real scared."

"You know me, Oz. I don't break that easy." Janiyah slowly turned to face Oz. "I've been through worse than this and I survived." Janiyah tried to force a smile through the pain.

Unfortunately, Janiyah had had a very rough upbringing growing up. She never liked to talk about her past, but in the two years she'd been there, she and Oz had grown close enough for her to share her history. She had grown up in a very abusive household. Her stepbrother started molesting her when she was six. He was fifteen, a wrestler, and weighed a ton. Janiyah looked like one of the kids that could've been on the *Barney & Friends* show. She didn't understand what was going on at first. When she started to feel uncomfortable and she tried to push him off, he used her as his personal punching bag.

Her stepbrother wasn't the only man in her family to take advantage of her. Her father did too. He and her stepbrother used to pass Janiyah around between the two of them. Every now and then, her father and/or her stepbrother would invite their friends and have her do strip tease shows and then make her sit on their laps and rub their pants until she felt something poke her. Her father and stepbrother would take money from their friends afterward.

As she grew older, they would lay on the floor and tell her to straddle them. Her father used to whisper to her that he was teaching her how to ride a horse and that one day Janiyah would be the best jockey in the world. Janiyah didn't care about becoming a jockey. She didn't even know what a jockey was, but she always did what she was told because she knew if she complained, she'd get beat and punished for days. They would punch, kick, and push her around as if she were a rag doll.

For years, as Janiyah's body grew, so did the men who invaded her body and her mind. Janiyah thought it was normal, that other girls got touched the way she got touched. One night, when her stepbrother had Janiyah lying on her stomach, she accidentally coughed in his face, and he completely flipped out on her. It was one of the worst beatings he had given her.

"Don't you ever disrespect me like that," he said as he kicked her on her side.

"I'm sorry. I didn't mean to do it," Janiyah cried out as she balled herself up in the fetal position to try to protect herself somehow. When her father came home and saw her all bruised up, he made her promise to say she fell down the stairs if anyone asked anything in school.

Sure enough, the next day when she went to school, she was immediately sent to the nurse's office. Her father was called in, and he told them the same story she had given them. They weren't too convinced, but there wasn't much else they could do at that time.

Janiyah always wondered why they treated her the way they did. She daydreamed a lot about how her life would be so much better if her mother was still around. Her mother died of cancer when she was five years old, so she didn't remember much about her, but it didn't stop her from imagining how different things could have been.

It was the PE teacher who figured out what was going on. She saw punch marks on Janiyah's back while she was changing for gym class in the locker room. At fourteen, Janiya got placed in her first foster family, and by the time she graduated from high school, Janiyah had twenty different mothers and about six or seven fathers. She had about three sets of grandparents too.

"Yeah, you did. But you ain't never got stabbed up like this. Thank God for always looking out and protecting." Oz interrupted Janiyah's thoughts.

"God? You want me to thank God for this?" Janiyah sucked her teeth. "Yeah, okay. Thank you, God, for letting me get beat up and stabbed. Thank you, God, for putting me in this hell hole. Thank the Lord for looking out." Janiyah knew her sarcasm was going to piss Oz off. The rolling of the eyes and the fact Oz balled her hands into fists only confirmed what she already knew. If Janiyah weren't laying in the bed, Oz would've punched her in the face by now.

"I'm not gonna sit here and let you disrespect the God I serve." Oz leaned closer, her lips inches away from Janiyah's. "I think you need to learn to be more grateful and realize that the reason you are still breathing is because *He's* been looking out for you all your life," she said as she pointed toward the ceiling. "Like the fact that I'm the only one in here who gives two cents about you or cares about whether you make it out of your sentence alive. But you don't care to see none of that, huh?"

"I care." Janiyah defended herself, making another attempt to lift her body off the bed. She failed miserably. "I am grateful, Oz."

"Yeah? You have a funny way of showing it, with your stuck-up behind. You need to learn to humble yourself and recognize when grace is given to you." Oz hurled the insult.

Now Janiyah wanted to punch her in the face. Oz knew good and well she had struck a nerve. Janiyah hated whenever anyone called her conceited. But she couldn't punch Oz if she were handing her a bag with a million dollars in it. Janiyah didn't have the strength to. . . . Never did.

"You're cold." Janiyah turned away from Oz.

Oz reached and turned Janiyah's head and pressed it into the pillow so she was forced to face her. "I'm not cold, baby girl. I'm trying to be your friend. It's called tough love."

"Is that what this is?" Janiyah struggled to ask as she forced her mouth to breathe in and out for her. The massive amount of air coming into her chest cavity only made her upper body feel like she'd been bitten by a bunch of fire ants at the same time. "Get off me, girl," Janiyah half whined, half cried. Oz was hurting Janiyah, and she couldn't do anything about it.

Amazingly enough, she complied without Janiyah having to ask her again. "I'ma back off for now, but I'm never gonna stop praying for you. God's gonna get you on His time," Oz said as she backed up and took her seat.

"I need to figure out who the hell did this to me." Janiyah shook her head. Janiyah still couldn't remember who had violated her. She could remember hearing a whistle being blown, but that was all that came to mind. She'd been trying to figure things out ever since she regained consciousness. Janiyah couldn't even remember the event that led her there, or how she'd ended up in the shower.

"And what are you going to do when you figure out who did this to you?" Oz demanded. It was like they'd rehearsed this script and went over the answer a thousand times.

"Fuck them up and not get caught doing it," Janiyah said between clenched teeth.

Janiyah gave the wrong answer for Oz. She could see Oz's face tighten with frustration.

Janiyah continued, "C'mon, Oz. You really want me to just get up off this bed and act like nothing happened? Whoever did this to me has to pay. I stabbed somebody and I got three years for it, but I get stabbed and I'm supposed to just shrug it off and let bygones be bygones?"

"Janiyah, I get that you're angry, but revenge is not the answer. Even if you get your revenge, you're not going to feel any better. You need to learn to forgive!"

Janiyah could see the sincerity in Oz. She appreciated Oz for always trying to make Janiyah see things differently, but she was getting tired of Oz's constant talks about God and forgiveness.

"I'm sorry to let you down Oz, but I just can't do that. I hope you don't hate me for it," she said without looking at her friend.

"I can't have hate in my heart. I've done enough sin to make me sit at the right hand of Satan on Judgment Day. I'm still trying to live for Jesus because no matter how dark the road may seem, I know I will be living eternally with Him when this is all over with."

Janiyah thought her head was going to explode. She was done listening to Oz go on and on about all this God stuff. It was not that she didn't believe in God. She believed that God existed, but she didn't believe him to be this supreme higher being that people made him out to be. If God was so powerful and loved all his children, how could He have allowed her to suffer the way she had when she was a little girl? How could He allow all the bad that was in the world? It didn't make sense to her that there was such a god that was merciful and loving, yet there was so much hate and suffering.

"Jesus may love you, but He damn sure doesn't care about me, because if He did, this right here wouldn't be happening to me! I'm happy for you being saved and all, but please, just stop trying to change me into something I'm not. I know right from wrong. I've never stolen or cheated. I'm know I'm not a bad person, Oz, and I don't need you or God to validate that for me."

Oz felt sorry for her friend. Years ago, she had the same mentality. When she first arrived at this prison, she was an atheist. She didn't only not believe in a supreme being; she hated the Jesus Christ, Son of Man, God's son story. Oz hated the fact that people were dumb enough to believe any of that crap. For almost all of her life, Oz had the theory that if she was miserable, then everyone had to be as well. She vowed to never give in to that kind thinking or pressure. But years of imprisonment and having nothing but time to think about things will do a lot to a person. Back when she was about thirty-one, she kept getting invited to a Bible study. She always said no, until she learned that they served all kinds of snacks and they were given an extra half hour in the recreation room for prayer. She decided she'd fake the funk while she was there, load up on snacks, and enjoy her extra half hour once a week.

As time passed, she caught herself getting more and more interested in reading the Bible. The stories the women talked about in Bible study really intrigued her. She took out a Bible from the prison library, and the more she read, the more she started to believe in the power of prayer and God's love and healing over people's life. She eventually made the decision to give her life to God, and it was one of the best things she could have ever done for herself. She could never take back the crime she had committed, but she knew she was forgiven.

"I know you've been hurt." Oz brought herself back to reality. "And I'm gonna stop trying to convince you of things. What I'm not gonna stop doing, though, is praying for you."

Janiyah inhaled. Wasn't anything she could do about that. She knew Oz had good intentions for her. Oz was the only friend she had in there, and even though she was annoying her right now, Janiyah cared a lot about her.

"Get some rest, Janiyah." Oz leaned in and got close enough to whisper in Janiyah's ear. "Before I go, though, let me remind you to watch your attitude with me. I may be a Christian, but I will lay hands on anyone that comes at me sideways or tries to disrespect me or the God I serve. The girls around here know better than to test me, and you out of all people should know that too."

Oz quietly walked away from Janiyah and left the infirmary just as a nurse was coming over to her bunk to give her some meds.

Janiyah recognized the nurse as the one from earlier in the day. Janiyah got Oxycodone and a muscle relaxer to help her cope with her situation. She also gave her Xanax to deal with her anxiety. The nurse then pulled out a red pill crusher and made Janiyah's meds as fine as the china-white powder they float on the streets. She poured the powder into a small bottle of orange juice and encouraged Janiyah to swallow the whole thing in two minutes or less. Janiyah chose to drink it down within thirty seconds. The faster it got in her system, the faster Janiyah would begin to fall asleep. Right before she went fully out, she could hear Oz's voice telling her to pray.

Chapter Four

"Wade—you ready to make your call?" Janiyah heard the officer ask her outside of the closed door. She was back in her cell after spending a few weeks healing in the infirmary. She was still sore but was thankful that her face didn't take so much damage that it altered her looks.

"Yes," Janiyah mumbled.

Janiyah heard the cell opening. Once opened, she walked outside.

"Girl—who are you going to call?" the CO asked.

The CO, Kendall McCall, looked a lot different in her light brown correctional officer's shirt and dark black slacks than she did when she was struttin' around the neighborhood. She was buttoned up and all business right now, but when she was outside the walls, she was a freewheeling girl who liked to show her shapely body. Her pecan-colored face was smooth, aside from the small scratch that appeared below her left eye, a mark from an earlier incident with an inmate who got out of line. Kendall may have looked pretty and sweet, but she knew how to throw down when the time called for it.

"Gun better pick up the phone since he couldn't show up for visitation," Janiyah grumbled as she and Kendall walked side by side. She was hurt that Gun had cancelled his trip at the last minute. After his last few letters, Janiyah was ready to see Gun's face in person.

She picked up the old-school tan phone and watched the circular apparatus move as she dialed the numbers. After the customary collect call message, Janiyah heard Gun accept the call.

"Janiyah?" Gun said.

"Hey, baby, it's me."

"I heard about the stabbing. What happenend that you ended up getting stabbed?"

"I don't want to talk about it."

"Okay, I can respect that. I'm so sorry I wasn't able to go see you. How are you feeling, baby?"

"I'll be fine. Still sore, but I won't allow whoever did this to break me or think they got to me. I'm gonna stay strong."

"That's my girl."

"I was hoping that you were going to come and see me soon."

"I don't know if I can go this week coming up, but I will do my best to make it. It's been a lot of shit going down on my end, and I have a lot of things that need to get taken care of. I got some people stepping out of line, and I need to make some moves to show them I'm not one to be played with."

Janiyah got a little tingle between her legs at that last comment. She loved it when her husband bossed up like that. She was still disappointed that Gun couldn't find the time to come see her, but she recognized that he had a business to run.

"I understand, baby. Go do what you gotta do. I'm not going anywhere. Just come see me as soon as you can."

"You know I will," Gun replied.

"Well, I gotta go. My time's almost up."

Before Gun could say anything, Janiyah hung up the phone. She wasn't mad that he might not be able to visit this week, and she knew he had a valid reason. For some reason, though, she couldn't help but feel some type of way about it. She couldn't tell if she was sad, upset, hurt, or disappointed that Gun wasn't going to visit. She walked back to her cell, confused and defeated.

***

The envelopes falling onto the concrete floor broke Janiyah's concentration. She had been putting the finishing touches on her plan for her comeback. She had just under a year to get everything together. She had spent the last hour plotting and re-writing the touches of her plan, thinking of contacts and finalizing the designers she wanted to work with when she got out.

Janiyah got up from her bunk and picked up the envelopes from the floor. There were two envelopes, one from Gun and one from the prison financial department. Wanting to get the bad news out of the way first, she opened the letter from the prison. Janiyah grinned widely when she read that Gun had deposited $200 into her account. It had come at just the right time. She couldn't believe he hadn't said anything to her when they spoke on the phone. That man was always ready with a surprise for her. The money was enough for Janiyah to buy her personal needs, as well as food, paper, black pens, envelopes, and stamps.

The letter from Gun had been postmarked four days ago. Her heart beat fast as she stuck her index finger under the flap and slowly moved it across the edge.

Janiyah,

How are you, beautiful? I wish we could've had more time to talk on the phone that day. There's so much I wanted to talk you about. And I miss hearing your voice.

I'm so happy to know that you are okay. My heart dropped when I found out you had gotten stabbed. I don't know what I would do if something ever happened to you. Since the stabbing, I've been thinking about making some major changes for when you get out. I know this is probably gonna come outta left field, but I'm thinking about getting out of the business. You know what business I'm talking about. I put in a lot of years, and I think I'm ready to walk away. I been lucky that nothing has happened to me after all these years, and before my luck runs out, I'd rather walk away on top. The more I think about things, the more I realize that I'm putting you in danger too. You are my everything, and I don't ever want to get a call saying you got hurt or killed because of shit that has to do with me. You've been through enough already.

I want us to focus on getting your career back on track when you get out. With me out of the business, I can give you my undivided attention and we can take over the modeling world!

I have spent some time researching Nisa Isley and the Omoria Hampton Collection. I think Nisa Isley is really going to pull it together and have something ready by the time you get out. I haven't reached out to her yet, but I think that she is going to be your best bet. Omoria Hampton is a bit conservative. She don't have many black or plus-sized models, but that don't mean she won't work out for you. You could be her breakout star if we do it right.

Getting the DBA for Janessa Tatum was easy. I decided to get a limited liability company for Gun Wade Entertainment, LLC because that was the better option. In case something happens to me, the company's money is protected, and if something goes down with the shows, then we're not losing personal money. So saying that, I paid more than I initially thought, but the LLC fees and the DBA filing fee is chump change compared to what we are going to make from your return to the runway alone. So don't sweat it. I got the IDs, the licenses, the bank accounts at Capital One, and street addresses through the UPS Store, so everything is set on the business end.

One piece of advice before we move forward: Nisa said you would probably have to do some shows for little to no pay so you can rebuild your portfolio. With Instagram growing popular, models are making career moves based on how many likes and shares they generate. We'd have to hit the ground running with fresh pics and rebuilding your audience. You got sentenced right before people really started blowing up on the Internet. Nisa suggested we stage your return this way.

You need to find some books on acting so we can possibly place you in a Web-series. The shows don't pay nothing but free food and maybe some free clothes, but you can use one of those shows for exposure. The more people see you, the more likely the audience will follow you, and we can really use whatever show we create or put out to benefit you. A good Web-series like "RoomieLoverFriends" or "Black Boots" can get you a long way.

You've never been a chick with low self-esteem, so you got this. We counting

*down. One more year and I'll be able to
see you outside of those walls, hold you,
make love to you. We'll get this money,
and my love for you will remain true.*

    Love,
    Gun

Janiyah wished she had a mirror so she could
see the grin on her face. She was sure that it was
as wide as the Mississippi.

She was amazed at how deep his love was for
her. She couldn't believe he was really thinking
about quitting the drug game. Gun had been in
the streets since he was practically a kid. She
couldn't imagine him not having to make runs
in the middle of the night or his phone not going
off constantly. She wondered if it would really be
that simple for him to walk away from the world
he'd been living in for so many years. He hadn't
said he was definitely doing it, though, so she
decided not to put too much thought into it for
now. She was going to stay by his side regardless
of what he decided to do. Either way, she looked
forward to having her freedom and being with
her man soon.

Janiyah was looking forward to what the
future had for them. She was confident that she
could trust Gun to be loyal and true to her, and

she felt in her heart that nothing would ever change that. The worst had already happened. He could have easily bolted after she was sent away, but he continued to stayed by her side and was even willing to end his career to help get hers to the top.

Janiyah sat down and began to write a note with the instructions on how her social media was to be set up, and what kind of comments she wanted to be posted about her release.

From that moment forward, she was Team Janiyah & Gun for life.

Chapter Five

"Ayo, Niyah!" one of the inmates hollered at Janiyah during her hour of freedom.

Janiyah was using her time to lift weights and do some calisthenics. The exercise helped her to blow off some steam. She had been stressing the fact that her attackers remained unidentified, and that she could be facing any one of these broads who was trying to mess up the months of her time in jail. The only inmate she dealt with and trusted was Oz.

Janiyah took getting back into shape and reclaiming her life seriously. Gun was going above and beyond in helping her with things. Gun had turned into a living information super-highway. If she needed a confirmation on some information, Gun got her answers within twenty-four hours, then delivered it faster than the carryout drivers delivered pizza, with or without the walls separating them.

Before she was released, Janiyah knew she was going to have to address the assault. She needed to find out who the bitches were that did her wrong. And she had seen enough behind bars to know that she was going to be tried again. The first contestant on the "Let's Try and Step to Janiyah Show" was front and center. Janiyah was going to have to deal with this and quick. She couldn't have some random girl getting to the media and spreading all kinds of vicious lies about what they had done to her. Janiyah wasn't a killer, but like anyone, a little provoking could go a long way. There were bigger fish to fry, and Janiyah needed to batter this one up and put it in the pan.

Janiyah sized up the inmate. They were the same height. The other girl was a couple of shades darker and had more muscle mass, but that didn't scare Janiyah. She was never one to back down from a fight. "If you want it, you could get it," was her motto.

"Can I help you?" Janiyah mentally prepared herself to beat this bitch's ass.

She really didn't want to get into a fight; she'd rather finish her workout and get back to the screenplay she was writing. This was in addition to the ideas she was coming up with for a Web-series. She figured that if she were going to pimp herself in a Web-series, at least one of the shows could be a reality-like situation that would show the work and effort it would take for her to rebuild her career. At first, she was against any project for YouTube. She thought it was beneath her. But Gun had convinced her that as long as she didn't put her ass and titties on display and she maintained full control of her image, she could make the show, which would allow her to gain a new following and put her in the position to keep shit going the way she needed.

The screenplay, which for now was titled *Love and War,* was something serious. She had about sixty pages drafted, featuring a strong male lead who would be Romeo mixed with OG from the *Menace II Society* movie. Her female lead would be a short, plus-sized, darker-skinned version of Beyoncé, much like how she saw herself.

"Actually, I'm here to help *you* out. I heard you been looking for me!" The broad lifted her voice to let others around them know there was about to be a showdown. "It's your lucky day today because here I am. I don't hide from nobody, ma."

Janiyah carefully observed her enemy. She had tats from the base of her neck down to her torso. She didn't appear to be holding a shank or any other homemade weapon, but that didn't mean that one couldn't be slid to her.

"Hey, Nat," Janiyah responded. She really wasn't trying to get anything going with this girl. She didn't want to do anything to risk her getting more time on her sentence. "I don't know who you been hearing shit from, but I ain't looking for anyone. I got eleven months left on my time, and I ain't trying to stir my pot. Whoever you got in your ear damn sure ain't looking out for you by feeding you lies. Me and you get to fighting right now, and I promise you nobody out here is gonna give a single fuck about neither one of us."

The broad talked some more. "Bullshit. You just saying all that to get me to turn against my peoples. I know my real niggas in here got my back."

Janiyah realized that the young lady really wasn't a threat. If she really was about that life, she would've made her move by now instead of bumping her lips. Janiyah caught the eye of the CO who was moving closer in their direction.

"Oh, is that what you really think? Look, little girl, I'm going to give you a piece of advice and I hope you're smart enough to take it. These so-called niggas of yours are only gonna have your back as long as you do whatever they tell you to do. The second you say no, you're gonna see they don't give two shits about you. You're wasting your time trying to get me riled up.

If you wanna scrap, then let's scrap. Now, if you're all bark and no bite, then do me a favor and go do your time somewhere else and stop wasting mines." Janiyah tried to give the broad one last chance to get out of her face.

"Bitch, fuck—" the woman started.

Janiyah took no chances. Before the broad could bust off, Janiyah delivered a bone-crushing uppercut to her jaw. She was a lover, not a fighter, but today, Janiyah was going to do the best she could and imitate Floyd Mayweather as she continued the assault with a left hook that not only broke this bitch's nose but sent the young girl reelin' backward. Janiyah let them hands rock that head like they were supposed to, delivering nothing but menacing and deadly face blows. If they had been locked up in a UFC cage fight, the referee would've pulled Janiyah off and given her the victory via knockout.

Instead, a few COs jumped to the girl's aid. Janiyah was thrown on the ground with her hands behind her back.

"Oh, now you COs wanna do your job. Where were you when I got jumped, huh?" Janiyah yelled as they were lifting her up. The cuffs seemed to tighten behind her back.

Inside, Janiyah knew that beating the youngin' to a pulp might not have been her best move.

She was supposed to get out soon. Now this protective custody situation was going to turn into a segregation situation—no freedom, little peace, and a lot less sleep. She would probably get some more time tacked on to her sentence. Damn, and she was almost home. Only good thing she could think that came out of the situation was that she'd have more time to plan her career move and get her gameplan going with Gun.

In the back of her mind, she prayed to God that Gun kept the letters they wrote one another. After watching *Love and Hip Hop* the other night and seeing how Remy Ma and Papoose still held it down, a woman like Janiyah felt inspired. With the right person helping her, she could turn their beyond-the-beast love and marriage into a bestseller. As she was led away from the fray, Janiyah kept repeating the idea in her mind.

She prayed that by the time she got out, Gun would be down for turning their love affair into a book. She halfway thought Gun had the ability to at least come up with a first draft if she coaxed him and wrote him letters along the way. All Gun had to do was be receptive to the memo and get that smart brain of his in gear and get to work.

Chapter Six

Janiyah was thankful that the young broad didn't steal her time by forcing her to fight. The judge saw it for what it was, some girl trying to make Janiyah's situation worse, but she was sentenced to spend the next ten days caged like a crazy woman. It didn't sit right with her, but it was either that or get more time, and screw it, how hard could ten days be?

Janiyah had privacy and time to think about how deeply Gun loved her, and she accepted that. After she was officially put on seg, Janiyah's twenty-four-hour protection evaporated. She was left to face the other inmates on her own, and after her fight, she wished she had done it sooner. Janiyah didn't want prison changing her, but she had to face the fact that it had.

Getting the news that Gun had gotten her message, was down with her ideas, and may have found some people who wanted to put her on as soon as she was released in the next few months kept Janiyah ecstatic. She couldn't wait to touch ground. Her goal was to rock out harder than Lil' Kim and Martha Stewart ever did. Janiyah Wade was going to get her spot back in the modeling industry, and this go-round, she would show that she was more than a beautiful face and a big smile. She was multi-faceted.

With no mirror in sight, she ran her fingers across her big mane. She felt the thickness and fullness that hadn't touched some good grease or metal in years. Janiyah was convinced that with the right styling, she could actually pull off Chaka Khan's look when she first touched ground. When she left, the target would be off her back, and on someone else's.

Janiyah held the letter with Gun's uplifting words. Her eyes scanned over the letter.

I love you. I don't know how to put into words the kind of love I have for you. I say it again: I love you, Janiyah.

Janiyah smirked when she read those lines again. She thought of their last dinner date in which they feasted on turkey breast, greens cooked with a turkey wing, yams, dressing, some cranberry sauce, and a strawberry cheesecake on the side. The meal was meant to celebrate

Christmas, Thanksgiving, six birthdays, and a few Easters at one time. As Gun wined and dined Janiyah, she took pleasure in watching him devour the food they slaved in the kitchen to make while she was in her lingerie and his boxer briefs barely stayed on his ass.

They say you don't know what you got until it's gone, and they're right. You're behind those walls with no one to talk to, no makeup to put on, or me trying to get into your pants after a long day's work. I come home to no woman to spend my time with, and that makes a man two seconds from losing his mind. My head has been spinning in circles lately just thinking about everything.

After giving things a lot of thought, I've made my decision. I'm leaving the business. I ran into Big Shirley the other day. I don't remember if I had ever mentioned her to you, but she was my mentor when I first came into the business. Big Shirley was a real OG gangster back then, and one day she left her business too. She told me it was the best decision she ever made. She's a big part of a church now. She invited me to go, and I went last Sunday. Janiyah, it was off the chain!

I had never felt what I felt that day. It's like a part of me woke up. A part that I never even knew I had. Listen, I know how you feel about God and everything, but if you experienced what I did last Sunday, I know you would change your mind. Talk to your friend Oz about it. She's the one that's always trying to get you to go to Bible study with her, right?

Anyway, I'm gonna keep going to the Sunday services and see where it takes me. I hope when you get out that I am able to go with you by my side. I'm going to stick with you because from now until I meet my Maker, there is nothing I ain't willing to do for us, and I promise I'm always going to take care of you. I'm looking forward to growing old with you, Janiyah.

Janiyah sat back, closed her eyes, and thought about his last statement. She didn't want to imagine herself being old and gray, but it was a reality she was going to have to face eventually. She pictured herself with salt-and-pepper hair and subtle wrinkles at the corner of her eyes. In the modeling business, Janiyah often saw women who lost their youth and their mind because they put so much emphasis on their age and not embracing the changes in their physical appearance. Janiyah promised herself right then and there to not become like those women. She was confident that she'd embrace the aging process and she'd wear it well. She decided she'd put more effort into keeping up with her health and physical shape so she'd have sex appeal into her fifties, sixties, or until she took her last breath!

My days will be spent doing pushups, situps, crunches, and any other exercise to keep my heart racing and my limbs warm.

Janiyah had already been applying herself to more exercising for a while now. She had read a self-published memoir of an ex-con on one of her first months behind bars. It inspired her to get on some weights and to work out, not to lose weight, but so she could stay in shape. She was thankful for that book, because the exercise had really helped with releasing a lot of pent-up frustration, not to mention the lonely nights when she missed feeling her husband inside of her.

Janiyah thought back to when she would see Gun standing naked in the bathroom after a hot, steamy shower. He looked so sexy standing there with drops of water sliding down his silky, smooth skin. She used to love to stare at his flaccid penis and how it hung between his legs. She would sneak up behind him as he dried himself off and glide her hands up and down his back. A soft, low moan would escape her mouth as she made her way down and gently took his member into her hands. Soft, it was about two fingers thick and the length of his middle finger. His tip was about the size and shape of a large mushroom head.

Janiyah lay on the bunk as she felt a throbbing sensation take over between her legs. As her hand traced her body, Janiyah closed her eyes and stroked herself. More thoughts of her and Gun's lovemaking sessions flooded her mind. God, she missed him. She'd had decent experiences with other men in her past, but none made her move and feel the way he did. In her mind, she pictured Gun doing the same thing. Janiyah pictured him grabbing his meat and squeezing it. She envisioned helping him and teasing him, making the blood rush to his member before he let it go.

Keeping her eyes closed, Janiyah slid her fingers inside herself, pretending her fluids lubricated his member. She pretended Gun was sliding into her nice, tight pussy.

Janiyah could've used that jail head. Instead, she was rocking her hips, clenching her ass, almost close to busting the first nut she'd had in months. When Janiyah's body trembled, she felt like the room was shaking.

Fuck, Gun, fuck me, fuck me, fuck me, Janiyah thought as she felt herself near her moment. The nut was feeling good. She could feel her fingers curling, and a deep, lustful grunt wanted to escape her lips. She knew she had to stay quiet so she wouldn't get caught. She didn't want to do anything that would make them keep her in seg any longer than she needed to be.

As Janiyah's eyes flicked open, she quickly grabbed a soda bottle off the toilet and put the rim at the opening of her pussy. She rubbed the rim of it around her clit, pretending she could feel Gun coming inside her.

Chapter Seven

The door of her cell opening broke her concentration. She was in the middle of doing a set of military-style pushups when she saw a pair of black boots entering her cell.

"Wade." The officer addressed Janiyah. "It's time to go. You will be released in one hour. Grab your personal possessions, and we will take you to holding shortly." The CO handed Janiyah a copy of her release papers.

A smile crept across Janiyah's face. She couldn't wait to get out of this hellhole. She couldn't believe her release day was finally here. The last six months had been a whirlwind. After her fight with Nat, the Nietas stopped chasing her. It seemed her showing she was willing to fight for hers took the fun out of the stupid little cat and mouse game they liked to play with inmates. It seemed her three-year nightmare filled with fights, negative thoughts, a vicious beating and stabbing, the modeling career put on hold . . .

all of that was coming to an end. The judge had promised her the fight with Nat would not affect her release date, and today the judge proved to be true to her word.

Janiyah had kept a very low profile these last months. She did not want to put herself in any situation that could possibly get her more time on her sentence. She had been doing a lot or reading, exercising, and mental preparation for when she got out. She was ready to hit the ground running. She couldn't wait to see Gun, to hold him, kiss him, make love to him.

Gun had been a very busy man over the past months too. He had officially retired from the drug game. He did one last major shipment that helped him go out with a bang. That last job was one of the largest paydays he ever did. Aside from his business life, he had also made huge changes in his personal life. He had continued to go to church every Sunday and had even gotten baptized. He had been attending Bible studies and retreats, and had really become a dedicated member of Big Shirley's church.

After letters upon letters from Gun encouraging and pushing her to go to Bible study with Oz, Janiyah finally agreed to go. Although she felt she hadn't really experienced a life-altering moment the way Oz and Gun had, she did open her eyes and heart to making changes in her lifestyle. She did have a better understanding of who God was now and had promised Gun she was willing to work on developing her spiritual relationship when she was released. Gun had faithfully stayed with her through everything in the past three years. It would only be fair to him that she stand by him with his new lifestyle change too.

As she left her cell, she looked around for Oz. Janiyah was going to miss her friend, but truthfully, she was glad she was going to be free. She hadn't been able to receive a letter from Gun in ten days, and she was given five days' notice of her release date, so she didn't know if he knew she was getting out today. She wrote him a letter to let him know, but the COs sometimes didn't send letters out until the end of the week, so she wasn't sure if he had received it or if it had even been sent out. Because of everything going on with his drug business three years ago, she hadn't listed him as the person of contact for her, so she was sure he hadn't been reached out to by any administrators to notify him of her release

As she made her way through holding, she looked for Gun. She wanted to hold him, kiss him, see him. She was deeply disappointed when she didn't see him. Her disappointment disappeared the second she spied her friend Grelle waiting for her.

"Girl, you're coming with me," Grelle called out and pulled Janiyah in for a hug.

"Grelle, what the—" Janiyah couldn't believe she was facing her best friend. Or *was she* her best friend? Janiyah didn't know, since she hadn't heard from her in the last three years.

Grelle looked good. Her white tank top hugged her tight and showed off her full D cups, and her Apple Bottom jeans made onlookers drool at the ass women paid good money to inject cement into their behinds to get. Her pink work boots gave a thuggish edge to her otherwise feminine look.

"We need to talk now, and we aren't going to do it here." Grelle jerked Janiyah back and made her way through the exit.

There was no way in hell her friend was about to come at her in broad daylight, but Janiyah noticed in Grelle's other hand was the holster of her Smith & Wesson M&P Shield. In Janiyah's mind, the fact that the state slipped and let Grelle slide in a weapon could only mean her happy release day was abruptly taking a turn for the worse.

***

Janiyah tried to free herself from Grelle's tight grip.

"Bitch, really?" Grelle questioned as she shoved Janiyah inside her obsidian black BMW 760 Li sedan. Three years was too long to go without seeing one of her best girlfriends. The six-foot, copper-skinned beauty was only a few pounds heavier, but she still made being a tall black woman look good.

In the back of her mind, Janiyah wondered what happened to Grelle. When her boyfriend, Trap, was alive, Grelle looked and acted the part of a dime piece. Top of the line clothing and jewelry was standard, even for a jog in the park. If Apple Bottoms were her version of dress down, Grelle still wasn't bad. She looked like she was dressed to beat a bitch's ass, and unfortunately for Janiyah, that bitch might be her.

"Why the fuck haven't I heard from you in three years?" Grelle jerked her head toward Janiyah.

"Grelle, I meant to check on you, but " Janiyah tried to explain, but she was cut off when Grelle started her engine and quickly backed out of her parking space.

"Girl, you haven't been checking on me since I told you that Trap got shot up in that hotel in

Greensboro." Grelle told the truth as she found her way to I-40. "I mean, you were there for me for the funeral and shit, but then you went ghost."

"Okay," Janiyah said, "you do realize that I was locked up?"

Janiyah looked down and realized she had Grelle's iPad in her lap. She looked through the Kindle app to see if her girl had any good e-books to read. Other than *Carl Weber's Kingpins* series, she didn't recognize any of the authors her girl was reading up on. That was one thing she had missed about Grelle: They used to talk about hot books.

"All right, you have a point there. But how come you never even told me about you getting locked up? And then I had to go about things myself to find out about when you were getting out." Grelle blew her frustration on the horn as Raleigh traffic came to a slowdown. The cars surrounding her were moving slower than molasses, and the cars were literally bumper to bumper. "And you know my uncle is one of the COs. I heard they were trying to do some real damage to you in there."

"They tried, but they didn't succeed." Janiyah wanted to reveal her plan, but she didn't know Grelle's true motive just yet. She wanted to think she wasn't in danger because her arms and feet weren't bound and her mouth wasn't taped shut. Grelle had her gun in her lap, but Janiyah didn't want to take the risk of trying to get it.

So she tried a different approach. "Why did you grab me? How did you know I was getting out today?" Janiyah looked at the skyline she had seen a thousand times between *The Real Housewives of the Triangle* and the numerous local romance movies that played on BET in the prison rec room.

"I just told you my uncle is a CO. He always kept me filled in on the shit going on with you in there. I showed up today 'cause I wanted you to look me in my eyes and explain to me why you kept me in the dark. Bitch, I coulda kept money in your commissary and had someone telling you how to make makeup from Kool-Aid packets so you coulda stunted on them bitches like *Orange is the New Black* and shit. And please tell me one of those bull-dyke bitches didn't try to slip their dusty fingers all up in you, 'cause I can go back and shoot a bitch," Grelle answered as she reached in the backseat and grabbed a copy of *Watch Out for the Big Girls* by J. M. Benjamin.

"Well, I . . ." Janiyah tried to come up with a lie on the spot but found herself tongue-tied.

Normally, she'd be able to spin a story off the cuff, but she couldn't get her facts straight in front of Grelle for some reason. Truth was, the only person she'd kept in contact with over the last three years was Gun.

"I thought we were friends, Janiyah, but I gotta go and hear about you stabbing a photographer and getting arrested from that rusty-ass assistant Brianna. Even though I don't like her, she knew the whole story, so my ass had to sit there and pretend like we cool and all just to get the scoop on what's going on with *my* best friend."

"You know what, Grelle? The knife cuts both ways. If you're telling me you knew all this and was even keeping tabs on me in there, how come you never came to see me?" Janiyah snapped and focused on the iPad. She opened the e-book and started reading a few pages. When she had first heard about the electronic devices, she wasn't interested in them, but while she was in the women's prison, all she could think about was getting her hands on an iPad so she could read books, play music, and try to get her business plan in order. Janiyah had no plans to sit on her ass and wait on an opportunity to come to her.

Traffic started to pick up a little, and Grelle guided her BMW west. "Because I was hurt that you left me out of it. Why did you keep it a secret, was what I'm trying to get at. I'm supposed to be your friend, and a bitch didn't like being the last to know."

"Okay, so I didn't reach out to you and you didn't reach out to me, so I guess that makes us even," Janiyah responded. She really wasn't in the mood to sit there and argue back and forth, "Yes, you are my best friend, and I should've filled you in on everything. What's done is done, though, so let's just move on. We good?"

"Yeah, whatever," Grelle said after sucking her teeth. She wasn't ready to stop talking about it, but she knew her friend had a point in that they needed to just let things go and move on.

"Where are you taking me?" Janiyah questioned.

"Against my better judgment, I'm taking you to Nisa Isley in Greensboro. She asked Gun about you, and she offered to help you get your career back on track. I only found out she was in town because she called Gun to check on you."

Janiyah felt like a bad friend now. Grelle had done all of that just to help her get her life back together, even though Janiyah had pretty much written her out of her life the last three years.

Not too many people in the industry reached out to her to find out how she was doing, if she was okay, or anything like that. Janiyah knew Grelle kept it one hundred and told the truth. Janiyah's plan was coming together much sooner and in a way she hadn't expected. Grelle was doing for her what Gun always did: saving her from her enemies. Grelle really was a good friend, because Janiyah could picture in her head how much money she must have turned down. Janiyah was grateful to have a friend like Grelle.

"So what do we do?" Janiyah asked, exhausted. In the back of her mind, she was trying to decide if she should go back to New York, and if so, how she was going to get in touch with someone who was going to help her.

Chapter Eight

"Watch where the hell you're going!" a woman screamed at Janiyah after bumping into her. The woman was barreling down the busy sidewalk of Friendly Avenue, pushing people to the side like a bulldozer.

The walkways of Greensboro stayed busy at the right time of the year. Being pushed, shoved, pulled, and grabbed was not an uncommon occurrence. In the few days Janiyah had been home, she'd grown accustomed to the fast pace and often rudeness that came with being in G-Boro. She refused to let the haughty and mightier-than-thou attitudes make her break a sweat. She needed to keep the focus on her goals, not the petty stuff these people were dealing. As long as none of these street thugs tried to snatch her purse or openly cop a feel, she didn't have a single care to give. And even if someone did try to do something, she doubted she'd do much about it. With her being so fresh out of prison, there wasn't anything important in her purse, and a little butt-grabbing never hurt nobody. It would feel a whole lot better than those strip searches she was forced to endure during her time away. Walking down the street, these people must have thought they were New Yorkers as they walked around as if the world belonged to them, and there was no way of telling who the punks were and who the aggressors were. Both wore the same outfits.

Janiyah quickly turned to look at the woman. Her impulse was to "accidentally" push the woman back. The problem was that Janiyah couldn't actually be sure who the perpetrator was. The night skyline concealed her identity as she walked past. There was a full-figured white chick in a loose-fitting blue blouse and skin-tight jeans who was on her phone talking shit to somebody about how she was going to beat somebody's ass. A part of Janiyah wanted to run up on her and trip her and watch her jelly roll down the block. Yet, Janiyah couldn't prove that it wasn't the skinny black thing with a huge Afro who appeared to be sashaying like she was RuPaul. It occurred to Janiyah that whoever it was that bumped into her might just have been in a hurry to get somewhere. She cut her eyes and shook her head, deciding to just keep it moving.

The sounds and smells emanating from the various restaurants along the street reminded her of the great times she'd had with Gun. There were so many different cuisines being represented: Indian, Jamaican, Spanish, Italian. Janiyah had missed this while she was locked up. It reminded Janiyah of all the fabulous trips she and Gun used to take. From the first day they met, he treated her like a queen and loved to wine and dine her. A trip to a luxurious island in the Caribbean, or the Straits of Gibraltar between Spain and Morocco, or any of the locations off the Mediterranean Sea were regular vacation spots. She tried to discourage him from spending so much money on her, but Gun swore up and down that it wasn't setting him back. He was adamant about taking her around the world. Janiyah was known to royalty and the world's wealthy alike, and she and Gun were never alone when they decided to travel the world.

The infectious reggae tune blaring from a barber shop competed against horns coming from impatient cars and Uber drivers waiting to get to their destinations. The $20 bill rubbing against Janiyah's breast reminded her she couldn't afford a cab even if she wanted to. Janiyah thought about the few fives and tens crumpled at the bottom of her purse. It was literally all the money she had at the moment. She was in dire straits and needed a come up, right quick.

A vendor hawking copies of the latest urban fiction and other African American books caught her attention. Her eyes zeroed in on the copies of *Whose Life II* stacked front and center on the table. While one man had two copies of the book in his hand, handing over some bills for the exchange, Janiyah noticed three young black girls scanning the pages. Janiyah smiled. This was all the confirmation she needed to know her next move was to make her story go to print. Dollar signs danced in her head.

"I see my wife."

Janiyah heard his voice. She turned around and was so happy to see her husband. She ran to him and gave him a hug.

"Girl, it's been too long."

"Yeah, it has." She hugged him tight. "How come you had Grelle come and get me instead of you picking me up?"

"Because I knew if Grelle picked you up, your money would have been your focus. If I had picked you up, we'd be screaming and hollering in some hotel in Raleigh somewhere."

"True." Janiyah didn't bother to deny it. Just holding him had her wanting to get him inside of her. She needed to feel her husband throbbing inside, pulsating, confirming that she was still wanted as a woman.

"And I trust that your meeting with Nisa Isley went well," Gun said.

"Yeah, I got a photo shoot tomorrow." Janiyah still couldn't believe it. She had met with the elderly oriental lady, who was impressed that she kept her figure while she was locked up and that she didn't have too many battle scars to worry about. "She even likes my mane. . . . You know I call her Chaka." Janiyah patted her hair.

Gun chuckled. "What am I going to do with you?"

"Get me into a room and you won't have to wonder."

Gun grabbed her hand and gave her a kiss. "I'm glad I talked Grelle into bringing you to her shop in the Friendly Shopping Center. I felt that if you came here and saw all the stores and really had a chance to sit down with her, you'd make a decision you wouldn't regret."

"And trust me, I don't." Janiyah kissed him back. "Now, can we head to the hotel?"

Chapter Nine

One Year Later

Flash, flash, flash.

Janiyah worked to time the blinks of her eyelashes so that the sharp beams emitting from the photographer's Cannon T5i DSLR camera wouldn't blind her. She wanted to rub her eyes to deal with the burgeoning headache that seemed to get bigger by the second. Janiyah needed an ibuprofen, but since it was her first shoot since her release, she wasn't about to stop in the middle because of a little headache. She needed to make sure she left a great impression so this job would lead to many more

Her arm was getting tired of holding onto her hip, and the four-inch red bottoms were working a number on her spine, legs, and feet. Janiyah had forgotten the stamina needed for an entire day-long photo shoot.

And plus, a big girl needed a break.

"Good, Janiyah! Keep up the pose!" the photographer shouted over the noise of the huge fan. Her hair had taken flight and moved as if it were going to fly off her head.

Why don't you strike a pose? Janiyah wanted to ask, but she kept quiet. Her focus was on making sure she didn't break a sweat. She could still smell the Rogue Love by Rhianna lotion that she wore, and Secret was keeping her secret under her arms. With all the heat in such a compact space, she didn't want to give out and have to take a break to freshen up.

Janiyah found it funny that most of the people behind the camera couldn't do poetry with her body the way she could, yet they were able to command her like a drill sergeant giving orders to a private.

"Okay, to the left," the photographer directed with both a verbal and a visual cue.

Another order. Janiyah quickly followed the prompt and got into position.

Flash, flash, flash.

Janiyah really wasn't enjoying her photo shoot with this particular photographer, but for now she was going to keep her mouth shut and her temper in check. She was in no position to start making demands. It had been a year since she'd been back in the real world, and she had been getting a lot of jobs to get her career back on track, but she still wasn't quite back at the top. A lot of things had changed during her three-year stint in prison. Vine and Instagram had seen the birth of many overnight sensations. Regular, round the way girls were now "Insta-famous" and being offered modeling and endorsement gigs based on the amount of followers they had on Instagram, Facebook, and even Vine. Some girls were even getting paid just to post amateur pictures of themselves using company products.

Right before the situation happened with Janiyah, she was gaining a large following on her Instagram page. With her being gone for so long, Gun deactivated her account because there was little she could do to keep it going. This past year, her primary focus had been to get back on the pages and become relevant again. Her Instagram page was booming again, and her phone was ringing constantly. She was proud of herself for getting back out there, and she was being extra careful to keep the momentum going for herself. The last thing she needed was to get snippy with a photographer and for rumors to start circulating that she was difficult to work with or too much of a diva.

She couldn't remember the photographer's name at the moment. Since he wasn't all too friendly, she had forgotten his name as soon as he introduced himself. In Janiyah's opinion, the photographer was inexperienced. He was rushing shots and not communicating clearly. As the man would ask her to get into this position or that pose, he'd be snapping random shots. She thought the flash was on too bright, and he could've turned off some of the lights. Still, Janiyah continued smiling and posing, working diligently to follow the nonverbal cues the photographer continued to give her.

"We're almost done. You're doing great." The photographer encouraged her and gave a visual prompt to turn around.

That was the nicest he'd been to her throughout the shoot. Janiyah felt herself tremble as her heel started to sink into the floor. She wanted to look down to see if it was broken, but she didn't dare break her stride.

"A couple more pictures. Maybe we can get some of you and your husband before the day is over," the photographer suggested.

They'd been at this shoot all day, and after fifteen outfit changes, she was happy it was almost over. They were shooting for a magazine that catered to full-figured career women, but

Janiyah couldn't remember which one. She did remember that she'd collect a check after the shoot and that the magazine agreed to highlight women of faith—full-figured women of faith, that is—single ministers and power couples who were moving up and pushing fame and faith to their limits.

Janiyah looked at her husband. The appeal of another photo shoot with one of the most popular up and coming, well-respected youth pastor in the state brought a smile to her face. Gun had undergone a full transformation over the last year and a half. He had found his calling as a youth pastor, and aside from helping with his wife's career, his job as a youth pastor was his priority. Because of his past and his "rough around the edges" type of attitude, young adolescents were very drawn to him. They loved to hear about his life experiences and were very receptive to hear what he had to say about God, Christianity, and how they could make better choices for their lives.

Janiyah, too, had become a member of the church and was also dedicated to supporting her husband in this new chapter in his life. She had also made a decision to give her life to God and had developed a true passion for serving in the community. Like Oz and Gun, she had been enlightened and awoken to a newfound faith.

Her mind, heart, and soul had been reset, and she loved working alongside her husband in the church. She was amazed at how fast things had developed for them in the church congregation. Gun completed his six-month course to become a certified youth pastor with such ease, it was as if he were born for it.

Flash, flash, flash.

"I just need one more angle and you are done, Janiyah."

And that's when the photographer's name hit her: Cable. It was actually Jeriah Cable, but he preferred to go by his last name. The man was surprisingly thick, not rotund or overly obese like the Fat Albert cartoon character, but Cable had a little stomach pouch that a few crunches, situps, trips to the gym, and a small diet could cure. His arms were rippled like a G. I. Joe action figure, which Janiyah found complemented his square face.

Cable pointed his finger at Gun and motioned for him to join Janiyah in front of the camera. Janiyah shook her head at his unprofessionalism. Pointing then directing was not the way one asked for something to be done. Janiyah took note of that as the heat continued to rise, and she noticed her foundation breaking as she started to sweat on her cheek and jawbone.

Every woman in America fantasizes about what it would be like to be with my husband, and in an hour, I'm going to get that experience again.

Motivated, Janiyah suffered through the increasing temperature. The fan only seemed to push the hot air around and make the studio feel like she was working in a sweathouse, but she remained professional. The end results, collecting a check and contributing to the household, were worth the minor pain and suffering.

Gun flashed his award-winning smile. His teeth shone as if he were doing ads for a teeth-whitening commercial. His cinnamon-colored skin shone, and his softer cheekbones, clean-shaven face, and round facial features gave him a baby face.

Gun's non-verbal actions gave consent to participate in the photo shoot, and for that, Janiyah was grateful. While Cable continued to take pictures, Janiyah watched as Gun headed to the dressing room. In her eyes, Gun was perfect. He didn't need to straighten his green and-blue silk tie, which was in the perfect Windsor knot. She loved the way his sea green button-up shirt and black three-button suit draped across his tall frame. In another life, Gun could've been a model for *GQ* or *Complex*.

"Okay, Rev, you're in." Cable was very informal with Gun.

Janiyah saw the look in Gun's eyes. The way his eyes scrunched closed and his lip twisted up quickly let her know that he was pissed. Gun hated being addressed as Rev, and preferred to be called Gun when he was away from church. Gun once told her that being called Rev was the church equivalent to being called Duffle Bag Boy, Junebug, or whatever ghetto name he wanted to leave behind in the hood.

Gun got behind his wife and wrapped his arms around Janiyah's curvaceous body. She could feel him take a deep breath. She knew he loved the smell of the lotion and couldn't wait for the opportunity to get closer to the scent intimately.

"Um, Pastor, I need y'all to loosen up and have fun," Cable suggested as he walked up to the couple. He reached into Gun's personal space and started undoing the buttons on the cuffs of his shirt. "Unbutton that suit jacket and take it off—and loosen the tie." This was another reason Janiyah thought he was unprofessional. On a bigger budget shoot, there would have been a person in charge of wardrobe who would have handled anything to do with the clothes.

Wardrobe people are very particular about how buttons are undone, sleeves are rolled, and jacket lapels placed. Seeing Cable start messing with clothes was low budget in Janiyah's eyes.

Janiyah was shocked to see her husband follow the photographer's directions. *Loosen up?* The request was the complete opposite of the demeanor Gun Wade was known for. Janiyah was grateful that her husband wasn't the same man he was over a year ago. Cable had no idea who he was talking to. If he had known that Gun used to be a big-time drug kingpin that wouldn't hesitate to pistol whip someone for disrespecting him, he'd be handling this photo shoot with a lot more care and respect. The old Gun Wade was dead and gone now, though. Gun had received his revelation from God, turned his life around, and was happy where he was. It would take a lot more than a rude photographer to get him to break.

Gun took his new role as a church leader and minister of the Word seriously, and he made sure that his dress reflected his outlook on life. Gun wasn't so uptight that he couldn't wear the popular brands sported by today's athletes and artists, but he understood that image was everything, and as a man of God, he felt his dress should reflect his walk.

"Yeah, man." Cable flashed his ugly yellow teeth.

Janiyah shook her head. For as much money as the magazine was paying this man, she couldn't believe Cable couldn't get his dental needs taken care of. But that was none of Janiyah's business, and she felt a pang of guilt for judging the man. She'd only just met Cable, and Janiyah knew the publication was giving him a chance, as they were also giving her one. There weren't many black photographers who shot for well-known publications, and Janiyah had always felt that everyone deserved a break. Who knew? Maybe Cable had some gems in his collection of random thoughts and picture-taking. Only time would tell. She'd have to give him a chance.

The camera continued to flash, and the wind continued to blow, as Cable directed Janiyah and Gun through a few poses. Some were even slightly suggestive. Janiyah didn't mind the world knowing that she and Gun were in love or that they promoted a healthy, intimate relationship to their congregation. It was her opinion that more couples, even those who led a flock, should be in tune with one another.

When the shoot was over, the fan was turned off, and Janiyah stepped out of her stilettos.

Thankfully, they hadn't buckled or sunk. She looked for an available chair to sit down and rub her feet. A foot soak complete with jet-stream bubbles with a strong lavender scent would have soothed her nerves and her spirit. Janiyah could've used a nap, but there was no place for her to sneak away to. The studio definitely wasn't as nice as what she was accustomed to. There were no fresh fruit trays or vegan-friendly spreads that most models nibbled on for nourishment, no purified water imported from Italy or France, not even a can of La Croix sparkling water. Janiyah couldn't believe the magazine had been so cheap. Then, when she thought about Cable and the old warehouse they were in and the portable equipment Cable had to bring with him to make his setup work, she wasn't surprised. She knew it was just something she had to endure in order to build her career back up.

"Baby, how do you think I did?" Gun asked nervously.

Janiyah found this question cute because Gun usually wasn't the vain type. He only cared about his looks when he was preaching the Word to the youth during Sunday service. Other than that, a torn-up shirt, some jersey shorts, and some athletic slides suited him fine.

"You were sexy to me." Janiyah kissed him on the cheek. "Besides, I don't think the magazine is going to use any of the pictures we took for this spread. I doubt anyone will see them."

Out of the corner of her eye, Janiyah saw the door open to the only room available for changing. Her biggest rival in the plus-size model market, Brianna Clarise, rushed out of the room. In the back of her mind, Janiyah wondered if Brianna had been in the room when her husband was getting himself together. Janiyah watched as the diva struggled to keep her blouse buttoned, and the enhancements Brianna had flown all the way to Peru to get done cheaply fought with the fabric to stay in place.

Brianna saw Janiyah looking at her as she exited the room. "The room is yours, honey," she said. "Please leave my purse on the counter and don't touch nothing!"

"I don't need—" Janiyah started to entertain her but felt Gun quickly escorting her five-foot-seven, two-hundred-pound frame to the room. This elevated Janiyah's temper a bit, as she felt stung by the insult. The implication that she would need or want anything that belonged to Brianna was offensive.

"Gun, slow down," Janiyah snapped.

"Oh, no." Gun continued his pace, and as he and Janiyah crossed the threshold of the door, he promptly shut it. "I didn't forget the black eye I got from the *last time* the two of you had an altercation. Never again."

Janiyah thought for a quick second and guilt overshadowed her. *She* was the one who had accidentally punched her husband, instead of that no-good, man-stealing hussy. In fact, her last altercation with Brianna had started because she made an inappropriate comment about Gun being a prude in the bedroom. Even if though it couldn't be further from the truth, she didn't want Brianna spreading rumors about them.

"Okay, baby." Janiyah exhaled as she took a step up to sit on her throne. The leather plush swivel stool moved as Janiyah maneuvered to get comfortable. "I hate when they put me and her in the same photo shoot. Folks should know by now we can't stand one another."

Janiyah tilted her head to the left to remove the huge silver, disco ball–shaped earrings. She couldn't wait to take them out. They were so heavy they were pulling on her earlobes and making them sore, and she thought they made her face look more round. As she did the same to her right side, she felt a weight being lifted off her shoulders, literally. She exhaled as she looked at her reflection in the mirror. She was surprised her makeup had held up despite feeling like it was going to drip from her face.

"That's not the way a youth pastor and his lady should handle things," Gun said as he lowered his body to massage Janiyah's feet.

Instead of arguing, Janiyah said nothing as Gun elevated her leg and continued to knead her foot as if it were dough. Soon, Janiyah forgot everything as Gun turned up the heat, making the dressing room their own personal bedroom. It seemed as if Gun had taken the photographer's advice and loosened up a bit.

Gun stood up and walked to the door to make sure it was locked. Once he felt secure about them being safe and alone in the room, Gun put a finger to his lips, encouraging her to remain quiet. Next, he unbuckled his belt, and Janiyah smiled as Gun's pants hit the floor. She was equally surprised that he not only stepped out of the pants, but that she had easy access to everything in front of her.

It wasn't easy, but she stayed silent as a clam as Gun began to work his magic on her insides.

Chapter Ten

"I wear the best eye shadow, lip-liner, and foundation that money can buy," Janiyah preached before a group of about two hundred youth. Janiyah was at a speaking engagement talking about fame and success in the church's school auditorium. The church was located in in Greensboro, and aside from the building temple, they also ran a private Christian school. Gun worked there on a full-time basis as the youth pastor and counselor for the students. She looked back at Gun, who nodded his head and subtly nudged her to continue. "I wear expensive perfumes, nice clothes, and y'all know I can keep my hair tight whether I'm all-natural or if my hair is dyed or fried."

Janiyah spun her hair in a circular motion. The windmill effect brought a slight breeze to her face and thunderous laughter from the crowds. Sistas were standing up and giving her encouragement, and she knew that a few guys were intrigued too.

"I get paid to look beautiful." Janiyah took a sip from her water bottle and placed it on the podium. She snatched the microphone from the stand and began walking down the middle aisle. "My day job is to sell beauty—I get that makes some of you uncomfortable. But I always keep in mind that Peter, chapter three, verses three and four say, 'Do not let your adorning be external—the braiding of hair and the putting on of gold jewelry, or the clothing you wear—but let your adorning be the hidden person of the heart with the imperishable beauty of a gentle and quiet spirit, which in God's sight is very precious.'"

A chorus of *amen* followed.

"I sell an image. That's why some of you are here." A few of the girls in the school were laughing, but before she could let them get far, Janiyah continued. "And I am not ashamed, because I know that He has made everything beautiful in its time. The difference between my image and the more popular image that you see on television is that while I sell physical beauty, I speak and promote about maintaining a positive spiritual image. When I meet little girls—especially young, thick girls like myself—I encourage them to move forward with their plans.

"Lose the weight so that you can live in good health and continue the mission that God put in your lives. Don't starve yourself so that you can fit into a bathing suit and capture a man's attention. Now, I'm not going to lie; I can make a two-piece or one-piece look good."

Janiyah was on a roll as she saw the young ladies' eyes on her. She looked up at the sound booth and was thankful that the members running the visuals were keeping up with the message she wanted to send. They emphasized the passages and, most importantly, showed pictures that highlighted different points of her message. They had been kind enough to give her a topic to speak on, and Janiyah and Gun had spent the night perfecting the speech in between lovemaking sessions.

"But the important thing is that I'm not vain. I don't sell hurtfulness. I don't need to put another model down so I can make a dollar." Janiyah almost choked as her spirit convicted her. She knew that her rivalry with Brianna was the one dirty spot in her otherwise polished career. It was not that she didn't try to get along with Brianna. Janiyah had hoped that two plus-sized models who professed to worship Jesus Christ could get along. She had extended an olive branch more than one time, but after being shunned, dissed, and outright blackballed from certain photo shoots because of the increasingly bitter competition, Janiyah had learned to love every plus-size model *except* Brianna.

"I love that when young girls see me, it's with my clothes on. I'm not twerking to some hard-thumping, pulsating beat. Girls don't see me gyrating in front of some fully-clothed man who's waving dollars and rubbing his hands over my chest."

"Wait a minute, Janiyah."

A sharp voice stopped Janiyah in her tracks. She looked around and couldn't find where it had come from. Gun had stood up, and the teachers were walking around too, trying to figure out who had the audacity to interrupt her in the middle of her speech.

"Who said that?" Janiyah asked. After ministering the Word for a few months, Janiyah had mastered the art of comforting babies, engaging children, and educating adults while letting the Lord use her as a vessel.

"I said it." A voice was clear and came from the sound booth. It sounded like her ex-boyfriend, Rodji. She hadn't seen or heard from the man in almost seven years, right after he left her near some farm in Waynesville almost thirty miles from the city. Being a young, dumb, naïve woman at the time, before there was Gun or even Jesus, Rodji was her god. Whatever he told her to do and however he told her to do it, Janiyah was on top of it.

Janiyah was certain it couldn't be Rodji, though, because he had been murdered three years ago after a dispute with another man. They had been sleeping with the same girl, and their argument turned deadly. The shooting shook the black residents of Raleigh to their core because many knew both Rodji and the man who was eventually convicted of his murder.

"I have some pictures I want to share. I believe this ho out there and the crooked pastor standing in the pulpit have some explaining to do," the voice commanded, bringing her out of her trip down memory lane. Images of Rodji's ashes being sprinkled along Blue Ridge Mountain were replaced with the blank stares from the members of the audience.

Before long, images of Janiyah and Gun's intimate moment in the dressing room of the studio flashed on the screen. Admittedly, that had been one of the best lovemaking sessions the couple had ever experienced. It was impulsive, creative, and satisfying. What it wasn't, apparently, was private. Janiyah's face felt like it was sagging as image after image was broadcast from the teleprompter for the students to see.

"Someone turn that off!" Gun roared as he moved to push the screen out of the way. Another teacher helped him as a few school administrators raced into the sound room.

"Oh, there's more," another voice announced. "I'm going to get you, Janiyah Merrie Wilson Wade, if it's the last thing I do. And I don't mind destroying your career in the process. Play with me if you want to."

Janiyah was offended. She couldn't recognize the voice right away, but whoever it was came for her in a very public way. This was unacceptable. Janiyah ran down the aisle and up the stairs to where the sound booth was, only to face deacons coming down the stairs.

"Who is it?" Janiyah demanded an answer. "Who has the audacity to try to embarrass me in front of children?"

Janiyah tried to hold back the tears as she saw the teachers shaking their heads in confusion. Janiah was infuriated. She wanted to know who did this to her, and most importantly, she needed to figure out how she was going to get them back.

Chapter Eleven

Janiyah bombarded Gun the moment he came into their home. "Any word on who that was that put our business all up and through the school?"

She hated that she'd honored his request to go home and let the police and the other church administrators handle the investigation. How *dare* they tell her she couldn't handle or be involved in the investigation going on? It was her that was being viciously and verbally attacked.

The look on Gun's face said it all: there was no new information. He loosened his tie and the top buttons of his shirt, and his suit jacket draped his arm like it was on a hanger. As she looked down, she noticed that some New Balance sneakers replaced the Johnston & Murphy shoes that he had grown comfortable with.

He almost never wears tennis shoes with his dress clothes, she thought when she looked him over again.

"We don't know who pulled this stunt," Gun informed her. He walked to their plush leather couch and dejectedly plopped his six-foot-one-inch frame down. "Apparently, our computer system was hacked, and the person was able to bypass our computer security and control the board from a remote location."

"That sounds like some FBI level stuff," Janiyah acknowledged. She took a seat next to Gun and leaned her head on his shoulder.

"Truth is, any system can be compromised at any time. Anonymous taught us that," Gun pointed out. "Whoever did it was probably waiting on the right time to catch us slipping, and they got what they wanted."

"Ain't nobody did this but Brianna Clarise, and when I catch her—" Janiyah got up. She was getting ready to put on her fighting clothes and throw some blows.

"Sit down." Gun reached up and pulled her arm. He pleaded with his eyes for her to have a seat. "We don't know for sure whether Brianna was in on this. You don't know for sure if that girl was involved."

"She wouldn't come on here unless she had a way to embarrass me. I bet she's been plotting this thing since I beat her—"

"Janiyah, stop!" Gun commanded as he forced her down next to him. "This thing with you and Brianna has gone on long enough. You need to let things go and forgive her. We won't have any more issues with that girl if you just leave well enough alone."

"Well, you need to tell her to leave *me* alone! I may have been saved, but God ain't finished with me yet, and I damn sure ain't finished with *her*!" Janiyah shouted back.

Gun brought his hand to the bridge of his nose. Janiyah thought about saying something slick but decided to let Gun have his peace. She didn't want to fight Gun; she wanted to fight the person who had the gall to broadcast their intimate moments in the school.

Janiyah got up and retreated to her bedroom. There, she stepped out of her blouse and skirt and put on some pajamas. She looked around her room and saw her large, cream-colored teddy bear. She had had the bear since she was eight, and she always grabbed it and held it tight when she was in a crisis.

As she sat on the bed, she thought of her and Gun's lovemaking session and wondered: if the still pictures existed, what was the possibility that there was a video? What else did their nemesis have on them, and when would they release it?

"The room is yours, honey." Janiyah thought back on the last words Brianna had said to her. *"Please leave my purse on the counter and don't touch nothing!"*

Brianna had always been rude to her: bumping her here and there, stepping on her toes, throwing her personal items in the trash. That was the reason why Janiyah always demanded that she not only have her own dressing room, but that her door had a lock. If she couldn't get a locked door, she at least wanted security on the premises.

"She probably rushed past me because she planned on sabotaging me some kind of way," Janiyah told her teddy bear. "Probably had the whole thing planned all along."

Janiyah wished that her teddy bear was a sister-friend she could talk to. It had been a long minute since she'd hung around women on a social level. Seemed like ever since she married Gun, either every woman wanted him, or they couldn't stand her because of what she had with and without him. There were only two women she really considered friends, and neither one of them lived anywhere near her. Oz was locked up, and Grelle had moved to New York. There was no way she was about to board a plane to New York and leave Gun in this mess alone, and she wasn't scheduled for a visitation with Oz for another month.

"Only problem with this was that she had no idea that Gun and I were going to take it there," Janiyah admitted to herself. "She just took advantage of a situation."

Her reasoning seemed right to her. If she weren't saved, she'd set Brianna up in a compromising position and make sure to destroy her career in the process. She'd make sure Brianna would never work in the business again. A few pictures to the right people and violà, her Brianna problem would disappear.

Years ago, she and another model caught Brianna and one of the extras on a movie set pretending they were married in the ladies' restroom. The other model, who was waiting on the restroom, was ten seconds from reporting Brianna as she and her lover were leaving the bathroom. The other model had a problem with Brianna too, but it was Janiyah who quietly argued with the woman about letting it go. Janiyah was the one who said that they needed to be the bigger women and not seek revenge just because the opportunity existed. Janiyah was regretting that decision now. She wished she could go back in time and do it over again, this time making sure everyone on set knew what she was doing in the bathroom.

But she had vowed to be an example of God's love and mercy. She remembered being proud of resisting her *own* temptation. In the end, Janiyah decided she couldn't do to Brianna what she wouldn't want anyone to do to herself.

But had she made the wrong decision?

Chapter Twelve

"We are going to get through this," Gun promised.

Janiyah was facing him, making a Windsor knot for his black-and-green fatigue tie. She pulled the tie tight, stepped back, and looked at Gun. He was looking sharp in a dark green suit with matching vest, green button-up, and shoes. Her matching army-green suit gave them the appearance that they were dressing up for an ROTC drill. It may not be war they were about to attend, but it was definitely going to be a fight. The church board had called an emergency meeting where their very existence as church leaders was at stake.

"Yeah, we are." Janiyah gave a limp smile.

For the most part, Gun and Janiyah had received an outpouring of support. Some of the teachers understood that there was never an intention to publicly display their affection. A few felt they were liberated, and that Gun and

Janiyah had encouraged them to spice things up in their own lives. As news and other media sources picked up on their story, members of their church came out in support, saying they were doing what married couples were supposed to do—have sex and have it abundantly.

Still, there were others who called for their resignation from their ministry positions. A few of the elders thought that sex at the work place was *highly* inappropriate. Some questioned the motive for their escapade being filmed. They argued that Gun and Janiyah had intentionally shown the pictures to sensationalize and bring unwanted publicity to the church. There were a few who thought they had leaked the photos because they were exhibitionists who got off on people watching them have sex.

Then there was the outside interest. Three adult entertainment companies had offered close to a million dollars each to sign off on the distribution of the film. A few of the companies offered extra money for the negatives. One company even offered a ludicrous sum of money if they'd do another session inside the church sanctuary.

Those who weren't trying to defile their marriage bed made every intention known that they, especially Janiyah, should have resisted the urge. Talk show hosts criticized the two for being irresponsible and accused them of not having respect for themselves or other people's property. Two of Janiyah's endorsement deals were in jeopardy, and one company had already pulled their planned ads featuring her image.

Janiyah and Gun pulled up to the church and walked through the sanctuary doors. Their future with the church was hanging by a thread. They both decided to let go and let God. Whatever happened was all a part of His plan.

"It is well." A response came from an older lady.

"Mother Shirley." Gun smiled and gave her a hug. Janiyah did the same.

"Yes, my children." Mother Shirley wiped tears from her eyes as she carried her Bible in one hand and her purse in the other. She was almost six feet herself, yet she maintained a slightly slender frame. She towered over Janiyah and was closer in height to Gun. Janiyah could imagine the fear she instilled in people back in the day when she was dealing in the streets. From the first day she met her, she immediately understood why they used to call her Big Shirley back in the day. Now in her later years, mother Shirley was a peaceful soul. Her smooth, chocolate-colored skin seemed to radiate from the love she'd given.

"You need help with those?" Janiyah offered.

"That's all right, darling." Mother Shirley adjusted herself. Her purple hat was tilted slightly to the right and was home to several faux violets and orchids. The hat complemented the blouse and skirt she wore. "The two of you need all the strength and prayers you can get. Satan is in the building, and we are getting ready to do battle."

Mother Shirley was right. This ordeal with the pictures had brought out some ugliness within the church.

Janiyah and Gun followed Mother Shirley into the auditorium. They were surprised to see many teachers in attendance. The meeting was important to them. Whatever happened to Gun would set a precedent for them, and they wanted to make sure that everything was being handled fairly.

Now that the meeting was a reality, Janiyah could feel her body tense up.

"Take your place at the front of the church." Mr. Ross, one of the assistant principals of the school, escorted the two of them as they continued to receive a standing ovation from a large group in the crowd.

Janiyah fought back tears as she internalized the words of encouragement many of the women were giving to her. Of course, she heard a few of the detractors too. She stayed strong and tried to deflect the negativity. She was ready to face the crowd.

As she and Gun took their seats, she spotted Brianna and her assistant, Danyelle, as they flashed their fake smiles and applause.

Lord, please don't let the two of them start any mess, Janiyah prayed as she took her eyes off them and scanned the crowd. Janiyah wasn't naïve, and she knew that some of the people had come to see a circus. Her job was to make sure she didn't give them one.

As Gun and Janiyah took their seats, the principal of the school, Paul Kenyatta, took the podium. He looked sharp in his black suit. His bald fade was recently done, and his sideburns and goatee were sharp. His looks betrayed the fact that the man was almost fifty.

"We're here to talk about what happened and how we can prevent mishaps and personal matters from happening again." Principal Kenyatta addressed the crowd. "Normally, and what may still happen, is that any time a teacher, counselor, pastor, or administrator is caught in a compromising position, even if that is not their intent, they are removed from their position.

In some cases, their licenses are suspended. While it was obvious that the pictures were not taken on school property, we can't ignore that a few hundred students were exposed to Mr. and Mrs. Wade's private and intimate moment."

Mother Shirley stood up for Gun and Janiyah. "I say they should be allowed to apologize, and of course, Mr. Wade be allowed to be reassigned, or at least be given the opportunity to resign."

Others appeared to agree. Some of the teachers were curious if any effort would be made to find the person who had perpetrated the crime on school grounds in the first place. A few teachers mentioned encouraging Gun to find work in another church without prejudice. A few were concerned about the news and media publicity coming from this situation.

Janiyah felt helpless. All she could do was sit in front of the crowd and hear their words, even the negative ones. As well as their joint troubles—they were both in danger of losing their positions as church leaders—each had their own personal burdens to worry about. Gun had to manage and deal with the school front, and she had to face the sponsors and advertisers she dealt with. Most of them had stuck by her, but that didn't mean that they would stand with her if they were petitioned or threatened with boycotts. They remained with her after she went to jail, but now with a second scandal, they might have a change of heart. Would a sex scandal be too much for them? Janiyah had no way of knowing.

Chapter Thirteen

After dinner a few nights later, Janiyah decided she needed to step out. Specifically, she needed to catch up with Brianna.

With the help of a few well-placed phone calls and a bribe or two, Janiyah tracked Brianna to a local art studio off Battleground Road, near the Friendly Avenue intersection. The late hours didn't bother her, as plenty of people walked the sidewalks visiting bars, walking their dogs, or attending art openings at the small, local art galleries. Janiyah had almost forgotten how lively Battleground Road could be, and the smell of fruity-flavored hookahs and synthetic cannabis gave the air a distinct smell.

Janiyah waited patiently at the crosswalk for all the pedestrians to finish navigating the streets and holding conversations that brought traffic to a halt. She was surprised that the traffic and the hustle and bustle of West Greensboro calmed her.

The building she had sought was an older brick building painted white that had a mural of a young black girl blowing dandelion seeds in the air while holding the hand of a young, blonde-haired girl. Janiyah pulled up behind the building and was glad she did not have to fight for parking. She parked in one of the spaces behind the building then entered through a back door and walked up the stairs.

The stairs moaned as she ascended, announcing her arrival. Janiyah needed to gather her composure. She wasn't nervous, but she definitely felt in her spirit that she needed to be cautious with her words. The last thing she wanted was another physical confrontation. Janiyah and Gun were still waiting to find out their future with the church, and she didn't want to give the board any reason to press for their removal.

The studio was open, and Brianna was posing against a green screen. Judging by the bathing suit that Brianna had on, Janiyah concluded that Brianna was doing some sort of summer catalog for a plus-size clothing store or label.

I wonder if this is the Catherine's ad we were both going out for, Janiyah asked herself as she stepped into the studio. A part of her didn't think this would be the spread for a major chain, but with the way graphic designers could manipulate backgrounds with Photoshop, she wouldn't rule it out.

"You came to see me, Janiyah?" Brianna was loud as she reached for a towel that one of the production assistants handed her to wrap around her body.

"Something like that." Janiyah chose to keep her tact. She didn't want to cause any drama with Brianna, but she did need to level with the woman and find out what was going on.

"Well, come have a seat," Brianna offered. She moved her purse and overnight bag off the extra chair. Brianna put her belongings in one of the rooms that was being used as a dressing room and re-entered the studio. "I wish Danyelle was here. I'd have her do all this random stuff for me."

Janiyah had to give Brianna her due; very few plus-sized models had assistants, and Brianna did enough business to pay Danyelle good money to keep her around. Janiyah missed the days of having an assistant. She could have really used one now to help with the church endeavors and for her modeling, too. Janiyah was sure that the iPhone in her pocket was tired of doing the work of three or four people, but that was why she paid good money for it.

In the background, the horns and haunting keys from "Drip Drop" began to infiltrate her ears. Janiyah recognized the track from one of her guilty pleasures, and current favorite television show, *Empire*. Remembering the task at hand, she resisted the temptation to nod her head.

"I'll get to the point," Janiyah started as she and Brianna worked their way inside their chairs. "Why did you come and vote at our church meeting? And how did you know about it?"

Brianna sighed. "Listen, listen, listen. I came out of support. Regardless of how I feel about you, I wouldn't want Gun to lose his day job."

Janiyah sucked her teeth. She didn't want to give Brianna any fuel to light her fire. "You and Danyelle voted for me, but you know your votes don't count. You have to be members of—"

"Town Mountain Baptist Church. I know." Brianna waved her hand as if to dismiss Janiyah's thoughts. "Danyelle and I have been members of the church for over a year now. We usually attend Bedside Baptist or order the recording of the sermon so that we listen to the Word while we're on the road, but when we're in town, we usually go to Town Mountain or this smaller non-denominational church Danyelle found in Arden."

She's a member of our church? Janiyah wanted to explore the idea further but chose not to. *How come I didn't know about it? Should I overlook the fact that she seemed to have joined around the same time Gun began attending there?*

Suddenly, the fact that she *didn't* know made her feel a twinge of guilt. Who else was at the church that she wasn't aware of? As she saw how quickly the production assistants and the photographer were moving things around, Janiyah knew she'd have to get to the point of this visit fast.

"Well, I'm glad to know that you and Danyelle are an active part of our church family," Janiyah responded in her attempt not to come off as rude.

Then she got serious.

"I did want to find out if you had anything to do with the pictures that were leaked at the school this past Sunday."

Brianna dramatically leaned back and put her hand up to her chest, as if to clutch her pearls. Then she shook her head and pointed her finger at Janiyah. "I knew you were going to ask that."

"So did you or not?" Janiyah got to point.

"No." The pitch in Brianna's voice had changed. She sounded as if Janiyah had insulted her.

"We may have our differences, but sabotage has never been my way to get things done."

That's a lie. Janiyah thought back to when she and Gun were first dating and how Brianna did everything but throw herself naked on the kitchen table to get him. Brianna was waiting naked for him on their sofa a few weeks after they got married.

"I only ask because you were one of the few people who knew that my husband and I stepped into the dressing room, and while things didn't turn out as planned . . ." Janiyah stopped when she noticed the production assistant motioning for Brianna to return to the shoot.

"I know," Brianna told her. "I'd help you get revenge against Cable because between me and you, that overweight lard gives me the creeps. You know he tried to touch my butt the other day. Talking about, 'it was an accident.'" Brianna stood up, looked in the mirror, and moved some of the loose strands of her shoulder-length hair back in place. Then she reached down and grabbed a piece of her behind. "I wouldn't call grabbing my butt like this no accident, if you get what I'm saying."

Janiyah nodded her head as she watched Brianna walk back to her spot in front of the green screen. A part of her wanted to believe that

Brianna and Danyelle had nothing to do with the pictures being exposed, but a part of her felt like the only reason she brought Cable's name up was to take the shade off of her. Sure, Cable was a likely candidate because he had possession of the camera. The pictures broadcast at the church were high quality pictures that couldn't have been taken with a cell phone camera or a disposable. Some of the shots felt like the photographer was in the room with them. Even though Gun had locked the door before their festivities began, Cable did have a key to the room. Janiyah did find it odd that she and Gun were able to spend more than five minutes in the room uninterrupted.

Janiyah decided right then that while Brianna and Danyelle were not off the hook, it was a possibility that Cable could've done the deed. Yet, as she pondered that thought, Janiyah hadn't the slightest idea what she could've done to make him come after her. Even though she thought him weird, Janiyah was still nice to him.

Janiyah would need to keep an eye on both of them. Besides her and Gun, they were the only other people at the photo shoot. Cable and Brianna could've been in on this thing together. One had the tools, but the other had motive.

Janiyah was sure that the culprit was between the two of them. She just didn't know who, or why.

Chapter Fourteen

Janiyah had a lot on her mind. Who had taken the pictures and was trying to destroy her? How was she was going to keep her sponsors and advertising money? Would they be asked to leave the church? It was almost too much for her to handle, but she wasn't going to give up easily.

She was getting frustrated because Gun was keeping the investigation of who took the pictures under wraps. He and the deacons of the church made it so the investigators only spoke to them. Janiyah desperately needed an update, so she decided to snoop around Gun's office. Unfortunately, the search yielded nothing; no pictures, no reports, no interviews, no evidence. It was like the incident had never happened. But she knew it had happened. The perpetrator had shown a slide show of various intimate poses and moments. A whole school saw what had happened, and it wasn't long before everyone in the whole world knew Gun and Janiyah's

business, talking about how freaky she and her
man were.

It was as if they had traded in one myth for
another. Instead of the wholesome, handsome
couple, they were now the undercover freaks. To
say that people were reckless was an understate-
ment. A predominant adult entertainment company offered them over $1 million to shoot new
scenes so they could repackage a sex tape. A lib-
eral arts college wanted them to do a seminar for
married couples to encourage them to get their
freak on like they were Missy Elliot. More photographers and magazines requested that she
and Gun do photo shoots together.

This was just too much for Janiyah.

Janiyah arrived at her go-see early, so she
went to the bathroom to freshen her makeup.
She placed her purse on the counter. Out of
the corner of her eye, she saw Brianna leaving the next stall.

Why this chick got to be everywhere I'm at?
she thought as she lathered her hands with the
creamy, non-fragrant soap.

Brianna stood at the sink next to Janiyah.
"Look, girl . . . I know you're catching a lot of flak
for the pictures of you and Gun."

"Pictures you assured me that you had nothing
to do with," Janiyah responded. She reached

across Brianna and pulled a paper towel from the silver dispenser.

"Trust me, girl, if I wanted you, I would have been got at you." Brianna snatched her purse off the counter and threw the strap over her arm. "I actually like and respect your husband. I would never do anything to bring harm his way."

Even though her flesh felt raw, in her spirit Janiyah knew that Brianna was telling the truth. She knew that Brianna had a level of respect and an unhealthy attraction to her husband.

"Well, I do know you like my husband—" Janiyah started to respond

"Well, Janiyah, try not to be catty." Brianna was blunt and to the point.

Janiyah leaned in closer. "I'm going to try this innocent-until-proven-guilty thing with you, just so I can keep my spirit at ease and so that I can believe that you actually didn't have nothing to do with the drama I'm in now."

Brianna closed the space. "If you think that I am your biggest competition, you're wrong. You"—Brianna pointed at Janiyah, and her fingernail was inches away from her chest "are your biggest competition. I don't see you as my biggest competitor; I see myself as my biggest competitor, because what I realize is that if I don't do a better job this time than I did the last time, there will be no next time."

Janiyah hated to admit it, but what Brianna said made perfect sense. Janiyah felt every full-figured model and every female model, for that matter, was competition. Maybe she did need to change her mindset.

She never really thought about herself as her own competition. Dora, the chocolate-colored Dominican beauty, always gave her a run for her money in the hair department. She was always saying that no matter whether her hair was short or long, Dora always had the right amount of bounce to it to make her be noticed. Then there was Candace, whose perfect vanilla complexion almost allowed her to pass for white. Candace was the one who had more business than both she and Brianna put together.

The difference was that Janiyah got along with Dora and Candace. Dora had been a bridesmaid during her wedding about five years ago, and Janiyah was recently contacted by Candace to do a job with her. And more so recently, Janiyah was being called upon by other models who sometimes struggled with what they wanted to do with their community, and who some felt God was calling them to be. They'd heard about Janiyah's newfound faith and were very inspired by it.

The modeling community, though slightly catty at times, was tighter knit than the threads in a pair of jeans. Models knew photographers, who knew graphic designers, who knew agents. Opportunities to model were endless, between the burgeoning crop of authors who seemed to come out of nowhere and needed cover models, to all the independent music artists who wanted fresh, unknown models for their music videos. Web series that were posted on YouTube, Hulu, and other platforms seemed to have made plenty of overnight celebrities.

If the culprit was someone within the modeling community, they'd suffer the consequences, too. The old saying of "loose lips sink ships" held truth, as advertisers wanted and depended on confidentiality agreements to protect their ideas. If someone couldn't be trusted to keep unauthorized pictures a secret, who'd trust them with their ideas?

Janiyah gathered her composure and entered the room for her go-see. After it was over, she felt like they really liked her, and she wouldn't have been surprised to hear from them soon.

As she walked to her car, she got a call. She thought for sure it was going to be the people she had just met, offering her a job. Instead, it was a casting director informing her that they had cancelled a shoot for a major telecommunications firm. Janiyah was shocked. It would set her back a few grand and any possible residual income opportunities. Her next scheduled shoot wasn't for a few days later with an old friend in Greensboro, North Carolina, for a few books she was putting together. After that, she was still waiting to hear whether she'd be going to Atlanta for the launch of another plus-size line. So, there was really no good money coming in anytime soon.

She knew that Brianna was a strong candidate for the Atlanta job as well, but unlike Brianna, Janiyah had scandal behind her, and not the kind that Kerry Washington starred in. Janiyah figured this probably gave Brianna an advantage over her. And if she didn't settle that, she wouldn't just need to find out who snapped the pictures and shared them with the church; she'd need to find another job.

At the moment, Janiyah had no idea what that other job could be.

Chapter Fifteen

The sound of Gun opening the door and entering the bedroom caused Janiyah's eyes to pop open. She smelled the subtle hint of the Axe body spray he'd applied earlier that day as it teased the hairs in her nostrils. Using her hands to push herself up, she rose and leaned her back against the headboard. Janiyah adjusted the sheet to cover her chest. She wore her favorite matching pink-and-black Fredrick's of Hollywood lace camisole and panty set, but ever since their privacy had been invaded, even around Gun in their home, Janiyah felt underdressed.

Flashbacks to the service still clouded her mind. How ironic that her speech on being faith fully clothed as a woman of God turned into a public exposure of her unclothed curves and dimples. Everyone not only saw Janiyah and Gun in the buff, but they got a peek of their most intimate moment too.

"So, I guess I can't be called a hopeless romantic no more, huh?" Gun said.

Janiyah sensed a nervousness in his voice. She reached to her right to turn on the lamp on the dresser. As her eyes adjusted to the light, she could see that Gun only had on a pair of black Calvin Klein boxer briefs.

She smiled, not because she found his attempt at humor amusing, but because she liked the way his underwear outlined his physical attributes. They seemed to highlight the muscle lines of Gun's upper body while defining the athleticism presented below the belt.

"I know you're my hopeless romantic." Janiyah forced herself to sit up straight. True, the video showed a much rougher side of their sex life, but she knew there were many different styles to his lovemaking. Of course, she didn't care or wasn't eager to show any other sides of that to the world.

"A little spontaneity is always good," Janiyah encouraged. "I just wish that everyone didn't have a glimpse of what that looked like for us. I'm sure the women of the church think I'm a whore."

"Naw, they don't think that," Gun assured her as he sank in the bed next to her.

Janiyah couldn't decide whether she should be offended by the fact that he seemed unbothered. Their reputations and their careers were at stake. Of course she was bothered.

"We are respectable members of our church. A married couple who got caught up in the moment." Gun made his case as he moved to the edge of the bed, lifted up Janiyah's soft, pedicured feet, and gave her a massage. He'd pressed a button that seemed to have released the tension in the air. "I believe that if I were with another woman or if you were with another man, the situation would be viewed more harshly."

Janiyah felt the heat coming off Gun's body. He moved and prodded her feet, careful not to press too hard. He was warm to the touch. After working her feet over, Gun made his way up her legs and to her waist. Strangely enough, Janiyah found that when Gun wrapped his arm around her, she was able to calm down.

Release. Thank God, because that was what she needed. *Release.* She exhaled, letting her frustration go with her breath.

"But we are leaders in the church." Janiyah stressed her point. "We can't just have sex anywhere we feel like it. We should've been more respectful of the establishment and waited to make love at home."

"Would we have made it?" Gun asked. "You are a model with a criminal background now; I used to be a thug that ran the streets. We are not, nor will we ever be, your typical ministers. Nothing about our life is supposed to be typical."

Truthfully, that was what Janiyah thought. They weren't *supposed* to be "typical." Yet in all their time together, all they did was the typical stuff. Well, except when they were dating and Gun would whisk her away on a fabulous trip to an exotic location—but that didn't count. He was trying to impress her then. Once they got saved, it became typical. They got dressed and went out on dates at dine-in restaurants; they drove up to forty-five minutes to catch some of the new Christian-themed films in the movie theaters in Greenville; they shopped in Charlotte, Raleigh, or Atlanta. Aside from their inability to produce a child at the moment, they were *typical*.

"Do you think the church will ask us to resign from our positions?" Janiyah was concerned. While she never looked at her ministry as a job, nor did she receive a salary for her role, she did value what she felt she brought to the church. In the back of her mind, Janiyah was concerned with how her outreach ministry would be affected. Would the relationship with the community organizations that worked with the church change?

Janiyah's mind clouded with visions of how the church would change without her outreach to the youth. She didn't want that to become a reality.

"At least now, if we eventually become counselors for couple's therapy, we have proof that we have and enjoy an active sex life," Gun replied.

Janiyah slapped him on his bare chest. The impact made him tense up a little. "That is not funny, Mr. Wade."

"It wasn't intended to be." Gun reached over and grabbed her sleeping mask and covered her eyes.

Janiyah could feel him moving around in the bed. Next, she felt a hand reaching up to throw the covers off the bed. As she felt around, Janiyah tried to figure out when Gun had time to slip the Calvin Kleins off. When he touched her, she felt the coolness of his wedding band. She liked the fact that Gun hardly ever took off the silver band that was a symbol of their lifelong commitment.

"Let's not worry about what the church thinks," Gun answered.

He positioned himself on top of her. He kissed her forehead, and all of a sudden, thoughts and opinions became foggy in her mind. She was very concerned and wanted to voice her opinion, but at the moment, Gun was making her understand his. His touches were beginning to manipulate her mind, and soon, she felt like putty under him.

Gun went about molding and shaping her, and Janiyah had no choice but to oblige. She fell into her feelings and let her worries leave her mind.

Chapter Sixteen

On a normal Wednesday, the only thing Janiyah would have on her mind would be noon day prayer, after-school programming, and Bible study. Most Wednesdays were almost treated like Sundays in the Wade household. Jesus and the agenda of the church came first. Town Mountain Baptist Church would sponsor a breakfast for the veterans that were staying in housing funded by the local Veterans Affairs office. Some of the church leaders participated in community outreach and civic-based meetings that put the church in the forefront of community affairs.

On a normal Wednesday, Janiyah wouldn't be posing in front of the camera. There were exceptions, and this Wednesday was one of them. The night before, Janiyah had gotten a call from an old friend confirming that she still wanted Janiyah to be the model for a three-book series featuring a plus-size heroine who was a highly sought after attorney. The author, Donya Mecklenburg, had worked with Janiyah at the local supermarket back when Janiyah was trying to establish herself. They were both struggling and had moved in together to help each other out. They shared a house with two other girls for about a year. Janiyah tried to change the day of the shoot, but Donya only had the photographer for one day and didn't have the money to reschedule. Janiyah understood and had agreed to help her friend.

The photo shoot would be her first since the scandal and would be shot in Greensboro, North Carolina. Janiyah loved to travel to various locations to shoot, and Greensboro was a welcome break from the dangerous gossips and rumor mills of Raleigh.

Donya was a statuesque five feet nine, one hundred and fifty pound, athletically built sister who could give Serena Williams a run for her money in the shape department. Janiyah respected that Donya was on one end of the full-figured spectrum, and she proudly represented the other. She knew that Donya valued all her brands and the people around her who worked hard to make sure that she could live her dream as a full-time author.

When Janiyah arrived at Battleground Avenue, traffic was heavy heading east toward downtown, as well as heading west toward some of the shopping centers and residential areas. She found the photography studio near the railroad tracks that served as a boundary for an older shopping center.

Janiyah hadn't parked her car and gotten out of the driver's seat before she could hear Donya yell, "Hey, Willow!" from across the parking lot. Only her friend was allowed to do that and not make it seem ghetto.

"Hey, girl," the young white lady with a deep, husky voice replied. Janiyah thought it was Winnie from the *Wonder Years* who greeted her back. Willow looked like she took her dressing inspiration from Marcia Brady from *The Brady Bunch*. Her long, brown hair, parted in the middle of her head, flowed like waterfalls past her shoulders. A big, synthetic dandelion sat on her right ear. Her one-piece green corduroy dress made her look like an oversized Girl Scout.

Janiyah sat in her car and watched as the two ladies greeted each other. As Donya hugged Willow, she spotted Janiyah. She released Willow from her embrace and waved at Janiyah.

Janiyah exited her car and Donya walked up. "It's so good to see you, sister girl." Donya hugged Janiyah.

"It's good to see you too," Janiyah replied.

"Where is that handsome husband of yours?" Donya asked.

"Hidden in the same place you stashed yours," Janiyah answered. "Probably at the church, meeting with some of the elders who are advising us on how to handle our scandal."

"Girl, I'm sorry to hear that."

They walked toward the studio as Willow followed behind them.

"I know what you mean by scandal. The way people look at me and my wife, you'd think we were on an episode of *How to Get Away with Murder*," Willow chimed in.

"If only I could," Janiyah joked.

Donya led them to a small room decorated with a psychedelic blend of blues, greens, and yellows. There was a definite Seventies theme happening. "Aurora worked with an interior decorator for a month to get this room ready for the shoot. It's supposed to resemble an old ice cream shop."

Janiyah looked around, and she could see the electric counters and the old jukebox, which not only worked but was playing Al Green's "Tired of Being Alone." The place had a youthful feel, complete with a giant disco ball in the center of the ceiling. The clothes that Willow continued to bring in the room seemed to make the whole decade come alive.

"You were always a Seventies freak," Janiyah pointed out as she rummaged through the outfits, pleased to find that many of the offerings were in her size or were close to it.

"I don't know what it is with me and this decade," Donya confessed. She too was looking for outfits. "But to me, it seems to bring about an innocence."

"No, let's keep it one hundred," Janiyah cut in. "You have always had a crush on what Michael Jackson looked like back then."

"That too." Donya chuckled.

After sharing their inside joke, Janiyah noticed two men walking in. They wore huge Afros, but that's where their similarities ended. The lighter-skinned one had on a pencil-thin, peach striped polyester button-up shirt with matching peach-colored bell bottoms. The dark one had on a black leather jacket with a teal shirt underneath, with black jeans and some combat boots. He looked like he'd just left a meeting with the Black Panther Party.

"Janiyah, I want you to meet the two models you'll be working with for this shoot." Donya made her way to the two gentlemen. "This is H. Keem Johson." Donya nudged the lighter one to move up. "He's the author of the *F Them Thots* series that stays on the bestsellers lists, and my writing partner."

"Nice to meet you," H. said. He took Janiyah's hand and kissed it.

"And this stern gentleman over here is Wanya." Donya motioned for him to move up. "He's the owner of the popular restaurant, Jamaica."

Janiyah smiled. She loved going to Jamaica whenever she got the chance. "What do I have to do to get you to open a location in Raleigh?"

"I haven't thought about it." Wanya's voice was surprisingly deep. "I haven't been to Raleigh before. We'll have to talk about it once the shoot ends."

Janiyah looked at the men again. Being around fine specimens that were as exotic as these two was sure to tempt any woman to leave her marriage and commit adultery for a little bit. H.'s Asian features competed fiercely with his African undertones. If it weren't for his name, one would have no idea he was multicultural. And Wanya's tight, compact body had muscles rippling in all the right places. She could tell by the way his jacket hung off him and the way his pants fit that his middle name had to be Trouble.

Donya handed Janiyah a blue dress, some light blue knee-high socks, and some blue platforms. "You'll find an Afro wig in the dressing room," Donya instructed. "Also, Willow will be assisting you in selecting accessories to bring this look to life."

"This'll be fun," Janiyah responded.

"Janiyah, I think this would look good on you." Willow held up a beaded, extra-long necklace that had violets glued to it. "It will match the violet that we'll place in the 'fro and bring out the light shades of purple and yellow that are going to be in the other accessories we'll match you with."

Janiyah reached for the wig that was hanging on the coat rack. She touched the violet and was surprised at how real it felt. She smiled as she felt she could relax and get into the spirit of playfulness and fun that Donya was trying to fit with the cover.

"I wish you'd let me read the series first before I shot the cover," Janiyah commented as she put the Afro back on the coat hanger.

"Now, you know I can't do that," Donya commented.

Janiyah began to take off her sweater and put on the blue dress. She pulled down and stepped out of her blue jeans and made sure the hem of the dress sat comfortably between her hip and her thighs.

"Are you still worried about the issue with your church?" Donya asked as she handed Janiyah the blue tube socks.

"No," Janiyah answered. She took off her shoes and socks and put on the tube socks. "God wants us at Town Mountain Baptist for a reason. I truly believe we are not done with our mission there."

"I felt that too." Donya placed the platforms on the floor so that Janiyah could step into them. "In these last days, Satan will always be busy, and he will always use things and people to keep us from focusing on our assignment, which is to put God first and to spread the word that He loves us."

Janiyah stepped into her platforms and made sure they fit securely and snug. She then walked around in them for a few paces. Janiyah was surprised at how comfortable she felt in the shoes. Janiyah walked back to the mirror and had a seat in the chair. Donya handed her the Afro wig, and Janiyah fixed it on her head, rearranging the violet so that it bloomed right over her ear.

"You're right," Janiyah stated as she reached for her purse and pulled out a brush and some foundation. As she beat her face, she replied,

"We are supposed to go out into the world and share the gospel, and if I can't do that with the church I'm with now, then I don't need to be there."

Janiyah spent the next few minutes chatting with Donya and applying shades of purple to her eyes, her cheekbones, and her lips. When she was done, she sparkled like the disco ball she soon would be sitting under. Once she finished her final look, she could hear the LaBelles crooning over a hard disco track. Patti's voice soared, and Janiyah could feel herself getting hype.

"I'm ready." Janiyah looked in the mirror one last time. For a brief moment, she could picture her mother wearing the exact same gear she had on, and she left with a smile on her face.

Chapter Seventeen

Gun and Janiyah walked into the church, arm in arm, to face the music. Together.

Janiyah was still feeling a buzz from her groovy Seventies-themed photo shoot, and she couldn't wait to see the book covers that she, H., and Wanya would grace. Donya offered Janiyah the Afro wig, and Janiyah gladly accepted the gift. She loved it so much that she was still wearing it, and she had gotten quite a few compliments from those who'd seen her when she arrived back in Raleigh an hour earlier.

The black leather trench coat and her black knee-high boots made Janiyah feel as if she belonged in En Vogue's "Free Your Mind" video. Ironically, she'd hoped that the members of her church were as free as she'd known many of them to be. She prayed that her indiscretion wouldn't cost her the position she'd grown to love in youth outreach at the church. She loved working with the young ladies and helping them see the beauty inside themselves and helping them overcome the obsession with dressing for the approval of others. Under her trench coat, Janiyah felt like she was trembling and moving back and forth worse than a broken church fan.

Gun looked like a boss in his sharp, double-breasted suit with a vest and a silk black tie to go with his white shirt. His Johnston & Murphy shoes continued at a steady pace as he and Janiyah greeted members of the church who were wishing them the best and encouraging them to stay prayed up in Christ.

Gun and Janiyah made it into the church, and they could feel the cool breeze. The smell of fried chicken tantalized their noses. Janiyah could picture the kitchen committee seasoning flour and making cornbread. She could smell the Applegate natural turkey bacon tempting her to come grab a piece, and the greens that were cooked in smoked turkey wings were Gun's favorite.

"I guess there is going to be a celebration of some sort after the vote is revealed." Gun smiled and flashed his heavenly white teeth.

Janiyah forced a smile. "I'm praying this is a church unification party and not our going away party."

Gun wrapped his arm around her waist and brought Janiyah closer to him. The smell of his cologne comforted her, and Janiyah felt that Gun was the protector she'd always known him to be.

"I believe we'll be fine," he said.

"I want to know who took the pictures and who embarrassed us at this church like that. I mean really," Janiyah started to complain as Brianna and Danyelle caught her eye.

"We will worry about that at another time." Gun pressed forward as he opened the door to the sanctuary and ushered Janiyah inside. "Right now, we still have a church to serve, and the last thing we have to worry 'bout is what Satan is up to." Gun turned to face her. "What I know is that God is in control now, and He'll continue to be in control of this Body of Christ whether we are part of it or not."

Janiyah continued her brave face as she walked toward the front of the church. The first pews were reserved for her, Gun, and members of the church board.

Once they were seated, a calm came before the church. One of the deacons led the deacon board and the trustees into the church from the adjoining room next to the sanctuary. He flashed a smile at Janiyah and Gun, and Janiyah returned a smile. As the deacon board and trustees were coming in, Mother Shirley led the elders of the church that were coming into the sanctuary. As the elders were seated and surrounded them, Mother Shirley took a seat next to Janiyah.

"You look really nice," Mother Shirley complimented as she gave Janiyah a hug. "No matter what, keep your head up."

"Thank you," Janiyah replied as the comforting words put her spirit at ease. If anyone made the process comfortable, it was Mother Shirley. Either way, Janiyah was thinking of a way to pay her back for her kindness.

The head of the deacon board stood in front of the congregation. "I'm not going to draw this out. This church has had some unwanted attention lately. There have been many spirited discussions. We are a family here. We do not turn our backs on anyone. With that being said, it is the board's recommendation that Gun and Janiyah stay with the congregation."

A sigh of relief left Janiyah's lips. Celebration could be heard. Many of her church family members reached out for hugs. Gun leaned over and gave her a kiss, and Mother Shirley hugged her tight.

"I knew God's will would be done," Mother Shirley said, rejoicing when she let Janiyah go.

"Yes." Janiyah felt the weight of the world lift off her shoulders. "His will is being done."

Out of the corner of her eye, Janiyah could see Brianna and Danyelle standing up and leaving. She didn't care.

"Let's go talk to the people." Gun got up and extended his hand to help Janiyah up. They walked to the podium, hand in hand, and the cheers only seemed to get louder. Once they reached the podium, Gun lifted his and Janiyah's joined hands, and pandemonium seemed to overtake the church. Janiyah could hear members of the congregation praising God and openly blessing them to continue in leadership. She could hear many say "congratulations" and "amen."

Gun took a step forward, letting Janiyah's hand go.

"Good evening, church." Gun's words silenced the congregation. "First, we want to thank all of you for your prayers, your love, and your support. Next, we want to say we love you. We love you, and we want to move forward with you to keep Town Mountain Baptist Church in God's will and to do the work He wants us to do. And with that, we say again, thank you all."

Gun extended his hand for Janiyah's again, and they walked side by side as they left the pulpit.

*****

Janiyah took a bite of chicken and immediately, she felt comforted. Southern cooking did the trick, and as she took the next bite, she didn't feel guilty about being a big girl, or that she had an abundance of food on her plate. After the ordeal they had just been through, she deserved to enjoy herself a little.

"I told you everything was going to work out all right," Mother Shirley said as she took a seat next to them.

"I believe you," Janiyah replied and exhaled. "Now, if I can find out who took the pictures and why they wanted to expose us and what's going on with the alleged videos and stuff. . . ."

"What you will find is that your mind is not to wander off and worry about those trivial things." Mother Shirley was firm. "God is in control. Let Him deal with the evil-doers. Contrary to popular belief, you cannot fight all the battles yourself."

Janiyah nodded her head. She tasted the potato salad and agreed with the others who said it was good. She made a mental note to herself to get the recipe from the kitchen committee once the festivities were over.

"Hey, Janiyah." Brianna had walked to their table. Gun and Brianna exchanged hugs. Janiyah and Brianna exchanged head nods.

"Good evening, Brianna." Janiyah was cordial in her response. She put her fork down so that Brianna would not see her eating.

"I just wanted to congratulate you in continuing your ministry here." Brianna addressed both of them.

"Thank you," Janiyah replied.

"Danyelle went home sick, but I did want to let you know that we voted for you and that we trust you will continue to take the church to new heights," Brianna told them as she looked around and waved at another parishioner.

"We thank you for the support," Gun said as he got up and gave her a hug. "Y'all come to church this Sunday. I'm sure we'll hear a message that will keep us moving forward."

"Thanks."

Brianna went on her way, and soon, another member of the congregation was congratulating and assuring them that they had their vote. A part of Janiyah wanted to know who had voted against them or who was indifferent, but another part of Janiyah accepted the fact that not everyone was going to like them. She was put in the position to praise God and inspire young girls. God did not put Gun and Janiyah in their positions to be liked by everyone or to be the most popular.

Janiyah was glad that she wouldn't have to worry about their ability to remain in the church, but the vote didn't answer two important questions: Who took the pictures of them, and what did they want from Gun and Janiyah?

Chapter Eighteen

The iPhone danced in its spot on the nightstand as Bando Jonez asked if anyone had had any good sex lately. Janiyah reached over and halted the alarm. She decided not to entertain the thought as she hopped out of bed. She looked at the mirror and smiled at her reflection, and loved the way she smiled back. While Janiyah wasn't narcissistic, she did enjoy her moments of self-love, because if she didn't love herself, she couldn't expect anyone else to. Janiyah flexed her muscles and nodded her head. The low-carb diet did its job as Janiyah did a self-examination of her frame. Like a skilled nurse, she scanned for new bruises, warts, or any other blemishes.

She had lost a few pounds since the whole sex scandal blew up. In order to relieve some of the stress she was feeling, Janiyah had begun working out more than before. The trips to the gym were starting to pay off. While she was getting fit, she still kept her full frame.

The church's support for her and Gun to continue in their ministry roles had lifted a huge weight off her shoulders. She thanked God for this blessing and couldn't wait to get before another group of young women. *I've come a long way from the angry non-believer I once was.* Janiyah thought. *If only Oz could see me now.*

As she took off her nightgown and put on some gray sweats and Fila athletic shoes, Janiyah glanced at her phone. Bando Jonez started singing "Sex You," and Janiyah shook her head. She must have hit snooze before. She quickly turned the phone off and chuckled.

"Gun, your sense of humor has gotten crass lately," Janiyah spoke as she looked in the mirror.

Gun wasn't in the bed, and Janiyah knew that when she got up. She looked at the phone again. It was six-thirty in the morning. She thought about where Gun could be. Normally he would be beside her, getting dressed so they could do the morning jog together. Janiyah couldn't recall a meeting that had been rescheduled. Wherever he was, she figured it was important and that she had probably just forgotten he told her where he would be. In all the craziness of the past few weeks, it must have just slipped through the cracks.

Continuing her morning routine, Janiyah shifted through a few yoga exercises to warm up. Then she got to the nitty gritty and worked on her reps of jumping jacks, push-ups, situps, and other calisthenics that helped her maintain her curvaceously fit frame.

Janiyah's motivation wasn't just tied to modeling. She always knew she wanted to become a mother one day. The thought of having children had been on her mind a lot lately. She glanced at the small picture of a young girl who bore a strong resemblance to Gun. That reminded her of the angry baby mama that was tied to her. Gun's daughter would soon be turning ten, and Gun had not been able to see her in months. Her mother used her as a weapon against Gun. He loved his daughter and would do anything for her, and his baby mama knew that. Gun had been giving her money for his daughter since the day she was born.

The mistake he made was that he always gave her cash. Since quitting the drug business, Gun's cash flow was not what it used to be, and he wasn't giving her as much as she was used to. Out of spite, she took him to court and claimed to have never received any money from him in years. The courts ruled in the mother's favor when he was unable to provide proof of payments, and he was now eight thousand dollars in arrears for child support.

Quiet as it was kept, it took some begging and some pleading to get the judge not to throw Gun in jail and instead set up back payments for child support. Gun had fathered two children during his time in gangs. He had his daughter that was turning ten soon, and another child that would have been turning eight had he not died within a year of his birth.

Janiyah often wondered if Gun's drama with his daughter's mother made him apprehensive to want to have children with her. Gun had assured her that it didn't.

Janiyah began to slow down her workout and headed to the kitchen. Ten minutes was enough time to warm up and get her heart racing. Not knowing where Gun was or how soon he'd be back, Janiyah wanted to welcome Gun back to their home with a home-cooked meal.

Keyshia Cole's "She" interrupted her.

"Aw, hell no," she cursed to herself as she scooped up her phone and saw TANISHA FRESH come across the screen. Janiyah shook her head. She couldn't *stand* Gun's baby mama. Broad wasn't anything but a troublemaker, and she knew that whatever it was she had to say would just be the cause of some mess.

Tanisha took great pleasure in running Janiyah and Gun up the wall, from forcing them to buy extra stuff for Nia, to attempting to violate their marriage by demanding Gun have sex with her in order to see his daughter. Tanisha knew exactly which buttons to push.

"Hi, Tanisha," Janiyah greeted. She tried to be nice—stay nice—because she wanted Gun to see his child without any mess.

"When am I gonna get some?" Tanisha asked as she made smacking noises on the phone.

"What are you eating?" Janiyah was annoyed. She usually ate after she took a shower from doing her workout—and because of Tanisha, she wasn't finished yet.

"Don't change the subject. I want Gun and a few of his homeboys to come and see me. I need to remind him why it was a mistake marrying you, and what we could have if he married me."

Here we go! Janiyah thought to herself. She put the phone on speaker and set it back on the nightstand.

"If I were to agree to some foolishness like that, who is going to watch Nia?" Janiyah decided to entertain herself with the nonsense to kill a little bit of time. She needed a good laugh anyway.

"I'll get my mom to watch her." Tanisha came up with a solution to her dilemma.

Janiyah shook her head as she headed toward her closet to pick out a suit to wear. She didn't have any major plans today, but she liked to be prepared in case she got called in for a modeling job, or if an emergency required her to be at the church or the hospital for one of their members.

"You know Nia gets bored over there," Janiyah complained as she decided on an outfit and grabbed her phone off the dresser. She took the phone off speaker and held the device to her ear. "Why would you even put that little girl in that situation? Real talk, Gun's mom and his brothers are coming from Goldsboro, and they planned on taking us out to eat. Maybe I'll have us all come by after dinner."

Tanisha smacked her lips. A slick grin came across Janiyah's face because Tanisha knew better than to mess with Gun's mom. Janiyah grabbed some light weights that were on the floor next to the dresser. She hated putting them there, but that was the only way she could remember to take them with her on her jogs.

"Can't that witch come another day?" Tanisha replied, frustrated. "Don't nobody got time for her and the rainbow coalition today."

"Why you gotta be mean and talk about Gun's family like that? You knew Gun's family was coming up to visit with us today. We will have to entertain your conniving ways another day." Janiyah's patience was running thin with Tanisha. She was pushing another button by talking about her in-laws.

"Girl, don't get slick," Tanisha quipped with attitude. "And believe me, Gun loves to be entertained by me."

"Tanisha, I hope you aren't calling to ask for any money outside of what we are already paying through the court." Janiyah was annoyed as she walked out of the bedroom into the bathroom. She looked on the shelf and grabbed a clean wash rag so she could rid herself of the sweat that was forming on her forehead. "Shoot," Janiyah vented as she realized she'd have to walk to the other side of their home to get the towels she'd left in the dryer and fold them.

"I have a good reason this time," Tanisha defended. "You know Nia got sick two weeks ago. I had to call out and didn't have any sick time left, so my check was short and now I don't have enough for my rent."

Lies, all lies, Janiyah thought but decided against calling Tanisha on it. She reached into the dryer to grab a rag, went to the other bedroom that she and Gun used as an office, and wiped her face off in the bathroom in there.

Janiyah was pleased that the bathroom still smelled like the multi-purpose cleaner and bleach she'd used to clean it the night before.

"Look, can I call you after Gun comes home?" Janiyah turned off the water. "That way you can talk to him before we have to meet his mom."

"Fine," Tanisha conceded. "Gun and I will be hooking up in another day or so—believe that. And I'm gonna have another one of his babies."

"Bye, Tanisha." Janiyah had had enough and pressed the END button on the phone. Janiyah rinsed the towel and picked up the bathroom cleaner off the floor, sprayed some in the sink, and put it back on the floor under the basin.

As Janiyah walked out of the bathroom, she saw that the front door had been left open.

"What in the world?" Janiyah said to herself because she knew something was up. The door had been closed when she walked from one end of their home to the other.

"Move and I'll blow your fucking brains out!" a voice commanded.

Janiyah lifted her hands. She could feel the cold steel at the back of her dome and knew she was in a bad situation.

"Walk back to your room and empty the safe," the voice commanded.

Janiyah wanted to ask how the intruder knew about the safe but decided against it. She moved forward with her hands still in the air. She knew that Gun still kept his piece of steel under the head of the bed, and the safe that her assailant referenced was in the closet at the foot of the bed. There was no way she could stop and grab a weapon without risking death.

Even if Janiyah could reach the gun, she had always been scared to touch it and wouldn't know how to operate it if her life depended on it.

Janiyah just wanted to see Gun, and her heart raced in fifteen different directions of worry about where he was and if he was still alive. She felt in her heart that he was, but that didn't stop her from wanting to be sure. There was less than two grand in the safe—rainy day money that she and Gun added to little by little. Janiyah and Gun were hoping to use the money to finance the week-long church conference they were planning to attend in the next month. They had also planned on being caught up with Gun's child support for Nia by then as well. Cash flow was not the same since Gun stopped dealing. He had a good payday on his last shipment, but they had used that money to pay off the house. They figured by paying off the house, they were guaranteed to always have a roof over their heads. Between her modeling career and him working at the school, they weren't struggling financially, even though they didn't have as much cash on hand as they were used to.

When she got to the closet, Janiyah knelt down and quickly put in Nia's birthdate and removed the paper. "This is all we got." Janiyah spoke the truth as she turned around and faced her assailant.

For the first time, she stared the barrel of his Glock down and shook her head. Janiyah glared at the partially masked man. He only had a handkerchief covering the lower half of his face. She immediately realized that the handkerchief he had on was exactly like the one Gun would custom order for his worker boys back when he was dealing. She remembered Gun telling her how he used to tell them to always hide their identities and how he taught them about getting down the "ski-mask way."

"Tell Gun congratulations—and I got something for him too." The man smacked Janiyah as hard as he could with his gun, knocking her out.

Chapter Nineteen

Janiyah lifted her hand and felt the knot growing on the back of her head where she'd been struck. She couldn't tell if it was bleeding, but she was definitely mad that it had started to hurt. She focused in on her surroundings and realized she was in the backseat of a car. She was surprised that she wasn't bound and gagged. Janiyah had no idea how long her lights had been knocked out, but she knew she'd been gone for a good minute.

Even more shocking, Janiyah's assailant had left a visual for her to see. He had removed the handkerchief covering his face. Her captor's skin was the perfect blend of milk and coffee. His tapered fade was fresh, and the strong smell of astringent invaded her nose every time she inhaled. He didn't look like he could walk out with a 12-pack of beer even if he had the proper ID.

"I'm driving; you're quiet," he commanded.

Janiyah was about to give him a piece of her mind, but the sharp glare from his dark brown eyes advised against it. The man had a full nose, much like the Sphinx. His thin lips would disappear when he pressed them together. His goatee was sharp and pencil-thin.

Where is Gun? she wondered. *God, let him be safe,* Janiyah silently prayed as she watched the driver navigate traffic on the busy Airport Road. He effortlessly guided the black Lincoln Continental on I-40 West, heading toward Winston-Salem.

Janiyah wondered if her kidnapping, if she could call it that, was directly related to the pictures and videos. What old scores did she or Gun need to settle?

As far as she knew, all of Gun's gang ties and street affairs were dealt with before he walked away from it all. He had reassured her that he had taken care of any loose ends and it was all behind him. If Gun was dead, she wouldn't be breathing right now. Right? They wouldn't have a need for her if they'd already killed him. Janiyah tried to reason with herself.

Her captor was focused on the road and didn't seem too threatening toward her now. Janiyah said a prayer in hopes that everything would turn out all right. She kept praying to God that her and her husband would both make it out alive.

Who is this and what do they want?

Her answers seemed to lie ahead, as her captor pulled into the Comfort Inn parking lot. Something about this didn't seem right, and her senses were heightened. As she looked down, she saw goosebumps on her arms.

After her captor pulled up to one of the rooms, he put the car in park. He reached into his button-up shirt and pulled out a plastic card that had an advertisement for Domino's Pizza on the front. "Go to room 232."

Janiyah exhaled, knowing that she had no choice but to do what he said. What if Gun was in room 232, and what if she had to save him? She gripped the card tightly in her hand and exited the car. Janiyah looked around and noticed that aside from a few cars parked at the motel and a maid at the other end of the building, the place was empty. Janiyah couldn't risk running to the gas station that was just a block over.

She walked up each step cautiously, making sure her feet were firmly planted on the slabs of concrete as she made her way up. Once she arrived at the top, she stopped. She was hoping she could find an identifying mark on the black Lincoln Continental so that she could notify the authorities. So many people in the area had black or white Lincoln Continentals. The make and model were popular for several people and firms who owned transportation services. Also, some of the well-to-do chose the model of car because it was more low-key than say a Lexus, BMW, or Benz.

She saw her captor talking on his phone and shook her head. Because the window was rolled up most of the way, she could barely see any more of the driver's face. Janiyah looked ahead and made her trek to room 232. When she got there, she put the card in the card slot and quickly lifted the card out. As the light on the card slot went from red to green, she pulled the door handle down and stepped inside.

Janiyah could hear water running and saw a pair of men's shoes placed near the foot of the bed. She could smell the preferred Jamaican cannabis, and it almost took her back to her high school days.

"I'm so glad you could make it," a voice called from the bathroom as the water was turned off.

The man had a raspy voice with a slower drawl. The voice calling from the bathroom was deeper and more authoritative. It kind of sounded like the voice that had invaded the school the day of the video.

Janiyah held her guard. All she had to protect her from her captor was the keycard that let her into the room. A part of Janiyah wanted to run, but again, she didn't know where Gun was, and she was determined not to leave the hotel room without him. "Who are you, and where is my husband?"

"Damn, you're beautiful." The man walked out of the bathroom.

Janiyah looked at this well-sculpted, six feet four, French vanilla–colored fine brother that walked toward her. The well-defined ripples in his chest told her that he worked out—a lot. The various tattoos on his chest told a story of lust and love as body parts seemed to come to life as he moved his body. The man had tattoos from the base of his neck to well below the thick white towel that draped his waist.

"Beautiful?" Janiyah got her senses together. "Who are you, and what have you done with my husband?"

"You don't remember me, ma?" the man asked as he flashed his boyish grin. He flexed his muscles as he put his hands on his hips.

"No." Janiyah caught an attitude. "The only reason you are relevant is because you have my husband. I hope you have my husband. Where is my husband?"

"Why don't you have a seat on the bed?" the man suggested as he moved closer to her.

Janiyah attempted to slap him into next week but found her right hand quickly blocked. She stared at the man but found that she was no match for his apparent brute strength. The way he blocked her wasn't forceful, but Janiyah didn't want to take the chance to find out how forceful he could be. She complied with his original request to sit on the bed.

"I'm offended that you not only don't know who I am, but that you tried to strike my pretty face." The man smirked as he dropped the towel from his waist. He leaned down toward her and their eyes locked. She could've sworn she recognized those eyes. She couldn't pinpoint from where she remembered them, though.

Janiyah couldn't help but scan the man's body, and she quickly covered her face when she realized he was completely naked. She couldn't believe this bold joker was standing before her in the same manner his mother had pushed him out of her womb. From what she could tell, the tats were all over his rump and extended down his calf and all the way down to his feet.

"Look at me," the man commanded.

"That's all right." Janiyah closed her eyes tightly.

"I said look at me!" the man commanded.

Janiyah felt her arm being yanked and her body being pulled up. She found herself leaning against this man, who exuded evil with every cell of his body. Janiyah remembered that in the Word, Satan was beautiful beyond measure. The man in front of her could give the supreme demon some competition. Or maybe he was Satan.

"What do you want?" Janiyah tried not to cry. The man still had a firm grip on her wrist, and she felt the spot where he was holding her start to hurt. His hold was tighter than a vise grip, and she could see her skin reddening under his fingers.

"I want Gun dead, but don't worry, I ain't gonna kill him without you being there to see it. And besides, I won't kill him until I get what I want first." The man flung Janiyah on the bed like a rag doll.

As she landed on the king-size bed, she looked up at the man as he was lowering his body on top of her. He wasn't so beautiful anymore.

"Please don't rape me." Janiyah winced as she attempted to push her captor away.

The man grabbed both of her arms and put them above her head. He applied all his weight to her midsection, pinning her to the bed.

"Now, why would I want to do that?" the man taunted. "I'm sure I can get you so fired up, you'll be beggin' for me to give it to you."

"Not in this lifetime." Janiyah couldn't believe her ears. "Me begging you . . . Oh, no, you got me messed up—I'm a married woman!" Janiyah let a few choice words slip. "Lord knows what diseases you got up on your nasty ass."

"I'll be as nasty as I want to be," the man whispered in her ear, "but I'm not here for sex."

"Then why are you on top of me?" Janiyah yelled, hoping she was loud enough for someone on the outside to hear her. Janiyah prayed that someone, perhaps Gun, would come to her aid. She continued to struggle to get the man off her, but she found that he was too strong.

"Because I don't want you to hurt me again," the man said as he let her go and rolled over on his side.

"Hurt you again?" Janiyah wondered what he meant by that, but she didn't care to stick around and find out. She punched him, her blow landing on his back. Before she could get another lick in, the man quickly grabbed her wrist in the same location he had gripped it earlier. Janiyah felt pain.

"Hey, don't make me hurt you now," he warned.

He got up, and Janiyah could see a name tattooed on his lower back. "Montez," she called out.

"And what if I told you I was him in the flesh?" Montez smirked as he walked toward the mirror. He looked straight at Janiyah through the reflection of the mirror. "I remember what happened the last time you and I were near a mirror." He made sure to look right at her, a sly smirk spreading across his face.

Janiyah gasped as she brought her hands over her mouth. *Montez!* she thought as she quickly hopped out of the bed and got on her feet. That's why his eyes seemed so familiar! She couldn't believe she didn't recognize her attacker. Here she was, face to face with the man that had caused her so much trouble and almost ruined her life four years ago. With all the changes her and Gun had undergone the past year, she rarely thought about that day anymore. She had come to terms with everything from that day and no longer dwelled on it.

Usually, a naked man didn't make her feel uncomfortable, as her profession put her in a position to be next to quite a few, but her history with Montez was different, and she knew for herself that this man would be just as dangerous sans clothing as he could be with clothes on.

"You're the one that tried to rape me!" Janiyah boldly accused him as she tried to make her way to the door. "I wish to God you would've been caught that day."

Montez was swift like a panther, and with ease, he blocked the door, preventing her exit. "You're not getting out that easy, bitch, and if you keep making moves when I'm telling you to sit your ass down, you won't ever see your pathetic little husband again. I promise you that," Montez threatened as he reached for a towel and concealed his waist, He walked to the bed and sat down.

"I hope they throw you—" Janiyah said as she was about to try to make a run toward the bathroom, but then she remembered Montez's threat.

"Your little tongue is bad, but I promise mine might be wicked," Montez teased as he made himself comfortable on the bed. He straddled the corner like he was riding a horse. "You're beautiful, Janiyah Merrie Wilson Wade."

Janiyah watched as Montez tried to continue to seduce her. She recognized men like him. They tried everything imaginable to lure women with their looks. Montez licked his thick, succulent lips like he was LL Cool J. He flexed his muscles as if he were a body builder standing in front of a judge. His presence was powerful and could draw most people in like a magnet.

Janiyah shook out of it. She focused on Montez's eyes as she looked at him. "And what do you want with my husband?"

"I want my money," Montez replied.

Janiyah took the opportunity to sit in the chair that was at the table next to the window. She was pleased when Montez got up from the bed and took a seat across from her.

"What money?" Janiyah questioned. In the back of her mind, she tried to remember what debts Gun may have had left. To her knowledge, before Gun got out of the drug game, he made sure he'd paid everyone, some even more than he owed. That was his secret to ensuring that he left the streets in the streets.

"Let's just say he owes me seventy-five thousand dollars for some Mollies that disappeared. That's the money I loaned him, and the interest." Montez was blunt as he reached across the table and put his hand under her chin.

"Montez, I can't come up with that kind of money by myself." Janiyah tried not to let the fear be revealed in her voice.

"Oh, you can come up with most of it, I'm sure." Montez smirked. "When my boy did his body snatching this morning, he found two thousand in the safe, and he relieved you of that gun you thought you still had at the head of your bed."

Janiyah cursed herself. The gun was the first thing she was going to reach for when she got home. Without it, she no longer felt safe.

"But some of the money I'd have to have him sign off on before it's withdrawn from the account," Janiyah told him.

"I'll let Gun go for two hours next Friday so y'all can go to the bank or whatever, so make your arrangements wisely beforehand. Whatever the two of you don't come up with, I'll have to sell you to the highest bidder in Venezuela to get that dough after I kill your husband."

Janiyah felt her soul jolt. She knew this man was serious. They said that before Satan got thrown out of Heaven, he was the most beautiful creature on earth. Montez had to be his earthly representative while Satan reigned in hell.

Now that she'd said his name, she remembered Gun telling her about him. Gun and Montez had partnered up on a deal. Something went wrong with the shipment, and the deal fell through. Montez had been rivals with Gun ever since. Montez was adamant that Gun was to blame for what had happened, and he refused to let it go. He was sneaky and ruthless, and Janiyah knew that Montez had the police force in his back pocket. Montez's mom was a sheriff for the county, and his father was a councilman. That was how Montez got away with all his crimes throughout the years.

Without warning, Montez grabbed Janiyah's neck and started giving it the same treatment he'd given her wrists earlier. "You'd like to have my money by six p.m. next Friday. Come to this same room with my cash, and I'll grant you his freedom and the negatives to the lovemaking session you and your husband had."

Montez let Janiyah's neck go, and Janiyah massaged it. "It was you," she strained to reply.

"My father owned the building your photo shoot took place in," Montez explained. "That's what brought Gun back on my radar. My father uses the building for many purposes and has always had security cameras placed in all of the rooms and outside the property. I saw the pictures you took, and then I saw the two of you in the dressing room. Watching the two of you did someth—"

"You're very nasty." Janiyah cut him off.

A smile appeared on Montez's face. "You're the adventurous type yourself." Montez complimented Janiyah. "I can't wait to see you again. Maybe I'll let you feel it next time, and we can make our own video."

Janiyah quickly got up and made her exit out of the hotel room. She wasn't going to let Montez feel anything if she could help it. She wondered where Montez was hiding Gun, and if he was okay. Janiyah wished she could talk to him so that she'd know for herself that he was safe. But Janiyah knew that Gun had to at least be alive if Montez was allowing her to get the funds together.

At least she hoped he was.

Chapter Twenty

It was two hours before school would start, and two days since she'd seen Montez. Janiyah had already told Principal Kenyatta that Gun had a family emergency and would not be in that morning. While it wasn't completely a lie, Janiyah hated the thought that she deceived the man just the same.

How was she going to get seventy-five thousand dollars all by herself? That was the question she had pondered over the last two days. There was sixteen thousand dollars in a joint savings account that she and Gun had established before she went to jail. Both of them contributed to the account equally. They had just discussed using the money from the account to the pay the arrears on the child support payments to Tanisha. That would leave them with seven thousand to start with when she was released.

Unknown to Gun and most people, Janiyah had her own money market account with about five thousand in it. That was where she put away a portion of her modeling money. She seldom touched the account, as she and Gun had learned to live well within their means. One of the perks of being a model was the ability to keep many of the clothes she modeled in, which was good for church because she didn't have too many pieces she couldn't wear there. Gun had suits from his past life, but Gun was the perfect size to get some of the new pieces that were left as samples from photo shoots.

The twelve thousand in cash was what she had access to at the moment. The rest was where it got tricky. A few years prior, Gun had purchased Janiyah and himself matching 2010 Honda Accords. His was an electric blue color, and hers was off-white. Both cars together could easily net them twenty-five thousand dollars, but the chances of finding a buyer for even one of the cars by Friday would be difficult at best. She probably would get less than half of that if they went to a car dealership that would give them cash for their cars. And Janiyah would need Gun to take out a loan on either car, since both cars were registered to them jointly.

Then there was their modular home and the land it sat on. Gun had initially had the house designed and built for one hundred and twenty-five thousand dollars, a year before he got the cars. The acre of land the house now sat on was bought for about thirty thousand dollars near Candler, which was a few miles from town. Gun had intended to farm vegetables and fruits, and he and Janiyah had talked about opening their own fresh market stand, but neither one of them had gotten around to getting seeds for their ill-fated garden. They did keep it mowed regularly and discussed where they were going to plant their garden. Also, there was talk of building a playground for Nia and the children they wanted to have together.

Their original plans had obviously all been put on hold when Janiyah was sent to prison. Since she'd gotten out, they hadn't had a chance to set any of them back in motion yet. The good thing was that Gun had paid off the house and the land when he retired from the drug game. The problem was that it would be practically impossible to find someone that would be able to buy the house and land in cash, and especially on such short notice. She was even willing to take half of what they had paid to get her husband back, but again, finding a buyer would be nothing short of a miracle. Also, the home and land were considered by many to be one fixture. They had been approached by a few banks to sell the property to them, but Gun had always refused. Selling the house would mean they'd have to start all over, and Gun didn't want the extravagance or the upkeep that could come with building a new house. Also, most of his neighbors owned mobile homes, so not having a modular home could possibly put him in conflict with those whom they were on speaking terms with. Janiyah considered going to the bank and asking if their offer to purchase was still available, but even if they said yes, the bank would probably take months to process all of the paperwork.

Janiyah exhaled deeply and tried to push her immediate troubles to the side. She walked to the closet and pulled out a navy blue blazer and matching skirt. She found a nice button-up, a dark blue ruffle tie, and complimentary heels that would go with the ensemble.

Janiyah walked to the bathroom and turned on the water for a shower. She disrobed, grabbed a wash cloth and a bath towel, and placed them on the counter. Janiyah found her hair bonnet on the back of the bathroom door and put it on to protect the relaxer she still had in place.

Once she stepped in the shower, she opened the canister that had some homemade lavender and vanilla body scrub she'd made. As the fragrance hit her nose, she felt herself calming and her mind being put at ease. The worry spirit was defeated and kept at bay—at least for a little while.

Chapter Twenty-one

"Your photo shoot was beautiful." Montez applauded as he followed Janiyah to a conference room in the church. The fact that he knew she had a photo shoot disturbed Janiyah.

Janiyah's heart skipped a beat. The Omaria Hampton Collection had called her at the spur of the moment to have her model some evening wear for an upcoming event. The pictures would be used for exclusive flyers and promotional materials they were making.

She turned around to face him. She could tell that his Giorgio Armani suit was custom fit to his frame. With his purple Burberry tie, VVS diamond cuff links, and Audemars Piguet watch, Janiyah was convinced that Montez had a direct connection to Beyoncé.

At first she wasn't convinced that meeting Montez in the church was a good idea, but Montez had her screwed. She either met with him in private and took the risk of him trying to rape her again, or she met him in a place where other people were around. Having them around made her feel a little safer, but then she took the risk of someone eavesdropping and gossiping about her even more. She chose the lesser of the two evils.

"Come in." Janiyah stepped aside and allowed Montez to enter the room first.

"Thank you for welcoming me." Montez was sarcastic as he plopped himself in the soft red leather chair that faced her. He comfortably lifted his right leg and crossed it over his left.

"This building isn't mine, and I have no choice but to welcome you." Janiyah took a deep breath to stop herself from saying more and making him angry enough to attack.

"I was wondering if you were ready to make a partial payment today." Montez reached into his suit pocket and pulled out a small sales receipt book. "I also wanted to give you the receipt for the two thousand I collected the other day."

"Okay, first of all . . ." Janiyah's voice was firm, like she was getting ready to tell his high and mighty tail off. "I'm sure I can speak for my husband when I say we did not *give* you two thousand dollars. You *stole* it from us. Let's make that perfectly clear."

"But Mrs. Wade—" Montez started to interject, but Janiyah quickly cut him off.

"Second, I don't have a payment to give to you today. I'm not about to give you the church's tithes and offerings to satisfy any debt we may have. That money belongs to God," Janiyah asserted. Just the thought of robbing anyone at the school or the students sent a shiver down her spine. Gun and Janiyah often donated twenty percent of their combined yearly salary back to the church to help fund its various ministries.

"I didn't ask you for the church's money." Montez forcefully leaned himself up and got in Janiyah's face. "I'm asking for *my* money that you and your husband owe me. Don't tell me you can't go to the bank and make a withdrawal."

"Yeah, tomorrow when the bank opens, I will see what I need to do. But let me tell you something." Janiyah walked around her desk and got in Montez's face. "I am not now, nor have I ever been, anyone's punk. And if you bogart your way into my house or my church ever again, I will have your ashes under your mother's office with a note that says this is what happens to misfits who threaten me."

Montez's face got red. "And how long did you rehearse that in your mind before you spit that line to me?"

"I—" Janiyah was going to say something else smart and borderline unladylike when Mother Shirley walked into the room. Janiyah quickly formed her lips into a smile as she slowly backed away from Montez.

"Good afternoon, Sis—" Montez was interrupted by Mother Shirley reaching up and grabbing a piece of Montez's ear. She twisted it and guided him out the door.

"Bye, young man," Mother Shirley said. "Janiyah and I have business for the church to attend to." Mother Shirley slammed the door behind him. Janiyah was shocked that the older lady had manhandled that brute. She made a note to herself to try that move next time.

"Mother Shirley." Janiyah tried to save face and offer her the seat Montez had been sitting in.

Mother Shirley lifted her hand up. "I knew that boy was trouble when I saw him follow you into the office. Now, outside, I arranged for some non-uniformed policemen to kindly escort him away from the building so you can work."

"You called the police?" Janiyah was shocked.

"Baby girl, have you forgotten about the life I've lived? Trust, he don't want it with me." Mother Shirley took a seat and put her purse on the desk. "Now tell me, sweetheart, what kind of trouble are you and Gun into with that man, and how much is it going to cost to get you out?"

Janiyah wanted to lie, but she couldn't. Mother Shirley was a church mentor and prayer warrior, and she truly had the gift of discernment. She'd read Janiyah like she wrote the book. "Seventy-five thousand dollars. Allegedly, Gun owes him some money for some drugs he used to sell back in the day."

Mother Shirley nodded her head. "That's some bull; I can tell you that much."

Janiyah was shocked. In the time she'd known Mother Shirley, she'd never known Mother Shirley to come close to cursing.

"Janiyah, let me let you in on some secrets. When you and Gun bring a baby into the world—and you will soon—you will develop what is known in the earthly realm as mother's intuition. I have four sons—two of whom played professional football and two of whom work for the State Bureau. I also raised half of the men on the deacon board for the church, as well as Principal Kenyatta. When he told me the story you told him about why Gun wouldn't be at service this morning, I knew something was wrong."

"I didn't lie to—" Janiyah started to defend herself.

"And I never said you did." Mother Shirley cut her off. "You probably don't know this, but I was with Gun or keeping tabs on him when he paid off several people he owed debts to when he quit the drug game. I explained to him that that was how I was able to walk away and never look back. If you wanna come out alive and not leave enemies behind, you got to suck it up and cut your losses. Gun did exactly what he was supposed to do and how he was supposed to do it. How else do you think the two of you got my blessings to be leaders in this church? I saw the action myself.

"Gun paid Montez fifty-five thousand. Fifty for the bad deal that went down for the Mollies in the Carolinas, the Virginias, and Kentucky, and he added ten percent interest. The truth is, Montez owes Gun twenty thousand dollars because Montez shorted him. Gun let the debt go because he was leaving the game for good, and he wanted a clean slate with everyone."

Janiyah was shocked that Mother Shirley not only knew Montez's name, but also knew so many details about Gun's affairs. She didn't even know as much as Mother Shirley. But she was relieved that Mother Shirley had so much knowledge and experience. She also appreciated that Mother Shirley seemed completely unfazed by what was going on and wasn't passing any judgment. The truth was Mother Shirley had nothing but love for them.

"Why does Montez need another seventy-five thousand, and why us?" Janiyah let a tear fall from her face. Her head hurt, and the last thing she wanted to do was pay money they *didn't* owe to anyone.

"Because Montez knew that Gun wasn't going to take it to the streets. But Montez doesn't know how I get down. He must not have been told about Big Shirley, otherwise he wouldn't be messing with my babies. Now, you and Gun are two of my children, and despite my age, I always take care of my own." Mother Shirley's revelation was making sense. Montez had pegged Gun as weak, and he thought that he'd be able to extort the money from them. "But don't you worry about the money. *I* will take care of it."

Janiyah stood up, and Mother Shirley rose with a quickness. "Mother Shirley, I can't let you do that. I have some of the money."

"And I have *all* of the money." Mother Shirley was firm.

Janiyah bowed her head. "Yes, ma'am."

"Now, this is what we are going to do. When are you supposed to have the money to him by?" Mother Shirley asked as she reached up and wiped a tear from Janiyah's face.

"Friday at six p.m. I'm supposed to meet him at a room at the Comfort Inn that he rented out in Burlington."

"Tell him you'll have the money on Tuesday at one p.m. He can pick it up at the church."

Janiyah didn't have an answer for that. She wanted to ask Mother Shirley how she came up with seventy-five thousand dollars, but she couldn't bring herself to ask. Janiyah prayed that Mother Shirley wasn't cashing out her retirement accounts, but she knew that whatever Mother Shirley had planned, she was going to follow through with it.

"Okay, I'll do it," Janiyah conceded.

"Good girl," Mother Shirley said as she opened the door. "Now, you go home and get you some rest. Don't think about Montez, and trust and believe that Gun is going to be okay. You are going to have to be ready to do war with Montez in a few days, and I need to make sure you're prepared."

"Mother Shirley?" Janiyah asked as she was headed out the door. "What makes you say Gun and I will bring a baby into the world soon?"

"Because you're pregnant, darling," Mother Shirley replied matter-of-factly.

"How are you certain that I'm pregnant? I haven't missed my period yet, and I have no symptoms."

"Let's just say I know you as well as I know my children." Mother Shirley smiled. "I can't wait to watch you and Gun be the model parents I know the two of you can be. Now, you just get some rest, and I'll stop by and check on you tomorrow."

Janiyah and Mother Shirley walked out of the office. Some plainclothes police officers were standing a few feet away, and a few other men from the force were standing at strategic spots down the hallway and at the doors leading to the sanctuary. Janiyah was impressed because she hadn't given a sign that she was in danger, but knowing they were ready brought her peace.

Without words, Janiyah reached into her pocketbook and took out the keys to her Honda and handed them to one of the officers. He led the way as he escorted them to their cars. The police officer took Mother Shirley to her car first, and another police officer got in the backseat of the car. Mother Shirley drove slowly, but eventually, she was out of the parking lot.

"I don't know where Gun is," the officer offered as he walked her to her car. "But I trust and believe he will come home soon."

"Me too." Janiyah gave the officer a hug. She felt like she was hugging an older brother who'd vowed to protect her.

One of the police officers opened the door and made sure Janiyah had her seat belt on before he closed it. He made himself at home in the backseat of the car and fastened his seat belt. She started her engine and headed out of the church.

When she turned down the street, she saw a white, unmarked patrol car following at a safe distance behind her. She leaned up in the rearview mirror to take a closer look, and she recognized one of Mother Shirley's sons. Janiyah realized then that God was not slack on His promise, and that He was taking care of her.

Chapter Twenty-two

When the phone rang and an audio recording of Donya Mecklenburg reading her novel *Resting in Peace* played in the background. Janiyah got excited as she rushed to pick up her phone.

"Hey, girl, how are you?" Donya sang after Janiyah hit the talk button.

"I'm good. How are you?" Janiyah asked as she lowered the sound on her television. It had been a while since she'd heard from Donya, so talking to her old friend was a welcome change of pace.

"I'm good," Donya replied. "I'm calling to ask you if you saw the pictures for the new trilogy I'm launching this fall."

"No, I haven't," Janiyah answered. She got up from the couch and headed toward her laptop. She flipped open the device. She stared at the picture that was taken a year ago that she used as wallpaper. It was a picture of Gun standing in front of the congregation, smiling.

"Here's to coming home soon," she said as she kissed her fingers and touched where Gun's face was on the screen. She went to her Internet browser and pulled up her e-mail account. "I'm clicking on the e-mail now," Janiyah spoke into the phone.

Next was a moment of silence. Donya had sent her three different emails, each holding a copy of the book covers. The first one was a solo picture of her working behind the register and getting ready to serve someone an ice cream cone. The second was of her and Wanya sitting at the back end of the ice cream store, huddled up in a conversation. The last e-mail had a picture of her dancing with Wanya and H., with the disco ball shining bright.

"Wow, Donya! These look hot." Janiyah was excited. She couldn't believe she was going to be on the cover of her friend's books.

"Yeah," Donya confirmed. "We're working on the marketing plan now because no one is coming out with an erotic suspense quite like this. We have the Seventies angle going and we have the food mystery. This is going to be a hot series."

"When do we get to go on tour?" Janiyah asked as she expanded one of the covers to take a closer look.

"As soon as you get done having that baby you got in the oven," Donya suggested.

Baby? Janiyah hadn't told anyone about what Mother Shirley had disclosed to her. She wasn't sure she believed it herself when Mother Shirley had suggested it.

"What makes you think I'm pregnant?" Janiyah asked.

"I've given birth to two boys," Donya reminded her. Janiyah had to admit to herself that it had been a while since she had seen Donya's sons. "I thought you were pregnant when you came to the photo shoot, but I didn't want to ask. For one, we had so much fun and were enjoying the music and fellowship, and two, I didn't want to ask you in front of everyone."

To Janiyah that made sense. She had heard of Wanya and H., but she didn't really know them like that. Plus, she didn't know Willow.

"What confirmed it was that I dreamt of fishes that same night, and you were the person that came to mind."

"So that dream about fishes is true?" Janiyah asked. She'd heard about an old wive's tale where if you dream of fishes, it's because someone you know is pregnant.

"Sometimes," Donya said. "But seriously, you move differently than you did when I saw you last. I just had the sense that you were. That's why I stayed so close to you, because I figured you were early, but I wanted to be sure."

"I haven't had a chance to take a test yet," Janiyah replied. "When do the books come out?"

"Hopefully January, April, and July. I'm not trying to waste no time getting this trilogy into the hands of my readers. With all I went through with the lawsuits and the starting to build a brand, I'm trying to write and drop books faster than T. Styles," Donya confided.

Janiyah nodded her head. She was a fan of T. Styles' *Pretty Kings* series and eagerly anticipated some of her other releases. The urban and street titles were one way she got to read about women who weren't like her, and she found a way to minister to those in the streets by staying on top of the popular reads.

The doorbell rang while Janiyah and Donya were discussing the *Pretty Kings* series.

"Girl, someone's at my door. I gotta go. I love the pics and can't wait to see all your success. Love you."

"Love you too, girl. Take care of that baby."

Janiyah walked to the door and was disturbed to see Tanisha Fresh standing there when she opened it. With all that was going on, the last thing she wanted to deal with was some baby mama drama. After taking a deep breath and quickly counting to ten, Janiyah let Tanisha in. She noticed that Tanisha didn't have Nia with her, and she hoped that didn't mean that Tanisha was there to try to start any mess.

"Oh, girl, this place looks nice." Tanisha was louder than an underage girl at the playground. "Nia and I should come to visit her father more often."

"How are you doing today?" Janiyah tried to be cordial. She figured that would be the best route of action to avoid conflict.

"I'm here because Montez said for me to get my money and his money." Tanisha threw her open palm out with the expectation that some cash was going to fall into it.

"Excuse me?" Janiyah had had just about enough. It was bad enough that Montez was trying to extort her, but to use Gun's baby mama to aid and abet had crossed the line.

"Bitch! Give me my money," Tanisha demanded.

Janiyah had to shake her head in order to keep from slapping the black off of Tanisha's bony frame. The nerve of her to call her out of her name in her house. Tanisha looked like the little girl from *Hey, Arnold!* and Janiyah still couldn't figure out what it was about her that had made Gun lay down with her and have a baby.

"You will get your money as soon as I get Gun," Janiyah fought back. "Did Montez tell you where he's at?"

"No, because if he did, I'd be trying to get him for myself. We need to go out on another date," Tanisha insisted as she continued to use her hands to help her communicate her points.

"Look." Janiyah decided to try reasoning with her once again. She prayed that once she'd gotten her point across, Tanisha would take a different route. "I'm giving Montez his money tomorrow. I've already called him and told him what I'd need in order for him to get his money. What I need you to do is to fall down ten or fifteen stairs so I can hand you some money too once I can get Montez's together."

"Why can't I get my money first?" Tanisha whined. "Technically y'all owed me my money before y'all owed Montez his."

"Technically," Janiyah corrected, "we really don't owe you a dime since Gun has been giving you money since Nia was born. You didn't complain all those years he was giving you two thousand dollars a month. And don't get me started on the amount of times he gave you extra because you claimed you didn't have enough to pay your rent, car note, and power bills. God knows what you were doing with the two thousand Gun was giving you that you couldn't pay your bills, considering you get help from the government too. And don't get me started on the weave money, Drake and Trey Songz concert ticket money, and the 'just because you are the baby mama' fund that I believe only Gun and I are contributing to. Do you go after your other baby daddies as hard as you come for me and Gun?"

"No, I—" Tanisha started to defend herself.

"No is right." Janiyah finished her sentence and walked toward the door. "You only come after me and Gun because aside from your other baby daddy Jeremiah, we are the only two who give you anything for the four children you have. Jeremiah and Gun should be able to split the children and put them on their taxes, but that would mess up your welfare dreams.

"Let me tell you something, and I want this to take root as you walk out of this door: All this craziness you're doing, this grandstanding, trying to make Gun out to be a bad parent when clearly he's not the one misusing the system, is making you look bad. And you make every black woman who's trying to do it with two or three jobs and no help from any baby's father look bad. You never stop to think about how the way you're acting affects not only Nia, but the other children you have. Your oldest daughter is twelve, and she's watching you and thinking this is the way to go.

"What you need to do is continue in your Work First program, spend the money Gun and Jeremiah give you on your children, and develop aspirations to move out of the projects. You'll keep more of your money, and your children will grow to love and respect you more."

Tanisha shrieked at the idea of not being able to get a word out. Last thing she wanted was for Janiyah to tell her about what she should and should not be doing. Janiyah pointed to the exit, and reluctantly, Tanisha turned to leave. Janiyah was glad that their interaction hadn't resulted in violence or arguments.

"Just know that you better have Montez's money, because I want *our* man to come home to us safely," Tanisha warned as she crossed the threshold.

"I will make sure *my* man comes back safe to me," Janiyah said as she slammed the door once Tanisha walked outside.

If Janiyah never saw Tanisha again, it would be too soon.

Chapter Twenty-three

The knock on the door had Janiyah on edge. The morning seemed to drag as she continued to lay in the bed.

"Who's at the door?" Janiyah asked herself as she placed her feet in her slippers. She grabbed the robe that was on the hanger on her door and rushed out of her room.

Janiyah wasn't used to people banging at her door at 7:45 a.m., and she prayed it wasn't the police telling her the worst. When she got to the door, she looked through the peephole and saw Mother Shirley wearing an all-black Baby Phat velour sweat suit.

I pray she is well, Janiyah said as she opened the door.

"Good morning, Janiyah." Mother Shirley greeted her with a hug.

"Is everything all right?" Janiyah guided Mother Shirley into the house.

Mother Shirley made herself comfortable on the couch. Janiyah didn't notice the tan, tattered leather bag she was carrying until she placed the ugly thing on her coffee table. Janiyah watched carefully as Mother Shirley unsnapped the bag, removed a stack of bills, and placed them on the counter.

"Seventy-five thousand dollars." Mother Shirley had a big smile on her face.

Janiyah was flabbergasted. She couldn't believe that Mother Shirley was able to get her hands on that type of money before the banks even opened. She picked up a stack of bills and then quickly dropped them like they were hot potatoes. "Mother Shirley, I appreciate what you're doing—"

"Good." Mother Shirley reached over the table and put the stack of bills back into the bag. "My son and I have thought everything out. Today and tomorrow, you'll make your runs to the banks, just like you would have on Friday. This bag of money will already be at the church. You'll meet Montez there, give him the money, we get our youth pastor back, and life will go on."

"Mother Shirley, that sounds too simple." Janiyah wasn't convinced that Mother Shirley had thought this through.

"It is simple." Mother Shirley sounded like she'd been insulted. Her mood tensed up, and she had that deep, angry look on her face that pierced Janiyah's soul. "I know you don't understand it now, but this is what I'm allowed to say. My son and his boys at the feds have been trying to catch Montez for a few years. They were hoping that they'd be able to get him for good with an attempted murder last year, but Montez's family is throwing their money around. Montez's lawyers and his mother's friends at the sheriff's office are doing everything possible to keep Montez from paying for his crimes."

"But what does this have to do with Gun being kidnapped?" Janiyah was losing patience. She didn't want to go off on Mother Shirley because she still wanted to ask how she was able to come up with seventy-five thousand dollars so fast. She'd never held onto that much money in life, yet Mother Shirley walked around with them like they were crumpled dollar bills.

"The feds want to track how Montez is spending this money," Mother Shirley answered. "When you make the exchange for Gun, all the bills that end up in the bag will have the serial numbers recorded. As he starts spending the money, we're hoping to find out how he pays for the drugs we know he's selling, how he's able to amass this wealth that he's spending, partying like a rock star.

"Montez is a trust fund baby, but he hasn't met all of the requirements to get the millions he'll inherit from his great grandfather by the time he turns thirty."

Janiyah scrunched up her face. She was confused. She didn't see how a man who already stood to gain it all would continue to live the kind of life she'd heard he lived. Men and women did anything for Montez at his beck and call. The selling of drugs and commitment to crimes was something that Janiyah just couldn't wrap her mind around.

"How do you know about all this?" Janiyah finally got the courage to ask. "About the trust funds and everything?"

Mother Shirley exhaled. She leaned back on the couch and got comfortable. "Montez's mother, Vanessa, and I used to be friends. *Real good friends.*"

"What happened?" Janiyah asked. "Do I need to get some coffee?" Janiyah got up to fix a pot. As the coffee brewed, Janiyah opened the refrigerator and pulled out the vanilla-flavored almond milk. She poured her cup half full before she yelled out, "You want sugar or cream?"

"No, I'm fine."

Janiyah kept an eye out for the pot as she got a cup for Mother Shirley. Finding one that had the church's name and logo, she rinsed it out of habit, and once the coffee got done brewing, she poured two cups.

Janiyah tried not to gasp when Mother Shirley took her cup and chugged it in one sitting. She'd never seen anyone down a cup of coffee like they were taking a shot of vodka. Janiyah slowly sipped hers.

"Well, I gave my life to Christ right before Montez and my second oldest son were born. I got tired of dealing in the streets and putting my life and my babies' lives at risk. I gave my life to Christ and found myself a Bible-based church, and I was so excited. I wanted to share my newfound wealth and love for God with my friend. Once I experienced the Holy Spirit and let Him live within me, I wanted to tell everyone. The first person I told was Vanessa.

"Being a new Christian convert, I thought she'd get it; that she would want the same experience I'd felt and that she'd want assurance of an everlasting life. So, we had lunch one day at Burger King, and I got to sharing my Bible and talking about God, but after five minutes, she stopped me. She told me that she didn't love God, and that she couldn't be friends with anyone who did."

The last sentence nearly broke Janiyah's heart. She couldn't believe that someone would disown their friend just because they believed in God. She remembered how rude she was to Oz whenever Oz tried to talk to her about the good Word. It annoyed her and she wasn't ready to hear it at the time, but she couldn't imagine not being friends with Oz just because of her beliefs.

"I'm sorry to hear that," Janiyah replied as she took another sip.

"Don't be." Mother Shirley's voice hardened. "I learned in all these years that I can't make everyone love Jesus. All I can do, despite my ministry, is to make sure I love Jesus. When we go out into this world and make disciples, we will always get told no. We put our lives on the line every time we boldly proclaim the name of Jesus. And when we do, God rewards us for doing His will."

"So, what about the money?" Janiyah was dying to know.

"What about the money?" Mother Shirley asked. "I am not now, nor will I ever be, a destitute woman. My husband was a good, honest man who made sure we had what we needed to survive. I met him in the church and he accepted and loved me despite my shady past and me having two sons already. God blessed me with a man that went above and beyond to provide for his family. I have money because I do not worship or give credence that a piece of paper is mightier than my God. I use money as a tool to take care of the Kingdom and to accomplish the few things God has asked me to do. I have always been a good steward over what is His, and that is why I have abundance.

"Before I spend a dime, I pray and I talk things through with Him. I get out of my way, and that can be a challenge. But when I submit to His will, I always do His way, and I'm telling you now, Janiyah, I was told months ago you would need this money—nothing specific in what the money would be for and how the money would be used, because I didn't know the information then, but I know the time is now, and like I said, this money can be tracked, and good will come out of this."

Janiyah felt at ease. It never occurred to her that Mother Shirley had wealth, and judging from outer appearance, she didn't seem like the type who'd manage money properly. Then again, there were people who had financial wealth who didn't want to flaunt it because they gave so much away

Mother Shirley handed Janiyah the bag, and Janiyah felt at peace.

"Tomorrow, go to the bank like you would, and make sure you get receipts for your withdrawals.

My son is going to be in the finance office, waiting for the cash you will give him, so that he can write you a check back for whatever you withdraw from your accounts. This way, you aren't walking around with a lot of cash for a long period of time. The church can lock the money up in the safe for a deposit that will be made later, and you and Gun will be able to get rid of Montez once and for all."

Janiyah felt at peace with Mother Shirley's instructions. It was as if God confirmed through her what she already knew—that everything was going to work out in her favor and that she would be all right.

Chapter Twenty-four

The cool day did nothing to soothe Janiyah's spirit. She was deeply concerned because while she didn't want to admit it, she did have some "what-ifs" that were close to the onset of fear. What if Montez tried to change the amount of money Gun owed him? What if Mother Shirley and her son's plan to give Montez money that could be traced backfired? What if after she paid Montez, he came back at them for more? What if something happened to her or Gun?

Janiya didn't want operate in fear, but it didn't mean she couldn't recognize the feeling. Yet the "what-ifs" were not strong enough to stop her from doing what she knew needed to be done. It was the only way to end the madness and return to a normal life.

She had already drained her personal account, and she now stood in front of the Fifth Third Building in downtown Raleigh, awaiting Gun's arrival. The only way for her to withdraw all the money from their joint account was for Gun to be there. It took a lot of back and forth with Montez in order for him to let Gun show up. Montez had finally agreed, but he warned that someone would be watching, and if there was any funny business, he would hunt them down.

Her phone buzzing distracted her from her thoughts. Without looking at the caller ID, Janiyah pressed the button to accept the call.

"The money is in the safe in the finance office." Janiyah was relieved to hear confirmation on the other end. "Once you and Gun arrive, the money will be placed on the bottom shelf."

Janiyah nodded her head as if he could see her. A black Lincoln Continental grabbed her attention. "Thank you."

"You're welcome, and know that we got your back, Janiyah."

The declaration brought a smile to her face.

The back door of the Lincoln Continental opened, and Gun stepped out. Janiyah wanted to scream because she had not seen her husband in days. She was excited and relieved to see that he was okay.

As Gun made his way to her, she tried to see who was driving the vehicle. She wanted to know if it was the same man who had first broken into their home.

Gun's strong arms wrapping around her and bringing her in for a hug distracted her. Janiyah noticed that Gun's usual sensual smell was not there. He had more of a stale, musty smell. It wasn't off-putting, but Janiyah missed the body spray that added that extra *umph* to his being.

"Baby, I missed you," Gun declared.

Tears fell from Janiyah's eyes. Being in her husband's arms again felt so good. With him around her, Janiyah felt whole. With Gun by her side, she felt she could face the obstacle that prevented this from being a happy reunion.

"I missed you too," Janiyah answered.

"We need to get inside," Gun commanded. "Montez is only giving us ten minutes to get this money, and then I have to do something else before I can meet you at the church."

"Okay," Janiyah answered.

She wanted to know what Montez would have him do. With Montez timing them, though, there wasn't any time to get into it. They had already lost three minutes due to their reunion.

Janiyah opened her purse and pulled out the checkbook. They walked into the bank and up to the counter. Janiyah had filled out the withdrawal slip. Gun signed his name first on the signature line, and Janiyah wrote her name next to his.

Janiyah was happy to see that no other customer was in line and they would be the next ones awaiting the tellers. The professionally dressed men and women were talking amongst themselves about Raleigh news and what they had planned on doing for the week. A young man invited the two of them to come to the counter.

Janiyah handed the man the slip.

"I need to see your IDs, please," he said.

Janiyah was relieved to see that Gun had pulled out his driver's license from his back pocket. Janiyah pulled out her wallet and slid her license from the card slot. They handed the man their licenses. The teller glanced at both IDs and then walked to the back offices. He appeared to be showing the IDs to the lead teller. Janiyah held her breath. She wondered what were they discussing.

They didn't have time for the bank to be dilly-dallying. If they didn't get out of there in ten minutes, there could be trouble. Janiyah started to pick at her fingernails and tap her foot. Her life could be ruined in mere minutes if this damn teller didn't hurry up.

Janiyah watched the head teller hand the IDs back to the young man. Soon, they were watching him withdraw money from a drawer. After the money was taken from the drawer, it was placed in a money counter that spun the bills forward real fast.

The teller placed the stack of bills in an envelope and handed it to Janiyah. She could finally breathe. Janiyah thanked the man and stuffed the envelope deep in her purse. They rushed outside and said their good-byes.

Janiyah felt a strong force pull her to the side. She relaxed when she realized she was back in Gun's arms again. "This isn't good-bye. I'll see you later."

"I love you," Janiyah declared.

"I love you too." Gun kissed her on the lips. "We'll see each other soon," he whispered.

"Yeah, we will," Janiyah said.

"I'll ask you how you got the other money once this is over."

She couldn't believe that their money was about to be gone and they were going to just hand it over to Satan with no accountability. Before she could process what had happened, the back door opened again and Gun jetted toward it. Janiyah took her phone out of her pocket and looked at the time. She had an hour to get back to the church to follow through with Mother Shirley's plans.

With that, she rushed to the car, knowing that the typically thirty-minute drive from the bank to their church would be met with rush hour traffic.

Chapter Twenty-five

As Janiyah was pulling up at the church, she could see an administrator opening the side door. She quickly parked her car, grabbed her purse, and sprinted to the entrance. She ran in her pumps as if she were wearing sneakers; part nervousness, part adrenaline.

"Janiyah, you are going to be fine." Mother Shirley tried to calm her nerves.

But it was no use. In less than thirty minutes, Montez would be in her presence. He'd collect seventy-five thousand dollars and do whatever possible to leave their lives in shambles.

"I'm ready," Janiyah promised as she crossed the threshold of her church. Once inside, she felt the spirit of the Lord. No matter what happened, Janiyah trusted that the Lord was on her side, and that she and Gun were going to be all right.

Janiyah walked to the auditorium and marched straight to the stage. Mr. Ross was waiting off to the side. Once Janiyah got to the stage, Mr. Ross stood up and pulled back the curtain. Janiyah was relieved to see the bag Mother Shirley had shown her the day before on the bottom shelf of the podium where she said it would be.

"I brought the money counter out here." Mr. Ross offered the small portable device in the chair where she sat. "I figured it would be best to do everything out in the open. We can verify the seventy-five thousand if you want."

"I trust you," she told him, putting herself at ease.

No sooner than the words left her lips, Montez let himself into the auditorium. With his suit from Burberry London, he looked like he should be leading the flock. The tie matched the suit and contrasted the light gray shirt he wore under it. His Hermès rose gold watch highlighted the rose gold setting of the diamonds in his ear.

Montez flashed his Colgate smile. "Good morning, Mrs. Wade."

Montez took a seat in the front pew. Janiyah smiled. The devil looked good today. "Good morning." Janiyah reached on the shelf in the pulpit and grabbed the bag with the money and the money counter.

"No need for that." Montez waved her off.

"Huh?" Janiyah was confused. She wanted to give the man his money and get him up out of her church.

"Let's socialize a little first," Montez suggested.

Janiyah gripped the money bag and the counter and made her way down from the stage to the front pew. "I would like to go ahead and get this counted so that Gun and I can attend the meeting that we have this evening."

"Relax." Montez tried to assure Janiyah. "Gun will enter the auditorium safe and secure. I promise."

"Well, let's get to it."

Janiyah sat down and put the money counter in front of her. She turned the counter on and made sure the amount read zero. Janiyah then opened the bag, undid the bundle of bills, and placed them on the counter. "Ten thousand," Janiyah confirmed as she handed the stack to Montez. She watched as he put the stack in his jacket pocket.

Janiyah unwrapped six more stacks and put them on the pew. When she was done, she confirmed, "Seventy thousand." Janiyah looked around and could see Mother Shirley standing at the door to the auditorium.

Janiyah unwrapped the last stack. "This should be five thousand," she told him as she placed the money on the counter. Within seconds, the money counter confirmed the amount.

"Seventy-five thousand dollars." Janiyah smiled as she passed him the last bundle. "My husband, please."

Montez pulled out a smart phone and pressed a phone number. The phone buzzed for a second before a voice greeted Montez on the phone. "The money is good. Bring Gun to the auditorium."

Janiyah faced the doors of the sanctuary, and when she heard Gun's voice, she stood up as well. Seeing him earlier had assured her that everything was going to be all right. She ran to him and they embraced. This entire episode made her realize that she was more in love with Gun than ever before. She never wanted to be apart from him again, and would do everything in her power to make sure that never happened.

"It was nice doing business with you." Montez flashed a smile and nodded to Gun and Janiyah as he stood up and made his way out of the church. His black studded loafers appeared to have smoke at the bottom as each step hit the aisle and flashed the red bottoms of his soles. The devil didn't wear Prada; he wore Christian Louboutin.

"So, Montez wins?" Janiyah questioned.

He exited the sanctuary and she took her seat at the pew.

"Not quite," Mother Shirley answered. She closed the doors to the sanctuary and made her way down the aisle. "We wait on Montez to do something stupid. He may not spend the money you handed him today, tomorrow, or even in the next year, but he will eventually spend the money, and he'll get caught from there."

"What if he puts the money in his bank account?" Gun asked.

Mother Shirley smiled. "Remember, we marked the bills. My son knows where he banks at, and there are agents at various branches waiting, just in case he does. It's highly unlikely, because Montez likes to flash and be flashy. He's been getting marked bills from his bank for some time. At the most, he'll put up twenty thousand, and that will only be to pay his lawyer. The rest he gives to his crew to spend, and he'll carry and spend some of the knots on his street gear."

"This sounds too simple," Janiyah complained. "Aren't you worried ab—"

"Janiyah, dear, what did I tell you about money?" Mother Shirley put her hand under Janiyah's chin and lifted her head.

"Money is a tool."

"Right." Mother Shirley continued to smile. "Trust me, sometimes karma has a way of handling people in ways we can't imagine. You helped me and others plant seeds, and sometimes, the job in being in God's good grace is watching the harvest manifest. If I couldn't afford to help you without expecting it back in return, I wouldn't have. Trust me, Montez will get his, and this robbery of sorts, he won't get away with. You can never spend money good if you didn't earn it. And with the way Montez is living, he will always be the type of man who will have to watch his back."

Janiyah closed her eyes. Deep down, she knew that Mother Shirley had spoken the truth. Gun was sitting next to her, and he'd be going home to her, not his baby mama. The church family still had their backs through the drama.

"Whoever digs a pit will fall into it." Janiyah heard a boisterous voice in her ear. She looked around and only saw Gun, Mother Shirley, and one of her sons in the room with her. The voice was none of theirs. Janiyah smiled. *The Lord works in mysterious ways.* Janiyah breathed a sigh of relief. Soon, she felt her stomach turn upside down and felt like her feet were in the air. She could taste the turkey sausage flatbread sandwich she'd gotten at a fast food restaurant earlier in the day come up from her throat and make its way to her lips. Janiyah jumped up and rushed to the trash can that was next to Mr. Ross's chair on the stage. Breakfast flowed freely from her lips. And that's when it hit her. She'd have no choice but to let time and God take care of Montez's life, because she would be occupied taking care of the life growing inside of her.

Janiyah was holding Gun's hand as she lay on the examination table. The nurse entered the room. "Good afternoon," she said

"Hello," Gun answered.

The nurse walked around the examination table and began preparing the ultrasound machine. "How are we feeling?" she asked Janiyah.

"Besides the fact that I have nasty heartburn every morning, I feel blessed."

"I hear you." The nurse smiled.

The nurse lifted Janiyah's shirt over her belly. "This might be cold." She pressed the ultrasound wand onto Janiyah's stomach.

All three stared at the monitor next to the table. A black and white image appeared. The nurse began pointing out the hands, feet, and head of the baby inside Janiyah's belly. Tears formed in Janiyah's eyes.

"Do you want to know the sex of the baby?" the nurse asked.

Janiyah and Gun looked at each other. No words were needed. They smiled at each other.

In unison, they said, "Yes."

"Well, it looks like you are having a healthy baby girl."

Tears of joy flowed from both Gun's and Janiyah's eyes. Gun leaned down and kissed Janiyah. "A baby girl. She'll be as perfect as her mother," he said.

Gun and Janiyah walked to their car, holding hands and staring at the printout of the ultrasound image. "A baby girl," Gun kept saying over and over.

As they got in their car, Gun's phone rang. Janiyah could only hear Gun's side of the conversation. He was doing more listening than anything. A quick *yes* here and there, but that was it. She had no idea what the call could be about. She tried to read Gun's facial expression, but he was stone-faced.

As soon as he hung up, Janiyah asked, "Who was that?"

"Mother Shirley."

"What?" Janiyah was nervous.

Gun stared expressionless for a few moments then burst into a huge smile. "They traced all of the money that Montez took from us. They have him and his drug supplier in custody."

"Oh, Gun, our nightmare is over. We are so blessed."

They leaned in and embraced each other. Janiyah felt safe and protected in Gun's arms.

They pulled out of the parking lot. Janiyah watched the world go by out the passenger's side window. She was thinking about all the trials and tribulations she had endured throughout her life and especially the last four years. She thought about how Montez had almost ruined her life. She had been through some dark storms, but she had survived it all, and she could see a rainbow on the horizon. *God is good,* she thought.

How Does It Feel?

Katt

Braylin

I really hope dude is about something, Braylin Smith thought as she got ready for her blind date with a guy she had met online. Her screen name was Honey_Dipped80. She thought it was a cute way to describe her complexion and the year that she was born. One day, out of boredom, she was browsing the web and happened on a site for BBWs and the men who love them. It was called www.BBWLOVERZ.com. It was there that she met DMAN76. They hit it off instantly, which totally surprised her. They exchanged e-mail addresses and communicated by e-mail for almost two weeks before she finally agreed to give him her phone number.

It didn't take long for him to call her, and they spent every free moment they had on the phone with each other for a week before he got the nerve to ask her out. She was a little reluctant at first, but, with actual hope in her heart, she agreed to meet him at The Lobster Palace at eight the next day. She took one final look in the mirror to smooth her hair and check her makeup, and once she was satisfied with how she looked in her Baby Phat denim cat-suit and matching stiletto boots, she grabbed her jacket and purse and headed out the door.

She arrived at The Lobster Palace precisely at eight p.m. The hostess asked if she was Braylin Smith. She was slightly taken aback, but she confirmed that she was indeed. The young girl then handed her a yellow rose and a note.

The note read: *My dearest Braylin, look down and follow the rose petals, and you shall find me. ~Donovan*

Hmm, she thought, *he's a romantic.* That was definitely a plus in her book.

So, with a seductive smile, she followed the rose petals until they stopped at a table and she looked up. One of the most handsome men she had ever seen stood, leaned forward, and they embraced.

Mmm . . . he smells so good, she thought. She had to let him go before she became more than just intrigued.

"These are for you, Braylin." Donovan handed her a bouquet of a dozen pink roses. Her favorite.

Throughout their dinner date, they had pleasant conversation, but she wasn't really thinking about his conversation skills. She liked him and knew that she wanted to take him home and have him wet the little man in the boat. For those of you who don't know, that means she wanted her clit licked thoroughly. And that night, she planned to have him do just that.

"Umm, Donovan, I want you to come home with me tonight," Bray blurted out before she meant to. But, oh well, the truth was out now.

"Damn, baby, I like that you up front with yours. No games, waiting periods, or all that other bullshit," Donovan replied, smiling like the Cheshire cat. "Hey, waitress, check please." His next action puzzled her, because then he was like, "Yo, shorty, you got da check? I'll get it back to you." She wanted to see what he was working with physically, so she paid the check, but she swore that she wouldn't ever do it again.

"Yeah, I'll get it this time, but I never pay for dates, and I never will again."

"Like I said, beautiful, I got you." He shot her a smile that wet her panties.

Once they were back at Braylin's apartment, Donovan made himself right at home.

"Hey, beautiful, do you mind if I work the stereo?" he asked.

"Sure, papi," Bray answered, thinking, *Forget the stereo, come work me.*

When Donovan slipped on Jodeci's "Freak-n-you," she knew that it was about to be on. "Oh, Donovan, how did you know to pick out my favorite song?" she cooed.

"It was just a li'l something I thought you would like. Do you?" he asked with a sparkle in his eye.

"Almost as much as I like you, Donovan," Braylin whispered as Donovan pulled her in for their first kiss. As his lips connected with hers, she could feel the passion ignite deep within her soul, and she knew that making love to him was something she needed. "Mmm . . . Donovan, damn, umm, wow." How could he leave someone who was paid to talk for a living speechless? She pulled him closer into her personal space.

"Braylin, you taste so good, girl," Donovan crooned in her ear as he began to kiss her neck and unzip her top to reveal her black lace see-through bra. "Mmm . . . see-through Vicky Secrets, my favorite."

"If you like that, just wait and see what else I have for you tonight." Braylin became bold and brazen. She normally wasn't this up front, but she definitely enjoyed the feeling. She couldn't believe that she was getting ready to make love to a man that she just met. She never did this, but everything about her was out of character tonight. Tonight, it was as if she was another woman, bold and confident, unlike her usually quiet and shy self.

Before she knew it, she was jumping up, answering the call of the dripping wet desire between her thighs, pulling her cat suit down, and stepping out of it. She stood over him, took his hand, and introduced Donovan to her love tunnel. The minute Donovan's thick middle finger nestled inside her, she felt her knees weaken. Her breathing became labored, and it felt as if he had opened the flood gates.

"Donovan, not here. Let's go to my room," she moaned in between trying to catch her breath. But before she could move toward her room, he inserted another finger, and, as if they had a mind of their own, her sugar walls locked him in. "Oh, Donovan!" She was gripping his shoulders and grinding and rotating her thick, luscious hips to match the rhythm that his fingers were creating inside her pulsating core. Her nails were digging into his back through his shirt, and they both knew that she was coming.

It seemed as if he loved the feeling more than she did, and he looked up at her and said, "Please, baby, come for me."

That was all Braylin needed to hear, because she pushed down harder on Donovan and happily complied. She was in complete bliss.

***

More than a year had gone by since that fateful night when Donovan first fulfilled all of Braylin's lustful desires. The bliss that she once felt whenever she saw him or felt his touch was fading. She still loved him, but it wasn't the same. The passion was long gone. Braylin wasn't sure how to get it back, but she was tired of trying to make a relationship work by herself. The days got longer, the nights got lonelier, and Donovan would often be nowhere near when she needed him most.

The flowers and candy and "I love you" notes became no more than a distant memory. The moment he decided that he needed to live with her full time, everything that made her fall for Donovan stopped. He waited until after he had moved in to even tell her the truth about having six kids, and then his disrespectful baby mommas were calling all hours of the day and night . . . and their conversations never had anything to do with the children. He was always getting fired from his jobs, but none of this fazed Donovan.

All Braylin could think was, *What in the hell have I gotten myself into?* She was the loving woman who believed in doing anything she could for her man. She made sure his child support was paid up so that he wouldn't end up in jail. She prayed that this would be enough to make him want to stay out of trouble, to hold down a job and do right by her, but sadly it only gave him an incentive to treat her worse.

I know he's cheating on me. She forced herself to erase him from her thoughts. His drama was the last thing that was needed on her crowded plate. Between studying for her promotion and her current workload, she had more than enough going on in her life already.

She stood up and walked out of the employee's lounge with her head held high. *I'll be damned if I let them two-faced heifers see me upset. Not me. Oh, hell no.*

Braylin's secretary buzzed her on the intercom. "Ms. Smith! You have a call on line one, and your two o'clock meeting is already here."

"Who's calling?" she asked her secretary.

"A Ms. Brown. She says she is looking to buy ad space."

"Thank you, Juanita."

Braylin picked up the phone. "This is Braylin."

"Hi Braylin, this is Sonya Brown. How are you?"

"I'm fine. How can I help you?" She put her personal feelings aside and went into professional mode. A potential client didn't need to hear any sadness in her voice. She did have bills to pay, after all, and worrying about a lying, no-good man was not going to get the job done.

"Can we meet tomorrow at three o'clock?"

"No, I'm booked up tomorrow. How is Tuesday, say, two o'clock?"

Ms. Brown answered without hesitation. "I'll take it. I heard you were a beast with the ad sales."

"Not to toot my own horn, but *beep beep*. You heard exactly right. I'll see you Tuesday at two."

"Thanks, Braylin."

"Thank you. Bye-bye."

She turned to see that her two o'clock appointment was none other than old, nosy, gossipin' Ms. Grant. Shit, she had to be about eighty-something. Braylin pasted on her brightest smile and walked toward the old bird.

"Hello, Ms. Grant, how are you doing today?"

"Hmph, I'm all right, even though you ten minutes late fo' our meeting."

Now, this mean old bird knew that her meeting wasn't until two o'clock, and it was only twenty minutes 'til two. She'd always been a well-paying client, so Braylin simply apologized.

"I'm so sorry, Ms. Grant. I had to take care of some business in the back. Will you come with me, please?" Inside, she was asking God for patience, because she was two seconds away from snapping on somebody after dealing with Donovan's lying ass. For a while she had thought that maybe Donovan was the one, but he was proving more and more that he was not.

As she finished up her meeting with Ms. Grant, she thought more and more about all the hurt that she had been through and grew more pissed off. But then again, she'd be damned if she let it show.

Braylin opened her laptop to document her meeting with Ms. Grant. Her cell phone vibrated, interrupted her concentration. She dug into her pocket to remove her phone. It was another text message from the trick who claimed to be Donovan's newest baby momma.

The text read:

I love what you've done to the apartment. It's really nice, and that leopard print and gold is the bomb.

Was that bitch in my house?

"I'll be right back!" she yelled to no one in particular as she bolted out of the office.

"But what about your next client?" The question fell on deaf ears. She was already in her Audi SUV, hauling ass through a red light. When she arrived at her apartment complex, she raced up the stairs and kicked in the door.

"Donovan, bring your ass out here now. You and that bitch gon' die today!" Braylin yelled as she ran from room to room. They were nowhere to be found.

Finally, she went into the bathroom. There was a note on the mirror written in red lipstick.

"'Chyna was here,'" Braylin read aloud.

Tears welled in her eyes, and Braylin realized she'd had much more than she could take. She sat down on the side of the tub and cried until she was sick to her stomach and vomit spewed forward. Seeing the vomit on the floor smacked some sense into Braylin. She was not going to fall apart. After cleaning the offending vomit, she took her time, took a bubble bath, and pulled herself together. After all, she was Braylin, and she didn't let shit like this hold her down.

She sat on the edge of her bed and called her best friend, Bronx.

"B! What are you doing?"

"Nothing much. What up doe, gurl?"

Braylin chuckled. Talking to her girl always tickled her. "Why don't we hit the mall?"

"Sounds like a plan to me, bish."

"Cool, see you in twenty." Braylin hung up, glad to at least be getting out of the house. She got dressed, left her place, and headed over to Bronx's apartment with her music blasting.

***

"Bronx, what am I going to do?" Braylin was walking through the mall with her best friend of more than ten years. They had been through a lot together, but usually it was Bronx seeking Braylin's help, not the other way around. Braylin prided herself on always having it together.

"Cheat on his ass, girl, or kick him to the curb."

Braylin hung her head. She knew that cheating wasn't the answer, and kicking someone that you loved to the curb was much easier said than done. "Bronx, girl, you know that isn't the answer. Seriously, what should I do about Donovan?"

"You really love him, don't you, Braylin?"

"Yeah, I do." Braylin looked like she wanted to cry.

Bronx began to feel terrible. Unbeknownst to Braylin, Bronx was seeing Donovan too. Bronx had dated her best friend's boyfriends before, but she had never known Braylin to admit to loving someone. Bronx figured that Braylin never knew how to please her men in bed, so, she always helped her out "Girl, he ain't doing nothing but using you. Braylin, c'mon. You need cheering up and so do I. I hate to see my best friend hurting."

"What good would that do, Bronx?"

"Let's go get some ice cream, and then we'll hit up that lingerie store you love so much."

Braylin tried her best to smile. It was obvious to her that Bronx, who had never stayed with one man more than a month, didn't have the answer . . . but at least her best friend tried to listen, and that was more than Donovan was willing to do for her lately.

"Hello, how may I help you?" the handsome server at Flavors Galore asked.

"Yeah, dude, let me get a rocky road waffle cone."

Bronx can be so rude, Braylin thought.

The man glared at Bronx for a moment and then turned to Braylin. "And what would you like?"

"Hi, could I please have a strawberry cheese-cake waffle cone?"

The server smiled at her then turned to fill the orders, grateful that she wasn't rude like her friend. After handing them their cones, he gave them the total of their order. "That'll be four dollars and seventy-five cents, please."

"Four seventy-five for two ice cream cones! Y'all crazy if y'all think I'm paying almost five damn dollars for two ice cream cones."

"Bronx, lower your voice. I got it. Damn." Sometimes her friend could be so ghetto.

Donovan had often told her she was a professional woman, and being friends with a "ghetto
bird" like Bronx could quickly ruin her image.
Not that Donovan was doing much with his life,
but he was always critiquing her life, her job,
and her friends.

"Here you go, sir. Keep the change." Completely
embarrassed, she handed the man six dollars,
grabbed her friend by the arm, and proceeded to
get as far away from the counter as possible.

In her attempt to get away from that end of the
food court, she ran smack dab into a huge, firm,
masculine chest—face first. As embarrassed
as she was, she didn't want to back away from
the man's chest; his smell was so intoxicating.
Slowly he stepped back and lifted her head.

"Braylin, are you okay?"

She was wondering how the man knew her
name, but then her eyes came into focus and
she quickly realized that it was Donovan's father,
David.

"Oh, hi, Mr. Jones. This is my friend, Bronx.
Bronx, this is Donovan's dad."

"Hello, Bronx, it's nice meeting you," David
replied. He didn't understand why Braylin was
wasting her time on his unfaithful son, or why
she was hanging out with a slutty thing like
Bronx. He had seen Bronx strip at a variety of

clubs, where he and his band had been the live musical entertainment for the evening. He also knew that she regularly propositioned several of his band members for sex. "Well, Braylin, I've got to get going, sweetie, but tell Donovan that I'll give him a call later."

"Take care, Mr. Jones."

Why can't Donovan be more like his father? Braylin wishfully thought.

"Y'all take care, and Braylin, please call me David. Mr. Jones was my father."

Damn, what I wouldn't give for a woman like her. Braylin is a beautiful young woman with a good head on her shoulders and a heart of gold. Donovan gonna keep playing and I'm gonna show him how to love a woman like her, he thought.

Just as David walked away, Braylin's business phone rang. "This is Braylin Smith."

"Hello, Ms. Smith, this is Nayla Anderson, CEO of Curvalicious. I've heard a lot about you, and I've seen your ad campaigns. They are fabulous. I'd really love for you to come in and talk about becoming the head of advertising for my company. What are they paying you at Motherland?"

Braylin was stunned and at a complete loss for words.

Bronx noticed her friend was speechless and nudged her. "Bitch! If you don't say something. Get that money!"

Well, that snapped Braylin out of her trance, and she prayed that Ms. Anderson hadn't heard her. Nayla, trying to stifle her laughter, told Braylin that she'd heard Bronx loud and clear.

"Please excuse my loud and crazy friend, Ms. Anderson." Braylin glared at Bronx. "I currently make ninety-five thousand a year."

"Oh, honey, I can double that. Whatever you'd need." Nayla was adamant about having the best team around her. "I know that you'll need time to make a decision. Did my number show up in your phone?"

Braylin looked at her screen and then placed the phone back up to her ear. "Yes, Ms. Anderson, it did."

"Okay, great. I hope to hear from you in a few weeks. Have a great day, Braylin!"

"Thanks, you too!"

One hundred and ninety thousand dollars . . . Braylin began to picture the possibilities of life with a salary like that as she hung up from the amazing phone call.

"What dey say, gurl?"

She'd temporarily forgotten that Bronx was even standing there.

"They want me to consider working for them instead of Motherland," Braylin calmly responded. She knew that if she told her about who it was, or what they were willing to pay her, Bronx would want her to adopt her and her kids. She did a lot for them as it was. Braylin loved Bronx and her babies, no doubt about it, but sometimes she felt like a grandmother instead of a play auntie when it came to them.

Nayla

Nayla was settling back in her chair, satisfied with the call she'd just made to Braylin Smith. She knew that Braylin was a force to be reckoned with in the advertising industry, and she felt that together they could be an even stronger powerhouse. Next on her to-do list was to hire a secretary that she felt she could trust. She had several interviews in the morning, but in the mean time she wanted to get home and get her pussy ate. She knew that her husband, Randy, would be down for some sex. He always was. Now, if only he supported her outside the bedroom, maybe they could have a great marriage.

Nayla knew when she married him she was just settling, but she didn't have time to look for real love. She certainly did not have time to wait to be hunted when she met Randy. The business was just getting off the ground, and love just had to take a back seat to her career.

***

"Oh, shit!" Randy was opening up Pandora's Box with his powerful tongue. All of Nayla's juicy secrets were being licked away as he stroked her clit with his tongue and wrapped his lips around her lower set of lips. Who knew a little pink flap could bring such pleasure?

Her thick body tingled all over as his tongue tangoed with her clit. She had never had a seizure, but the way her body was shaking and saliva was pouring out of her mouth, she just knew that she was about to have one. Nayla was actually scared that she was about to bite her tongue off! That's just how intense her much-needed orgasm was. She unloaded all her liquid ecstasy into Randy's open, waiting mouth.

That was just the beginning, though. He flipped her over, smacked her plush, round ass, and rammed his eight inches inside her wet pussy. Nayla was ready and willing to wrap her lips around it, but it seemed that Randy wanted the hotness that only her pussy could deliver.

The man pumped hard and fast. His thrusts were quick and short. Nayla attempted to speak, but every word got caught in her throat as his nuts slapped her behind. Then Randy slowed down. The slower, longer thrusts felt so damn good to her that she started speaking in tongues.

She didn't know what the hell she was saying. Randy didn't give a shit; he just kept on pumping, picking up the pace until the thrusts were short, quick, and hard again. Nayla felt his dick throbbing just before he screamed, releasing his white chocolate deep inside of her.

"Damn!" he said, almost out of breath. *Damn,* was right! Nayla's husband knew how to make him some serious love. Once upon a time, she thanked God for Randy each and every day, because he had brought it each and every day. No man had ever eaten her pussy or penetrated her as well as Randy did. He always left Nayla satisfied.

With a look of euphoria on her face, her elevator of bliss was rising toward cloud nine. Yes, his loving was like that! But just before she got past cloud six, Randy's ass had the nerve to ask, "So, have you thought anymore about having a threesome with Dalia?"

"Now I remember why I can't stand your country apple ass!" Nayla blanked on Randy. She wasn't as furious as she acted, but why did he always have to go and ruin the moment? Her sexual high quickly descended, and before she knew it, she was at ground zero again.

He had been bugging Nayla about the threesome bullshit for over a month. The more she said no, the more his dumb ass asked the question.

The only thing she felt she could praise about Randy was his sex game. Were it not for his tongue and his dick, she wouldn't have shit good to say about the bastard. Nayla knew then that marrying Randy had been a huge mistake. Besides the sex, she was totally unhappy. She was ready to do something about it.

He is constantly bringing that shit up at the wrong fucking moment, Nayla thought. *I mean, damn! I get sick of that bullshit. Plus, he doesn't take responsibility for his actions.* Nayla hated to get rid of her good dick, but she felt like he was cheating on her with the woman he wanted to have the threesome with anyway. Other than their sex life, there wasn't a relationship. She was always busy working, and Randy was busy being Randy. He changed jobs like decent women changed panties.

Nayla jumped out of her beautiful cherry wood king-sized bed. "Get yo' country butt up and get out. I mean it!"

Randy looked at Nayla in pure disbelief.

"Did you not hear what I said?" Angrily, she reached down, grabbed his clothes and shoes, and threw them at him. "Get out, I said! I don't wanna see you anymore. I'm also going to see the lawyer. It's time to end this mess." Nayla turned her back and waited for him to put on his clothes and leave.

When she heard the front door slam, Nayla felt more liberated than she had ever felt. She looked around the lavish bedroom, decorated in rose gold silk, and sighed. Stepping into the massive bathroom with the jet Jacuzzi tub and shower, she turned everything on before walking to the expansive walk-in closet that was reminiscent of Kimora Lee Simmons' closet.

She wondered why Randy wanted that other woman so bad. Nayla was a bad-ass bitch all by her damn self. Full-figured, yeah, but she was sexy as fuck.

After a long, relaxing bubble bath, she ate the fabulous lunch prepared by Chef Tahir, who looked as delicious as the meals he prepared each day. Then she got dressed, making a mental note to make a stop by and see her lawyer before going back to the office. As always, she had to make sure she was looking fresh in one of her custom pantsuits. Satisfied with her appearance, she headed off to her lawyer's office.

"I want a divorce! Everything is mine because he hasn't worked for shit. He will walk out of this marriage the same way he walked into it—ashy and broke!" Nayla skipped the cordial bull and got straight to the point. Besides, she and Randy were only married for a little over a year. Her thirtieth birthday was six months away, and she was looking forward to celebrating the milestone and her divorce to that trifling-ass Randy.

The very patient lawyer finally smiled, spoke up, and said, "That's fine, Nayla. If you are certain that's what you want, then I'll file the papers right away."

"Thank you, Clayton." Nayla slid on her Chanel shades and turned to walk away. She glanced over her shoulder and caught the handsome lawyer, Clayton Dean, looking dead at her juicy round ass. God knew what He was doing when He made full-figured women! Nayla knew that's why He blessed her to build her million-dollar company, Curvalicious, from the ground up.

Nayla walked out of his office and handed the valet her ticket. As soon as her car pulled up, she hopped back into her platinum-colored Lexus and drove to her office in the heart of downtown Atlanta.

The next thing to check off her to-do list was hiring an assistant. She hated having to leave the majority of her staff in New York to keep her first office running. She was excited to start a new chapter with a new team down south.

Judea

At 4:45 a.m., Judea awoke to the sound of her rooster alarm clock. You could take the girl out of the country, but you couldn't take the country out of the girl! Shoot, Judea wished she could have brought her rooster, Walter, to Atlanta, from her hometown of Altoona, Alabama.

She had an interview that morning for the secretarial position at Curvalicious. *I'ma straighten my hair special this mo'ning,* Judea thought as she was frying bacon and scrambling eggs. She leaned forward, almost burning herself on the grease.

"Lordy, I'm so nervous about gettin' this here job that I almos' burned myself!" she said aloud to the walls that surrounded her.

Having come from a big family, she wasn't used to being in a house alone. Judea was one of twelve children.

After having breakfast, Judea laid out her best Sunday dress. It was navy blue, with a white sailor collar. She had white stockings and navy blue shoes to match. Judea smiled to herself. She knew the outfit just might do the trick and land her the job she so desperately needed.

Judea Hamiliton had moved to Atlanta without much more than a suitcase full of dreams and eyes that still sparkled with innocence. At age twenty-five, she was still fairly young and tender, with thick thighs and a seductive smile. The youngest of her siblings, Judea was the first one in her family to ever venture outside of her home state.

Even though she loved her family dearly, Judea wanted to see what life outside of small-town Alabama was like. It was almost as if something was calling, or even pulling her, to Atlanta. She didn't know what it was, but she packed up her bags, kissed her family good-bye, and set out to discover what life had to offer. She'd been in the A for a few weeks with no job, and her money was running out. If Judea didn't get the job at Curvalicious, she'd be headed back to 'Bama on the first thing smoking.

After straightening her long, thick hair, Judea took a quick bath and slipped into her Sunday best. She stared at herself in the mirror and smiled, revealing deep dimples in each cheek.

She had turned her long hair under with a curling iron. It looked pretty, resting on her shoulders. Her size fourteen dress fit nicely. It was one of her favorites.

Judea closed her eyes and prayed. "Lord, please, let your will be done. If I'm to stay here, I've got to have a job. Otherwise, I can't 'ford to stay up here. So if it's your will, Lord, I pray for this job in your name. Amen."

Judea took a cab to her destination. She tipped the driver four quarters that he didn't seem to appreciate. He grumbled something obscene as Judea exited the cab. She said a quick prayer for him. She didn't understand why people had to be so rude and unhappy all the time.

Judea stared at the tall building in front of her before entering. She couldn't believe that entering this building every day might be her future. Her nerves went into overdrive. She looked up in awe; it had to have twenty or more floors. According to Judea's directions, Curvalicious was on the top floor.

Judea wasn't used to riding in elevators. In fact, she was terrified of elevators. The thought of cramming into a tiny box and having it potentially break down and trapping her inside, was enough to deter her from getting inside. Twenty flights of stairs was a long way up, but it was safer than the elevator. Judea took a deep breath as she followed the sign that read: STAIRS.

"Excuse me," a deep voice said.

Judea turned around to see a tall, dark man staring at her. He was wearing a uniform with the name "Lamar" stitched on the brown shirt.

"How far up you going?"

"I got a interview at Curvalicious," Judea told the stranger. She felt nervous as she noticed him staring at her. She read the approval in his eyes when he smiled.

"That's all the way up top. You'll be out of breath by the time you make it that far. Why you don't just take the elevator?" He pointed toward the stainless steel doors. "It's a lot quicker."

Judea shrugged her shoulders. "Ain't too comfortable in no elevator." She felt comfortable with Lamar. He didn't sound like all the other city folk. He spoke with a deep southern accent, just like her.

"I tell you what. I'll join you and keep you entertained. Before you know it, the ride will be over, and you'll be having your interview. What's your name?"

Judea extended her right hand to him. "Judea Hamiliton." The simple touch of his warm hand against hers sent chills up and down her spine. She couldn't deny that she was attracted to Lamar.

"I'm Lamar West." Lamar had already fallen in love with Judea's smile. Her eyes twinkled every time she smiled. And those dimples were as deep as the ocean. She was beautiful. Judea was curvaceous, and Lamar loved a full-figured woman.

"Come on. I don't want you to be late." Lamar extended his arm and Judea wrapped hers under and held his elbow.

Such a gentleman, she thought. Judea allowed Lamar to lead her to the elevator. He talked to her and told her jokes the entire ride up. And as promised, before she knew it, they had arrived at the top floor. Judea closed her eyes and thanked God. The elevator ride wasn't half as bad as she had thought it would be.

"Good luck," Lamar said as Judea stepped off the elevator. "I sure hope you get this job. I would love to see your pretty face every mornin'."

Judea blushed. "Thank you. I hope so too."

The doors closed, and Lamar disappeared.

Judea was twenty minutes early, so she got a magazine and took a seat. No sooner had she sat down than the elevator doors opened again. A beautiful, full-figured woman, who was fashionably dressed and carrying a briefcase, stepped off. She smelled like fresh Georgia peaches.

"Hello. May I help you?" the woman asked Judea.

"I got a interview with a Mrs. Anderson in 'bout fifteen minutes," Judea answered as she held tightly to her resume and purse. She didn't know the woman. For all Judea knew, the woman was there for the same job and may try to sabotage her.

"*Ms*. Anderson," the stranger corrected her. "Mrs. Anderson is my mother."

Judea looked at the woman strangely.

The woman laughed. "I'm Nayla Anderson. I'm the founder and owner of Curvalicious. And you are?"

Judea laughed nervously. "Judea Hamiliton. I'm here for the secretary job."

She handed Ms. Anderson the resume the woman at the library had helped to prepare for her. Judea didn't know much about computers and such.

"Well, if you would like, we can get started. Follow me," Nayla said.

"But . . . but don't you need me to get you some coffee or something?" Judea asked. "It's really no bother. I'll be glad to fetch you a cup."

"Thank you, Ms. Hamiliton. That's very nice of you." Nayla sensed that Judea was a good person. She didn't have the type of experience Nayla was looking for, though. According to the resume, Judea hadn't done much outside of farming and some bookkeeping for her father. "Maybe we can get a cup of coffee after your interview."

Judea followed Nayla into the large office. There was a beautiful view outside the large window. Judea kept looking to the window as they spoke. She had never seen a view like the one from Nayla's office.

"It's beautiful, isn't it?" Nayla asked.

"'Scuse me?"

"The view. I noticed you keep looking at the window."

"Oh, yes, ma'am. I ain't never been so high up in a buildin' befo'."

"Well, let's look at the view while we speak." Nayla got up from her chair and walked to the window. Judea followed and stood beside Nayla. The view was breathtaking.

The two women talked about the position and Judea's previous experience. "I know I ain't got a lot of experience, but I'm a fast learner. And I really need this job, Ms. Anderson," Judea pleaded. She felt at peace in Nayla's office. It was as if Curvalicious was where she belonged.

"Call me Nayla." She turned toward Judea. "Now, let's go have that cup of coffee so we can talk about when you start. Then we'll come back and fill out the paperwork."

Judea was so happy she wrapped her arms around Nayla's neck. "Thank you, Ms. Anderson—I mean Nayla. Thank you!"

Again, she closed her eyes. She thanked God above. He had a plan for her in her new surroundings. She wasn't quite sure what that plan was, but she was ready to find out. She had a hunch that it had something to do with her new boss.

Braylin

"Bray!" Donovan screamed as he stomped in and slammed her front door.

"My name is Braylin!" It was to the point where the small things he did, that she once thought were cute, she couldn't stand anymore, like him calling her Bray.

"Why I don't smell dinner, girl?" He pulled on her ponytail as he walked past her toward the kitchen.

Damn, no "Hello" or "How was your day?" Braylin thought. She was second guessing her marriage. *You cheat, you lie, you don't do any of the things you used to do, but you want and expect the same special treatment from me.* She was no longer fond of the familiar stranger who called her place his home.

"Get the burgers from Caesar's out of the refrigerator and heat them up. I'm trying to prepare my campaign for a new potential client," she said.

"Well, I guess it's something. Thanks." He had gotten so that he wasn't genuinely grateful for anything anymore.

Braylin sighed as she continuously noticed how Donovan used to say things to encourage her, or make her feel wanted and loved. *Maybe he never really loved me,* she thought. *Maybe he got tired of keeping up the charade. But I'm so tired of him, coming in at all hours of the night, and then always expecting a hot meal and for me to be waiting for him.*

Through her frustration, Braylin drummed her fingernails against her desk. Just as she was getting up to call it a night, her iPhone began vibrating its way off the desk. She started to ignore it, but it was Bronx. Knowing that this was Bronx's main night to work at the club, as she was always the strip club's Wednesday night headliner as Almondy Brown, Braylin figured something must be wrong.

"Hello?"

"Hey, girl. Whew, have I got some shit to tell you."

"What's up? I was just getting ready to call it a night."

"Well, honey-boo, you need to stay up for this one."

"Okay, what is it?" Fear began settling in Braylin's mind as she knew it most likely had something to do with Donovan. Bronx quickly confirmed her fears.

"Do you know where your man was up until about an hour ago?" Bronx continued without even waiting for an answer from her friend. "His ho ass was back here in the dressing room eating stank Toniya's pussy. No dental dam or nothing!"

What Bronx didn't tell Braylin was that while Donovan was sticking his tongue in foreign objects, he was pounding his manhood in and out of her scary pussy without a rubber. Bronx's only reason for telling Braylin about part of the situation was because she wanted Braylin and Donovan to fight so that he'd leave Braylin and come stay with her for a couple of days. This was what he would do when they got into it.

It was during those days that Braylin wouldn't hear anything from Bronx, and if Donovan called, it was always from a blocked number. Something never felt right about that, but Braylin refused to believe that her friend could or would be the one to ever betray her.

"Damn it, Bronx, I'm sick of this. I'm a good woman. Why in the hell do I continue to put up with this?" As Braylin's anger was bordering on rage, she thanked her friend for letting her know what was up and hung up the phone.

She knew that Donovan's two-timing behind had long since fallen asleep, probably dreaming of

Toniya. She never second-guessed her friend, and Bronx had always looked out for her. It was Bronx who would always stand up to the girls who tried to pick on Braylin in school, often getting suspended from school for fighting on Braylin's behalf.

Braylin stormed into her bedroom and walked right up to a soundly sleeping Donovan and slapped him dead across his drooling mouth. "Wake the hell up!"

Aw, shit, Donovan thought, *what is it now?*

"What you slapping me for, girl?" His nostrils were flaring and his light brown face was turning red.

"I slapped you because I'm sick of you! I'm the only one working, I'm the only one cooking, cleaning, and the only one paying any of these damn bills, including your child support, and you can't even keep your body parts to yourself? I'm sick of you, Donovan!"

"If you so sick of me, then get rid of my ass then. But tell me why you so sick of me. You know that can't nobody lay that pipe on you like I can." He smirked. He knew he was telling the truth about his lovemaking skills.

"Yeah, but why you always sharing the loving that you promised was mine and mine alone with all these sluts, especially the whores from the club?" Braylin looked as if she was going to cry, but she fought the urge to do so with all her might.

"Look, what you need to do is stop listening to Bronx's simple ass. I know that nobody told you I was up at the club but her ho ass." He walked toward Braylin, opening his arms to wrap around her, but she pushed him away. "The only reason Bronx called you is because she mad that I didn't let her give me a lap dance. You need to check your girl. She just mad because you got what she wants." He leaned forward to kiss her, but she walked away. "Whatever, but Bronx ain't your damn friend. The sooner you see that, the better we'll all be."

Donovan was telling the truth about one thing: Bronx wasn't Braylin's friend, but it would be some time before she would be able to see that.

"Donovan, I'm going to meet Mama. Please don't have any company while I'm gone. I really don't feel like coming home to any mess." Braylin had given him a second chance, but he was still on very thin ice as far as she was concerned.

"Don't worry, mami, I got you. I love you, girl." Donovan crooned the sweet nothings in her ear as he wrapped his arms around her. He felt his phone vibrate in his back pocket, and he knew it was probably one of his chicken-heads.

One of these days, I'm gonna settle down and marry Braylin, and I'll be done with all these hoes for good, Donovan thought as he temporarily ignored his vibrating phone.

"Have a good time, baby. Tell Moms I said hey." *What a MILF she is. Yeah, I'd fuck that stuck-up old crow.* Donovan's thought process was a twisted one, and the sooner Braylin saw that, the better off she'd be.

Braylin knew that her mother couldn't stand him, much less him calling her Moms, but she kept her thoughts to herself. "Bye, D, and like I said, *no* mess." She kissed him on the cheek and headed out the door.

Donovan couldn't even wait until she was down the driveway to reach for his phone and call his ho of the moment back. Unsurprisingly, that particular ho of the moment just happened to be Bronx.

"Yo, ma. What's good, Ms. Hood?"

"What's up, daddy?" Bronx gave her sickening imitation of a sexy laugh as she grinned into the phone.

"Waiting on yo' ass to come wrap your lips around my dick."

"Mmm . . . really? Well, open your back door and put it in my mouth."

The moment Bronx said that, Donovan became rock hard. He couldn't wait to show her that today he was going to hold her to her word.

Nayla

Nayla had just hired the sweetest and most country woman she had ever met. She was from someplace in Alabama that sounded like the countriest place in the whole world. And poor Judea was the epitome of country!

Nayla told her that she reminded her of Goldie from the *Flavor of Love* show, and Judea said, "I didn't know that love came in different flavors. Why in the world would somebody name their child Goldie?"

Nayla couldn't help but burst out laughing, and Judea couldn't understand what was so funny. She must have thought that Nayla wasn't going to give her the job or something, because all of a sudden she got the saddest look on her face.

"Pick your chin up, because employees of mine have to walk with their heads held high."

Judea seemed so excited. Nayla had never had someone who seemed so thrilled to be her personal assistant. Judea thanked Nayla with a hug that she didn't even know she needed until she got it.

No, Judea wasn't the most qualified, but in her heart of hearts, Nayla just couldn't send her back out on the street without a job. There was just something about her. Her simplicity and look of innocence was like a breath of fresh air. She knew that she would really enjoy working with Ms. Judea Divine Hamilton.

The first thing Nayla wanted to do was transform Judea's style. Actually, she needed a style to transform! She actually came in wearing a navy blue dress with a big-ass white sailor collar. That wasn't going to cut it at Curvalicious. All of Nayla's staff rocked her designs.

Most of the thick and plus-size celebs rocked designs by Curvalicious. Those who couldn't did what they do best, and that's hate.

Nayla couldn't help but yawn as she reared backward into her leather office chair. She was weary, as yet another day of running Curvalicious had ended. She loved running the exclusively full-figured clothing line. Sometimes she still couldn't believe that she was living out her dream from childhood. Now that she had accomplished her main goal professionally, her personal life had turned into days of painful boredom.

Every once in a while, she wondered why she had left her husband. If there was one thing he could do well, it was eat some pussy. But even with that said, he didn't do much else to make a sensible woman want to stay married to his ass. Nayla just needed to be touched and rubbed in places that the rest of her body had forgotten about.

She drifted off into another one of her stimulating daydreams. As she sat at her desk, she began to smile while rubbing her wet pussy. Nayla normally daydreamed of Palmer, the deliveryman, with his tongue buried deep inside her love tunnel. She was used to someone knocking on her door just as it would start getting good. She sure hoped that wouldn't be the case as her fingers started to do the walking.

Nothing pleased Nayla more than having her thick pussy licked and sucked. *If I didn't act like such a bitch, maybe would I have gotten some dick or tongue action already.* It was a huge adjustment going from getting some every night to being celibate.

She didn't want another husband or a baby daddy, but she sure did want some dial-a-dick that was only for her pleasure! While she enjoyed using her digits to dial up her own orgasms, she was ready to enjoy somebody else's manual labor.

Sometimes the simplest of daydreams turned her on in such a powerful way. They gave Nayla such a rush! They were what kept her going. Nayla didn't have time for love. Love would have to find her late in life when she didn't have shit else to do. For now, she would just continue to fantasize. . . .

"Won't you join me?" she boldly offered.

Without hesitation, Palmer eagerly pulled her into his arms. Not knowing where to begin, he took one of her large, dark nipples into his warm, moist mouth. Nayla squealed as she felt herself become hotter and wetter. She bit her bottom lip while Palmer planted soft, wet kisses all over her bronze skin. His kisses started at her full lips. His warm mouth then traveled south. Nayla reached out, grabbed Palmer, and gently forced his face into her hot, wet inferno. Her body shivered when she felt the heat of his breath blowing in the opening of Pandora's Box. She could hardly wait to feel his tongue inside of her. He eagerly licked cum from her pussy. He then stuffed his hand inside of her. Nayla's pussy took to Palmer's hand as if it were his dick. At that point, she began fucking his large hand harder and faster. She continued until she built the ultimate climax.

Palmer was holding her close, kissing her passionately. He had just made the most beautiful love to her. Palmer then looked at her with his dreamy eyes and whispered the words, "I love you."

Nayla snapped out of that daydream quick. As much as she wanted to feel that man's nature, she was not ready for love with anyone. Not even the beautiful chocolate Palmer. Still, she just couldn't stop thinking about that sexy man!

If only Palmer could have felt what she felt. Palmer Campbell was a widow and a single father. He had asked Nayla to join him for lunch, dinner, coffee, church, and everything else, but she just couldn't. He wasn't a man who would be satisfied with just fulfilling a woman's sexual desires. Palmer was looking for the one thing she wasn't ready give. He wanted love.

Little did Nayla know that across town, there was someone dreaming of her too. Palmer Campbell awoke with a seductive smile on his face as his heart raced and sweat poured from his brow. He had had another dream about Nayla, and as usual, right before he had the chance to make love to her, his alarm clock went off. He jumped up, took a long look at his wedding picture before kissing it, showered, and got dressed into his uniform. He had to get his five-year-old to school in time for breakfast.

"I don't wanna go to school today, Daddy," the younger version of Palmer whined. Five-year-old Jason looked more and more like Palmer with each passing day. "I wanna go on the deliveries with you!"

"Come on now, big man." Palmer couldn't contain his smile. His son sat beside him with his arms folded across his chest and his bottom lip poked out. Jason looked like Palmer, but his actions reminded Palmer of his late wife. How he missed that woman.

"You can ride with me on Saturday, the way you always do. But today, you have to go to school. Deal?" Palmer offered his hand to Jason for a shake that would seal the deal.

"Deal!" Jason chanted as he smiled, revealing his two missing front teeth.

***

After dropping Jason off at school and giving him a big hug, Palmer headed to a down-home diner not far from his office. He ordered his usual: scrambled eggs, cheese grits, turkey bacon, and a bowl of fresh fruit. A simple glass of milk would be enough to wash the meal down. He took his time enjoying his breakfast while talking to some of the familiar faces.

Palmer was in no hurry to get to the office. He knew once there he would be hit on relentlessly by his aggressive co-workers. And, of course, he was right.

The women in the office stared, mouths agape, as they watched the sexy, milk chocolate man load boxes into the back of the delivery truck. Palmer was sexy, simply because he didn't realize his own sex appeal. The man had lost his wife three years ago to cancer and was raising Jason as a single parent. Many of the women wanted to fill the void in his life, but Palmer never showed any of them any interest. He was never rude, but he was obviously not interested in a relationship with any of them.

"If only I could run my fingers through that wavy hair," said Amanda, a petite brunette. She chewed on her bottom lip while watching his six-feet-plus frame. Palmer possessed an athletic build that would make a blind woman see.

Amanda had tried seducing Palmer on more than one occasion. Though he was polite, he still turned her down. Amanda couldn't believe that Palmer wasn't interested in her. She was a young, beautiful woman in her mid-twenties. Her reputation preceded her. Most of the guys in the office marveled about her "oral skills." Surely Palmer wanted to know firsthand what all the talk was about.

"Tyson Beckford better watch out!" Selena, the bombshell Latina, whispered. She was another hot tamale who tried to get next to Palmer. She, too, had been rejected. They'd never understand that Palmer liked his women BBW.

Palmer could feel the eyes on him as he loaded his truck. The women in the office were gazing out of the window at him as they always did. They were all beautiful women, especially Selena, but none of them was as curvaceous or charismatic as Nayla. If only Nayla looked at him the way the women in his office looked at him. If only she wanted him the way they wanted him.

Palmer placed the last box inside the back of his delivery truck. He carefully secured the doors. The women were still watching, so he smiled and waved to them. He didn't want to lead them on in any way, but he wasn't going to be rude, either.

Eager to get through another day of work, Palmer hopped in the cab of his truck. Working wasn't a must for Palmer; it was a choice. He had been born into wealth, but no one outside of his family knew of his financial worth. Palmer wanted people to know and love him for who he was, and not what he was worth.

He had a ton of deliveries to make, and as

always, his final stop would be at Curvalicious. His mother had always taught him to save the best for last, and Nayla was definitely the best. Palmer couldn't contain his smile as he pulled out of the parking lot with naughty thoughts of Nayla racing through his mind. The things he wanted to do to and with that woman . . .

He couldn't deny his sexual attraction to Nayla Anderson, but there was so much more to his feelings for her. He wanted to do more than just make love to her. Palmer wanted to love the woman. He wanted to be able to let go of Karmen, his late wife. Three years after her demise to cancer, Palmer still cried himself to sleep some nights while clutching their wedding picture to his chest.

At times, he felt guilty for the way he felt about Nayla. It was almost as if he was cheating on Karmen in some way. That's something he would have never done. Palmer loved Karmen from the first moment he laid eyes on her, and he still loved her. He would always love her. But never again could he hold her in his arms.

In his heart, he knew that Karmen would want him to move on with his life. She would want a woman in the home to help him raise Jason, their only child. And he knew she would approve of Nayla. Even though they were as different as night and day, Karmen would admire Nayla's drive. At age thirty, the woman had established herself in the world of fashion design.

Palmer had asked her out on many occasions, but she always told him no. He didn't understand. The look in her eyes proved her attraction toward him. He noticed how her face lit up every single time he made deliveries. Maybe she just didn't think he, a deliveryman, was good enough for a professional woman like herself. If that was the case, she wasn't the woman that Palmer had thought her to be.

After a long day of non-stop deliveries, Palmer finally arrived at Curvalicious. He had not asked Nayla out since she had turned him down a few weeks ago. So, he decided he would ask her one last time. If she said no, he would somehow put thoughts of them together out of his mind. Somehow.

Judea

It was seven thirty in the morning when Judea hurried into the office building. She was wearing a red dress similar to the navy blue sailor dress she had worn to her interview. Today, she wore her red pumps instead of the blue ones.

Walking with her head down, Judea almost walked right into Lamar, who was posted next to the elevators. "I'm sorry. I shoulda been watching where I was goin'."

"Well, good mornin', pretty girl." Lamar smiled, exposing his gold tooth. "I was hopin' to see you again." They stepped onto the elevator.

"Ooh, I'm so nervous," Judea told Lamar. "I ain't never liked first days, but Nayla seem so nice. Maybe it won't be so bad."

"Ms. Anderson has always been nice to work for, and she give nice gifts to er'body at Christmas. I hope you'll like it here, Judea, 'cause I sho' like you!"

No one so handsome had ever made her blush. "Oh, Lamar, you makin' me blush." She giggled then nervously checked the time on her wristwatch. "Uh-oh, I'm 'bout to be late. This here elevator takin' a mighty long time. Back home, if you weren't fifteen minutes early, you were five minutes late."

"Oh, don't you worry yo' pretty self 'bout that. Ms. Anderson don't come in 'til 'round ten," Lamar reassured her with a huge grin. "You know," he continued, "you sho' is pretty!"

She smiled. "Oh, Lamar! You jus' sayin' that."

"Naw, Judea, I means it. I bet you done broke plenty of hearts 'round Georgia."

"No I ain't, Lamar!" Judea laughed. She thought that was the funniest thing she had ever heard. "I ain't never even had no real boyfriend befo'. I used to talk to boys on the porch, and every once in a while Momma would let me sneak and talk to them on the tel'phone, but that ain't no real boyfriend. I was still in high school."

Judea enjoyed talking to Lamar. She felt as if she had known him forever. She hoped that he liked her as much as he said he did, because she really liked him too.

"I'm sure you done left yo' share of broke hearts in Virginia, Lamar."

"No, ma'am. I ain't dated nobody since my ex-fiancée left me fo' some ball player. But it don't matter, 'cause he left her a year later."

"Well, that's what she get," Judea said, laughing. "You can't be mean and not get meanness back."

"Ain't that the truth," Lamar agreed.

The elevator finally stopped on Judea's floor. Reluctant to end their friendly conversation, she said, "I guess this here's my stop."

"Okay, pretty girl. I'll stop by and see you later." Lamar tried his best to hide his sadness. He hated to see her go.

Nayla was even later coming in than Lamar had said she would be, so all Judea had done all morning was answer the phone and take messages. *This 'bout easy,* she thought.

"Hi, Judea! How are you today?" Nayla asked as she emerged from the elevator. She looked so tired.

"I'm okay. How you doin'?"

Nayla responded with a weak smile and a shrug of her shoulders.

"If you don't mind me sayin'," Judea continued, "you look so tired." Judea truly was concerned. Her new boss wasn't wearing that bold mask of confidence she had seen the day before.

"I'm fine, Judea. I just didn't get much sleep last night," Nayla answered. "Has the delivery man come in yet?"

"No, not yet. Here's your messages, though."

"Thank you." Nayla accepted the sticky notes. She rushed into her office and shut the door.

Judea knew that it was more than fatigue bothering her boss. She spent the next couple of hours answering phones and taking messages. Nayla had buzzed her on the intercom and said she did not want to be bothered unless it was urgent.

When Judea went downstairs on her break, she never expected to see the handsome Lamar sitting there in the fancy coffee place called Starbucks as if he had been waiting for her.

"Hey, Lamar!" Judea was smiling and waving as she hurried to his table.

"Hey there, Judea! I thought that you might be coming down for a coffee break, and I got you one of those mucha lottos." Lamar was maybe even more country than Judea, but you could never tell Judea that. In her eyes, all Lamar was, was fine!

"Ooh, thank you, Lamar! I've always wanted to try one of those mocha luchas." She sat down across from him, but in her mind, she was sitting on him. She couldn't believe that she was already fantasizing about Lamar West, but she was, and didn't really mind it at all. In her mind, she was sitting in his lap, kissing his beautiful, full lips and licking his chocolate skin. Just tasting him and not caring who saw them.

"Judea! Judea! Earth to Judea." Lamar laughed as Judea snapped back to reality. "I was askin' ya if ya wanted to go to one'a these here restaurants fo' lunch."

"Lamar, I ain't used to all these different languages of food. We can jus' fetch something from McDavid's and watch the kids play in that playground over yonder." She didn't want no Italian, French, or any of them other languages. That food didn't set right with Judea. It sounded too fancy and complicated. She liked simple foods.

"Judea, McDavid's is nice an' all, but I knows a soul food joint not far from here. It's called Mama Soul Food. They got collards, chitterlings, neck bones, fatback, black-eyed peas, and all kindsa good eatin'." Lamar could see her getting excited as he told her about the restaurant.

Judea licked her lips. It was nowhere near lunch, but her mouth was now watering. She closed her eyes and imagined the hog chitterlings sliding down her throat. "I hope it ain't too far aways. I don't wanna be late comin' from lunch," Judea explained to Lamar. He assured her that he would have her back before the lunch hour ended.

Judea could hardly wait until the clock struck twelve. Not only was she looking forward to the good food, but she couldn't wait to be with Lamar again. "Thanks again for umm, uhhh, this here drink. That was very sweet of you, Lamar. I'll see you in 'bout an hour."

Shortly after twelve, Judea and Lamar were seated in his '79 Chevy pickup, headed towards Mama's Soul Food. The windows were down, and Judea was able to take in all the beauty that Atlanta displayed. The buildings were so tall! But nothing took her breath away more than the smell from Mama's Soul Food. She could smell the aroma in the air as they pulled up.

The people had to be from down on the Bayou. The food was awesome, and the iced tea was cold and sweet. Judea and Lamar talked about their similar upbringing as they enjoyed neck bones, rice, butter peas, macaroni and cheese, collard greens, and cornbread. Judea was so full that she had to get her dessert, sweet potato pie, to go.

"I sho' would like to meet the cook. She put her foot in that food," Judea told Lamar as they headed back to the office. She was rubbing her full belly and trying not to let out a loud belch.

"She's a sweet li'l lady named Ms. Sadie. I think she's from some place near Lousiana." Lamar was now pulling into the parking garage at their building. They spent ten minutes in the truck talking about everything to nothing. Even though they hadn't known each other long, Judea was falling in serious like with him—and the feeling was mutual.

After returning from her wonderful lunch date with Lamar, Judea had to spend the next three hours trying to type up a one-paragraph letter for her boss to send off to twenty different people. By the time she finished with her one-finger typing, it was four thirty, almost quitting time. After she gave Nayla the paper, Judea sat back at her desk to wait for the last-minute calls to come into the office. She decided to pass the time with one of her favorite crossword puzzles.

"Hi there!" The greeting startled Judea. She looked up from her crossword puzzle. "You must be the new secretary. I'm Palmer."

"Hey, Palmer. I'm Judea. It's right nice to meet you." Judea couldn't help but notice his nicely packaged body. "Nayla was expecting you. I'll let her know that you're here jus' as soon as I figga out this here system." Judea was now mumbling more to herself than talking to Palmer. "Aww, shucks! I'll jus' call her regular." Palmer couldn't help but chuckle.

"Nayla, the delivery man, Palmer, is here with your package." Judea noticed a change in her boss's voice and attitude when she told her that Palmer was there.

Nayla emerged from her office, smiling from ear to ear. Judea immediately sensed an attraction between her beautiful boss and the sexy deliveryman. She pretended to be engrossed in her crossword puzzle.

"Hi, Nayla. You look beautiful today," Palmer said.

"Tha-thank you," Nayla stuttered.

Judea couldn't help but smile. Nayla was acting like a nervous schoolgirl.

"Where do you want these fabric rolls?" Palmer asked.

"Just bring them here into my office, please," Nayla said, smiling at Palmer as they disappeared into her office.

Judea rolled her chair close to the open doorway.

"Nayla, I was wondering if you would go to dinner with me tomorrow night," Palmer asked, hoping that for once her answer would be different.

Judea was dying to hear her boss's response. *Say yes!* she almost screamed.

"No, Palmer. I don't think that would be a good idea," Nayla heard herself say.

"Are you sure?" Palmer asked, hoping that his smile and charm would change her mind. "I've got tickets to see *The Color Purple*."

"I'm sure, sweetie. Thanks for bringing up the fabric." Nayla pretended to busy herself inspecting the fabric rolls.

Judea rolled her chair back to her desk while shaking her head. She couldn't believe that Nayla would pass up a date with Palmer, especially when he had tickets to see *The Color Purple*!

Feeling defeated, Palmer mumbled, "Have a good day." He bid Judea farewell and wished her a nice evening before boarding the elevator.

Judea knocked briefly before entering Nayla's office. "Nayla, I ain't tryna get in your business or nothin', but why'd you turn that fine man down? Chile, he 'bout as fine as a golden egg laid by a prized hen!"

Nayla smiled at her and said, "I know, but he wants so much more than I do. I don't want a relationship right now. I just wanna get laid every now and then."

"Get what?" Judea was confused.

"It's just an expression. It means I'm not looking for a serious relationship. I just want someone who can . . ." Nayla didn't quite know how to put it. "I just need to release some stress sometimes. You know what I mean?"

"Hmm. Yeah, I know what ya mean, but life is 'bout mo' than just sex."

Nayla didn't respond. Judea didn't understand city life. She couldn't. Things were a lot different back home.

"It's 'bout time fo' me to go home fo' the evenin', but I just want to let you know that at the end of the day, your heart needs a lot more than this company can give you. Think 'bout that." She gave Nayla a sisterly hug and left her with strong words to ponder.

Braylin

"Mama, this would be perfect for you to wear to the company awards banquet." Braylin held up a gorgeous, semi-backless emerald green floor-length gown with lace sleeves. Braylin felt that it would look perfect on her tall and slender mother.

"Oh, Braylin, this is perfect. I saw the matching pumps and purse over in shoes. Sweetheart, you should have gone into fashion design for the stars instead of PR for these stuffed shirts from these corporations." Braylin's mother always saw and made note of what her daughter could have done, instead of what she did.

Braylin had just received a huge promotion and raise and was up for the Employee of the Year award out of the entire nationwide corporation. She was the youngest woman and the only African American to be named into her position, plus the awesome job offer from Curvalicious. Braylin was proud of herself and wished that her mother would show a little pride in her daughter's accomplishments as well.

"Mama, I love what I do. You know that." Braylin sighed, wondering what Donovan was doing. It would be so nice if he was home doing the dishes, but that was a "yeah, right" situation. Braylin laughed to herself at the thought.

"Come on, Ms. Bray, let's go to that big gal's store and get you the best dress possible. Especially if you're going to work for them soon."

Why won't my mother accept me and my size? I love my size. Why can't she?

"Ma, what do you mean, 'that big gal's store' and getting 'the best dress possible'? I love Curvalicious, and the designer is one of the fiercest plus-size designers I've ever seen."

I can't wait to be a part of their team, she thought. *Then I can show my mother and people who think just like her that every woman is beautiful, and that big women are winning.*

Braylin had gotten the catalog in the mail yesterday. "I'm going to see if they have this." Braylin held up a clip of a stunning, backless, single-shouldered beaded black gown with a see-through mermaid train. It was a Curvalicious original, and Braylin was in love with it, so nothing, not even her pessimistic mother, was going to stop her.

"It's nice. If that's what you want, let's go. My treat."

Braylin hated her mother's attitude, but at least she was generous.

"D, I better go before Bray gets back home. You know that she can only stand being around her mom for a few hours at a time." Bronx reluctantly pulled her swollen lips away from Donovan's long, agile manhood.

"Well, let me tap that ass right quick." Donovan was determined to get his now and worry about Braylin coming home later.

As soon as Donovan entered Bronx, she realized that Donovan didn't use a condom. Panic set in. She had stopped taking her birth control a few weeks ago. "Donovan, you forgot the rubber, daddy."

Never stopping the rhythm he had going, he said. "Oh, well. You on that pill, ain't you? We straight." As if he were on a mission, he began to pound even harder.

It was then that Bronx realized how Donovan could lay with her and Braylin, not to mention at least a few other women at the same time. He was coldhearted and careless. Oh, well. He could be as careless as he wanted as long as he kept giving it to her like that. He was moaning in Bronx's ear and it was driving her crazy.

"Damn, boo, you taste so good." He was licking and kissing Bronx's shoulders and her neck, and all she could think was, *If you love that, just wait until you taste this pussy.*

"So you like that, huh?" Bronx purred back at Donovan. Bronx's raunchy pussy was beginning to do some meowing of her own. "I think it's time that you meet my best friend." The trifling bitch who called herself Braylin's friend patted her twat as Braylin's man dug himself deeper into Bronx's overrun vagina. He sucked her nipples, driving her to the point of madness. She took his masculine hand and gently placed it on her womanhood.

Donovan's cell phone went off. The special ringtone let him know that he had a text message from Braylin. Bronx didn't even try to mask her disappointment when he pulled out of her and read the message.

"What it say?" Bronx asked, trying to pull Donovan back to her by his dick.

"It say that you gotta get yo' freaky ass outta here, bitch." He kissed her and smacked her ass. He grabbed her clothes, stuffed them in her arms, and pushed her out the back door. Bronx was trying to resist, but Donovan overpowered her.

Once Bronx was gone, Donovan commenced to cleaning up the condo before Braylin came home. Bronx stood naked outside the back door with an armful of clothes. In a huff, she put her clothes back on.

"Triflin' mu'fucka," she said then kicked the door before walking away.

Braylin was so excited, as this would be the first time that Donovan had accompanied her to any of her company functions. She stopped by the tuxedo shop and picked up his tux. It was the perfect complement to her gown. The following night was going to be an extremely special one for her. It was the most important night of her career, and everyone she loved and cared for was going to be in attendance. She couldn't believe that her boss had given her enough tickets for Donovan, her parents, Bronx, and she still had two left, so she had invited David and Nayla.

She was feeling so good that she decided to push all of Donovan's bullshit out of her mind. She simply wanted to make the night special. She called him to make sure he would be home.

"Hey, D."

"Hey, mami. What's up?"

"I just wanted to make sure you were going to be home. I thought we could make tonight special, just you and I," she said.

"A'ight, I'll see you later."

"Bye, baby."

"Bye, girl."

She hung up, satisfied that at least for the moment, things would be right between them. She stopped by The Lobster Palace, the place where they met face-to-face for the first time, and picked up her to-go order. For once, everything was going to be perfect.

When she got home, Donovan was nowhere to be found.

Why would he tell me that he was going to be home, and then run out? It didn't matter. She figured he would be back soon, so she went and made herself sexy for when her man came home.

***

Braylin had been at home, waiting for Donovan in a negligee with a plunging neckline, for more than three hours. She had put dinner in the oven to keep it warm, but she was hungry and just about sick of waiting. She had half a mind to eat her dinner and his too, but she wanted to be sure that she would be able to comfortably fit into her gown the following night.

Six hours after she had gotten home, she was lying in bed in her flannel pajamas. She heard Donovan easing the door open, trying not to wake her, but Braylin was far from asleep, and soon Donovan was going to know how awake she was.

"Where have you been, Donovan?" she said without emotion. She couldn't even yell. She felt drained of all emotion. If her eyes had been daggers, Donovan would have died instantly.

"Uh, hey, baby. I was out getting that wine you liked, and I ran into one of the boys and we just had a couple of quick drinks. I didn't mean to stay gone longer than an hour."

"Well, you apparently can't tell time either. You're six hours late."

"I'm sorry, boo." Donovan gave her puppy dog eyes—the same eyes that he always used to try to smooth things over between them.

"Where's the wine, Donovan?" She looked at him, knowing that he didn't have an answer.

Donovan pulled out the tiniest bottle of her favorite local wine, and it was half empty. "Right here, princess." He wrapped his arms around her and gently laid her down on the bed. He reached inside her pajama bottoms and grabbed her ample behind.

It was enough of a distraction for Braylin to forget why she was mad. "Baby, why do you play me like this? You know I love you and can't resist you." Her pulse began racing and her vagina became moist with desire.

"I love you, too, girl, and I'm trying to change. You still down to ride with me, girl?"

Of course she is, he thought. *It ain't another man this side of the Mississippi that can give it to her the way I do.* Donovan was a smug dog, and he knew it.

Donovan began easing her pajama bottoms off and slowly and methodically spreading her legs open, easing his open mouth to meet the thick lips below Braylin's luscious hips. Before she knew it, he was taking her mind and her body back to the place where he had made love to her for the very first time.

"Oh, Donovan . . . oh, D . . . oh, yeah! Tongue me deeper, D!" Soon, she was coming and releasing her juices all over his face. Her clitoris was swollen and pulsating, and she was so aroused that she thought that she would explode. "Donovan, hand me a condom, baby."

"Only if you'll put it on me with your mouth."

"Mmm . . . it has been a while since I've done that, hasn't it?"

"Yeah, girl, so are you?"

"Give it here." Braylin took the condom and placed the tip carefully in her mouth, holding the condom open with her thumb and forefinger. She placed the flavored condom on his swollen head, and swirling her tongue over and around his rigid penis, she slowly eased the condom up his shaft with her hand. There was something erotic and exciting about the way she was making love to him with her mouth. He was close to coming before even penetrating her vaginally.

"Baby, stop. I don't wanna come yet."

"Well, then, put it in, daddy." She leaned back and held her vagina lips open with one hand and beckoned to him with the other.

As Donovan filled her body, love once again filled her heart. He was blowing her mind the way he used to. Braylin wanted this potion of ecstasy to last forever. She wanted to taste herself on his lips, so she grabbed him and kissed her own juices off his delicious lips.

Damn, I taste better than I remembered.

He stroked her, she cooed, he went deeper, and after a couple of hours of steady lovemaking mixed with fucking, while staring into each other's eyes, they came in unison and all was right in their world—for once.

Nayla

Judea's advice about Palmer made sense, but Nayla still wasn't ready for dinner with him. She thought about having coffee with him, but to her surprise, he hadn't asked her out in weeks. Sometimes when you snooze, you lose. With Judea and Lamar hitting it off so well, Judea had a better chance of getting laid than Nayla had.

Nayla drove home with the top down, letting the wind massage her tense body. *If only I had a man to sit next to me in my ride*. Nayla wanted to be nearly naked in the passenger's seat while her man drove her to a secluded area. She wanted her thick, ample thighs to feel the wind as he hit it again and again and again. That would be so good right about now.

Damn it! She had to come to a screeching halt to avoid hitting the car in front of her. *Get it together, Nayla.* If she kept thinking about sex, she'd be on the six o'clock news. It was a damn shame that a grown-ass woman wasn't getting it on the regular.

Once she got home, she parked her coupe in the garage and entered her big, empty house. She prepared dinner for one. She sat down and took a long smell of her food. It smelled delicious, but it made her even more lonely knowing no one was there to share it. She picked up her mail, shuffled through it, and was about to throw it all down until she saw an envelope from Braylin.

"Ooh, she's being honored. I'll call in the morning and let her know that I'll be there . . . alone."

Now back to her lonely home. No man. No children. Even the workers were gone for the day. Nayla would've invited Judea over for dinner, but even she had a date. She and Lamar were really getting along. Even though Lamar liked Judea as she was, Nayla felt that she still owed her a makeover. *I'm sick of the sailor dresses in every imaginable color.*

Tired and alone, Nayla headed up the winding staircase. If only Palmer was up in her room waiting for her. The things she could do to that man. If only he would let her get her freak on without any strings attached. *I'm not trying to hurt him or get my heart broken while being a puppet in a show called Love.*

After a long shower, Nayla plopped down on her bed. With nothing else to do, she reached for the remote. Wouldn't you know the first channel that popped up was HBO, featuring a couple going at it. She quickly turned the channel. Damn cable TV wasn't much better. She turned to Animal Planet, hoping that maybe the crocodiles or whatever wouldn't be mating. Wrong. A species of animals she had never seen before were fucking the hell out of each other. Everybody was getting some except her. Frustrated as hell, she turned off the TV and sent the remote sailing across the room.

Her body said "call your ex," but her mind screamed "hell, no!" They argued back and forth. Finally, her throbbing pussy won the argument and commanded her hand to pick up the phone and dial D-I-C-K. He answered on the second ring. Nayla's pussy smiled at the sound of his voice. *We 'bout to get laid!* Her pussy cheered by automatically flexing her muscles.

"So, to what do I owe the pleasure of this call?" he seductively asked.

"Randy, you already know full well why I'm calling." Nayla could imagine him stroking his dick while they talked, because she was definitely massaging her knob. "I was wondering if you wanted to come over this evening." She nervously bit down on her bottom lip. "I have all the dessert you can eat in my bedroom." *Boy, do I miss that man's tongue. It is lethal!*

"We can be there in thirty minutes," he eagerly agreed.

We? We better be his ashy ass, his tongue, and his dick!

"Nina needs time to get showered," he said.

"Are you fucking kidding me?" *Un-be-fucking-lievable!* His obsession with wanting her to fuck another woman had led to their divorce, but he still thought he could get her in the bed with that fat, milky white bitch of his. Hell, no. Nayla wished that she'd never told him about her experience with women in college. That was college, though. She had chosen between soft and hard, and what she wanted was hard dick with no sides.

"Come on, Nayla. It ain't like you never done it before. Why can't you do it for me? Let me see your big, sexy ass eat Nina out."

She knew damn well he had lost his mind. Her mouth wasn't going nowhere near that skank's rank ass. Nayla's pussy-eating days were over. And even when she did eat pussy, it was sweet chocolate, not buttermilk.

As horny as she was, Nayla knew she wouldn't be getting any from that clown. "Fuck you. You go eat that raggedy bitch's ass." She hung up the phone and stared at it, daring him to call back. He didn't.

Nayla had no other options. The only way she was going to relieve her stress was with her damn vibrator. It wasn't the real thing, but it was as close as a couple hundred bucks could get. Nayla pulled it out of her drawer and put in new batteries; she wanted a fully charged dick. Turning on the chocolate dick, watching the vibrations as it hummed seductively, made her wet. Inserting the full girth inside of her wet tunnel, she felt like a virgin all over again. It sure had been a long time.

With thoughts of Palmer dancing in Nayla's head and her heart, she unleashed on her vibrator, almost fucking the latex off it. Just before she peaked, she pulled it out of her pussy and brought it to her lips, opening her mouth wide and taking it in. Nayla licked and sucked her juices from its shaft, all the while pretending it was Palmer. If only she had the new dildo that had the button that would shoot cum down her throat. If only.

She navigated her pretend Palmer back down south and called his name as she peaked. "Palmer! Aww, shit, Palmer!"

Nayla's body shook violently as the vibrator continued to hum and dance. She turned it off, turned out the lights, and fell into a short slumber. Just a few hours later, she was once again fiending for the real Palmer, and substituting for him would have to again be "Palmer the Dildo." Her pussy was already wet, but she still enjoyed touching her own pussy, so she just had to reach down and massage her swollen clitoris before "Palmer the Dildo" entered. It felt so good that she wanted to taste herself again. She thought about how good it would taste to Palmer and squeezed her pussy walls around her fingers, collecting her seductive cream, and bringing the sweet nectar to her full lips.

Damn, mmm . . . delicious as always! Nayla licked every drop of cum from her own fingers as if each digit were Palmer's dick. She put each one in slowly and pulled it out of her mouth the same way she longed to suck his massive dick. Then she inserted "Palmer the Dildo" into her fat, wet love tunnel. She plunged it in and out of her pussy with a passion. Dripping wet, she propped it up on the hands-free stand, climbed on top of all eleven and a half-inches, and rode it, while spreading her legs farther apart. Taking all its girth into her wetness, she saturated it with all of her love juices.

Nayla had repetitive massive orgasms as she did as many tricks as she could do solo. *God, I love this hands-free stand!* After coming for what felt like the twentieth time, she climbed down from Daddy Dick, kissed it, licked her own cum off the head, then went to sleep and slept well into the next day.

If only I could be in Palmer's arms after making love to him. Maybe Judea was right. I need more than the satisfaction of running my company. I should stop running from love and embrace Palmer.

Then and there, she decided that she would take the initiative of asking Palmer out. Maybe it wasn't too late.

The fine and sexy Palmer was sleeping soundly in the bed that he had shared with Karmen, his departed wife. God, how he missed that beautiful woman. At the same time, he longed for Nayla. Had Karmen been alive, he wouldn't see Nayla as anything more than a friend. As sexy as that woman was, his devotion to his wife was dear to his heart. But Karmen wasn't alive. Cancer had taken her away from him, and his attraction to Nayla was very real.

Palmer had dreamt of Karmen. She had given him her approval of Nayla, and no sooner than he took her into his arms, she disappeared into the same thin air from where she appeared. This time he wasn't sad, though. This time he felt at peace. And when a very thick, sexy, and sassy Nayla appeared, he felt horny as hell.

"Oh, Nayla, I love that pussy. Ride me harder."

"Oh, shit, Palmer, I'm comin'! Mmm . . . Oh, yeah! Oh, yeah! Yes! Yes! Oooh, yes!" Nayla plunged him deeper into her hot, wet, huge inferno. She then exploded all over his huge manhood. "Oh, Palmer! That was so amazing, baby."

"My queen, it isn't over yet," he told her as he turned her around and penetrated her wet pussy with his thick, long tongue. "Nayla, girl, you taste so damn good!" He stuck his tongue deeper and harder into Nayla, and the more she moaned, the harder his manhood got. Palmer didn't even know that it was possible for his dick to swell any more than it already had.

"Baby girl, I'm comin'! I'm comin!"

"Get off of me, Palmer! I wanna swallow every drop," Nayla instructed him, her voice filled with passion.

He loved her take-charge attitude. Just before he released his love juices in Nayla's mouth, Karmen appeared in the doorway with tears rolling down her face. Before he could run to her and grab her, she disappeared.

Palmer awoke in a cold sweat with tears running down his face. He looked over at his alarm clock. It was just ten minutes before time to get up and get Jason ready for school. He went to the bathroom to wash his face. The last thing he wanted was for Jason to see him crying. He then went back into his bedroom, turned off the alarm clock, and headed down the hallway to wake his son.

"Good morning, Daddy!" Jason exclaimed, as happy as he always seemed.

If only I could know his happiness. "Good morning, son. And how are you today?" Palmer asked his bright-eyed son.

"I feel good, Daddy. Today we gonna plant our garden at school, and the teacher said it's gonna be big!" Jason exclaimed, extending his little arms as wide as possible.

"That's nice, son," Palmer said, trying his best to hide his sadness from his son. He pasted on a smile and said, "Come on, let's get your bath."

"Aww, do I have to, Daddy?" Jason whined and laughed at the same time.

"Jay, now, you know the importance of being clean," Palmer said in a stern voice. The active child had been so tired the night before that he had fallen asleep without taking his nightly bath.

As Palmer was helping Jason out of the bathtub, the child looked up at Palmer with curious eyes and asked, "Daddy, what's the matter?"

"I miss Mommy," Palmer explained. He was trying so hard to blink back tears.

"Daddy, was Mommy pretty?"

"Jason, your mommy was the most beautiful woman in the world," Palmer told his son proudly.

"Daddy, can I stay with you today, please?" Jason asked, just as he did every school morning.

"No, son. You know that you can't go with me on the weekdays. But Daddy's off on Saturday, and we are going to the park. Just you, me, and Poopy."

Palmer's thoughts ran to Poopy, the dog, and how he got the name. Jason was two when his mother bought him the puppy. Jason could not say "puppy" so he was calling the dog Poopy and the name stuck. Palmer laughed to himself, remembering the happy moment. Then he remembered that Poopy came into their lives right before Karmen passed away. He tried so hard to get Jason to name the puppy something else, but Karmen reminded her husband that Jason was only two, and that if he wanted to name the dog Poopy, the dog should be named Poopy.

"Are you dressed?" Palmer asked as he was cleaning all the water off the bathroom floor. Sometimes Palmer did not know who left more water on the floor: Jason or Poopy.

"Yes, Daddy. I'm ready."

Palmer was hoping and praying that Jason did not have that same Batman shirt on. Palmer had been trying to throw that shirt away for a year, and every time, Jason would take it right back out of the trash and put it in the washing machine.

Just as Palmer feared, Jason had on the Batman shirt. He didn't even say anything about the shirt. He just didn't have the fight in him that day.

"Come on, son. Let's get your breakfast and get you to school."

After Palmer dropped Jason at school, he went to the diner to eat his usual: scrambled eggs, cheese grits, turkey bacon, and a bowl of

fresh fruit with a glass of milk. Palmer talked to
the other diner customers that he usually talked
to whenever he was at the diner. And, as usual,
he hated having to go into the office. He just did
not want to be hit on by the relentless women he
worked with again.

Palmer could not get over that dream of him
and Nayla where Karmen, his deceased wife,
showed up crying. He had recently dreamed of
her giving him her approval of his feelings for
Nayla, so why she came back sad and crying did
not register with Palmer.

Palmer made his deliveries with his beloved
Karmen on his mind. He had to slam on the
brakes several times that day due to not paying
attention to the cars in front of him. Finally,
after a long day of boring deliveries, he arrived
at Curvalicious.

Palmer stopped in the coffee shop before heading up to Nayla's office. There, he saw Judea and
Lamar. The two were sharing a grande mocha
latte with chocolate sprinkles. They seemed so
in love, and he envied what Lamar had: a living
woman who wasn't afraid to love him.

"Hi, Lamar. Hi, Judea." He pasted on a smile
when they looked up at him.

"Hey there, Palmer." Both Judea and Lamar
exclaimed at the same time.

"Palmer, Nayla is upstairs. She's been expectin' you directly," Judea told him in her adorable country drawl.

"Thanks, Judea." Palmer grabbed his black coffee and headed upstairs. The ride up the elevator seemed too short. Palmer needed time to figure out what to say to Nayla. If he did not try to get her to go out with him, then she would notice that something was wrong. If he did ask Nayla out again, he felt like he would be disrespecting Karmen.

As soon as he walked into Curvalicious, Nayla's beautiful face was the first one he saw. It was as if she had been waiting on him all her life.

"Hi, Palmer! How are you doing today?" Nayla sang, her thousand-watt smile beaming at Palmer.

"I'm good, Nayla. How are you?" Palmer smiled at her with his sexy-ass eyes. "You look beautiful as always." And she did. She was wearing a pantsuit that hugged her hips snugly. She looked professional yet sexy.

"I'm good, Palmer." He couldn't help but notice that she was wringing her hands as if she were nervous. "Listen . . . I was wondering if we could go out for coffee and dessert this Sunday evening." Nayla's eyes were filled with hope and joy.

"I'll have to make arrangements for my son. Can I call you in the morning and let you know?" Palmer asked, shocked that Nayla had asked *him* out.

"Sure thing. Here's my number. Call me." She kissed his cheek, handed him her business card, and took the small box of fabric samples. She disappeared into her office, switching her shapely hips as if she had no doubt that Palmer was standing there staring at her every movement. And he was.

Palmer was shocked, surprised, and mesmerized as he entered the elevator. He wanted to go out with Nayla. He'd wanted to go out with her for months, but now that he had his chance, he didn't know what to do.

When the elevator descended to the lobby, Judea was waiting as the doors opened. "What's wrong?" she asked Palmer. "You look like you just seen a ghost."

Palmer felt that way. He didn't know Judea well, but she looked like someone he could talk to. "Nayla asked me out."

"So why the long face? Thought you liked her."

"I do, Judea. I . . . I just. I had a bad dream about my late wife. I feel like I'm disrespecting her by going out with Nayla. I know it sounds crazy, but I loved Karmen so much that I feel like I'm cheating on her," he admitted sadly.

"Ain't nothin' wrong with a man lovin' a woman. But, you're still a young man wit' yo' whole life 'head of you. You got to figure out a way to let yo' late wife go." She took his hand in hers and patted it as if he were a child. "'Cause no matter how much you love her, she ain't comin' back." Judea took her leave by way of the elevator.

I know why Karmen came back. Because my heart still belongs to her. I haven't let her go.

Judea was right, and Palmer knew it. He just had to figure out a way to let Karmen go so that he could freely give his heart to Nayla.

Braylin

"Mama, are you ready?" Braylin was on the phone. She was outside of her parents' condo, waiting in the back of a limo with Bronx and Donovan. Nayla would be meeting them at the event, and she didn't want to be late.

"I'm coming Braye, calm down!" Victoria Smith's reason for taking so long wasn't so she could look nice for her daughter's big moment; it was so she could do her best to outshine her daughter on her special day. *After all, I've got to look perfect. I want them to see the fabulousness that Braylin came from.*

"Hurry, Mama. Please. I know Daddy is ready, and we've still got to stop and get Donovan's dad."

"Yeah, girl." Mrs. Smith hung up on her daughter. She had yet to tell her daughter that she was proud of her, or anything slightly positive.

Finally, Braylin's mother emerged from her condo, on the arm of Braylin's handsome father.

Robert Smith's chest was puffed up with pride; no father could have ever been prouder of his daughter than Robert was of Braylin at that very moment. Braylin jumped out of the limo and hugged her daddy's neck, and she knew that everything would be okay.

"Hey, kitten, how's my little girl?" Robert leaned forward and kissed Braylin on the forehead and held her close again. At that moment, she wasn't Braylin the businesswoman; she was Daddy's little girl.

"Hi, Daddy! I'm so glad you were able to make it tonight."

"Of course I made it, baby girl. Nothing was more important than being here for you tonight."

"You had no problem rescheduling our anniversary," Braylin's mother said. "I guess celebrating the thirty years that we've spent as husband and wife wasn't important enough for you to reschedule a client, huh?"

They had climbed back into the limo and were pulling off when Victoria decided that she would show the jealousy that she felt toward the relationship between her husband and her only daughter.

"Victoria Annell Smith, you know good and well that if I had canceled that client, you wouldn't be driving that brand new Jaguar with the custom animal-skin interior, so I don't even know why you're complaining. You weren't complaining when we were at the dealership and I was putting cash down for your Jag that I paid for and then put in your name. So chill. This is our little girl's night, and damn it, we are going to enjoy it, with or without you."

Braylin, Bronx, and Donovan sat there in shock. None of them had ever heard Robert stand up to his vindictive wife before.

"'Bout time you stood up to her stuck-up self, Mr. Robert!" Bronx began laughing hysterically and clapping her hands.

"Bronx, calm down, girl." Braylin was happy that her father had finally stood up to her mother, but she wasn't going to say so and give her mother anything else to trip about.

Donovan simply sat there in amusement. *Well, well, well, Bray's little perfect family ain't so damn perfect after all.*

"Yo, man! You passed my Pops' house," Donovan barked at the driver.

"Donovan, you didn't have to yell at him like that. I'm sure it was an accident." Braylin looked at her boyfriend sternly. "Sir, if you make this U-turn right here, Mr. Jones' place is just a couple of houses down."

"Very well, Ms. Smith. Thank you." The driver appreciated the young lady's manners. He thought that she was sexy as hell, in all her thick glory.

Hmm, Lord only knows what I'd do if I could get my hands on a sista like her, but I'm old enough to be her daddy. Young blood better watch out. He chuckled to himself as he got out of the car to open the door for Donovan's father.

"Hello, people!" Donovan's father, David, always had a cheerful disposition. "Hey there, Ms. Braylin. Congratulations, sweetheart."

"Hi, David. Thank you!" Braylin beamed as she reached up and hugged David's neck.

"'Sup, Pop? Hey, girl, don't be calling my pops David. That's Mr. Jones to you."

Donovan could be such an ass. Braylin simply rolled her eyes at him.

"Hello, son, and I told her that I prefer that she call me David. I'm not an old man, and I don't want to be referred to as such." He set his son straight without so much as raising his voice or losing his smile.

"Mom, Dad, I would like you to meet Donovan's dad, David Jones. David, these are my parents, Robert and Victoria Smith."

"Hello, it's nice to meet you both—and Bronx, it's a pleasure to see you again." He was a master at being polite, because he knew he couldn't stand her.

"Hey, Pop, how you know Bronx?" Donovan was trying to play innocent. He knew good and well where David knew Bronx from.

"I met her the other day when I ran into Braylin at the mall." He figured that he wouldn't call the young girl out. She embarrassed herself enough without anyone's help.

"Hi, David, how you doing?" Bronx uncrossed her legs, spread them open, and then slowly crossed them again, giving out the universal, silent booty call.

Everyone in the car noticed the stench of musty, sweaty vagina and immediately knew that it was Bronx. It was then that Donovan realized that Bronx hadn't even washed off the smell of the raunchy sex that they'd had earlier.

What the hell am I doing messing with a skank like her?

Then the sly dog smirked to himself. He knew what he was doing with her. She gave the best head he had ever had, and she loved being stuck in her ass and gladly took everything he gave her and begged for more.

When they arrived at the banquet hall, Braylin pulled her friend to the side and whispered in her ear, "Girl, do you need some of my baby wipes and body spray?" She loved her friend and didn't want anyone else to say anything to Bronx, especially Victoria.

"Oh, yeah, girl. I thought I felt a little sweaty." Bronx didn't seem embarrassed at all.

Braylin couldn't believe how comfortable Bronx seemed about walking around with an unpleasant body odor.

Robert noticed the look of discomfort on his baby girl's face as she walked toward the table. "What's wrong, princess?"

"Nothing, Daddy. I just felt a little dizzy for a minute. I'm fine." She pasted on a smile and hooked her arm in her father's and gracefully walked to the table. There sat Nayla in a ruby red, high-low hemmed gown.

"Hi, Ms. Anderson. Thank you so much for coming."

Nayla stood up to hug Braylin. "Hi, beautiful Braylin. Congratulations on such an accomplishment. And call me Nayla."

"Nayla, thank you so much for coming. These are my parents, Robert and Victoria Smith, my boyfriend, Donovan, and his father, David." Everyone said their hellos, and Nayla was immediately put off by Donovan. Just something about him rubbed her the wrong way.

After Donovan spent a few minutes looking Nayla up and down, he noticed that Bronx was gone. He texted her to see where she was, and when she replied that she was by the restroom, he rushed off to see if he could go sneak in some nookie.

They were serving the second course of the meal when Victoria announced to the table, "Donovan and Bronx have been gone an awful long time. Isn't that weird, Braylin, that both of them have been gone this long at the same time?"

"Mama, I'm sure that Donovan's just gone to smoke a cigarette, and Bronx's using the bathroom."

"Mmm . . . yeah, give it to me, Donovan! Yeah! Ooh, yeah!" Bronx was screaming even as Donovan had stuffed his tie in her mouth.

"Shut up, girl! Do you want somebody to hear you and walk in on us and then go tell Bray?"

"No, daddy. Mmm. . . ." He had Bronx with her back up against the bathroom stall door with her legs wrapped around his waist.

"Then shut up and take this pipe, girl." He plummeted in and out of her loose vaginal walls, and the thought that they could be caught excited him. "Yeah, girl, hurry up and make me come so I can shoot it down your throat."

Just as he was making one final thrust into Bronx, the bathroom door opened, and they knew that they had been caught. Donovan peeked through the crack in the bathroom stall and saw that it was their limo driver. By the look on Donovan's face, Bronx knew that it was someone who could easily expose them to Braylin, and she began to panic.

"What we going to do?"

"You gonna shut the fuck up until he leave. That's what you gonna do."

Donovan was a rude and crude bastard, but that didn't faze Bronx. She was used to, and liked, roughnecks.

"Better yet, you can stuff this in your mouth, ho. I'm not gonna let nobody stop me from getting mine."

The limo driver just shook his head as he washed his hands and hoped it wasn't that sweet young lady's boyfriend in there screwing around on her. Not that he thought for a second that he wasn't capable of cheating on her, but because she didn't deserve to be hurt like that.

***

I wonder where Bronx and D are, Braylin thought as they finished dessert. Both of them had missed the entire meal and were about to miss the award ceremony. Just as she was about to get up and go looking for them, Donovan made his way back to the table and kissed Braylin on the forehead.

"Where have you been, Donovan?" Braylin had a feeling that wherever he had been, he had been up to no good. She leaned over and took a whiff of him. All she smelled was weed.

"I ran into a friend of mine who is a busboy here. We sat out back and smoked some 'dro. That's all, no big deal." He leaned toward her and kissed her softly on her lips to distract her from Bronx approaching the table.

"I'm back! Y'all miss me?" Bronx could be so loud. Several people from the next table looked at her and wondered how she had even been invited to an event like this. "Girl, thanks for the hookup." Bronx winked at Braylin.

Braylin turned her attention from Bronx to the emcee on stage.

"Now, for the Public Relations Executive of the Year Award. And the nominees are: Joshua Gettinger, Braylin Smith, Haybert Fields, and Bill Coates. And the winner is . . . Braylin Smith!"

Braylin was overwhelmed and couldn't believe that she had actually won the award. She had felt honored just to be recognized. She waited for Donovan to help her up, but then she realized that would be like waiting for Christmas of next year, and she refused to let his insensitivity ruin her evening. Still, she couldn't ignore the fact that he didn't really clap or even seem happy for her.

"You go, girl!" Bronx screamed.

"Congrats, Braylin!" Nayla exclaimed, genuinely happy for her.

"Congratulations, darling. I knew you could do it." Of course Victoria had to get up and put on her show. "Mommy is so proud of you."

It felt good for Braylin to hear her mother say those words, even if it was just for show.

"I'm so proud of you, Braylin." Robert squeezed his baby and kissed her cheek.

"Congrats, Braylin. I'm so happy for you. May I escort you up to the podium, pretty lady?" David was purposely flirting with Braylin. If nothing else, he wanted her to see that just because Donovan acted like a dirt bag, didn't mean that he came from one.

As David took her arm, she got comfortable and let him guide her up to the podium to accept her award. *Damn, he feels good. I could get used to being on David's arm. Wait! What am I thinking? He's Donovan's father!*

"Thank you, David." She lowered her eyes and planted a soft kiss, which she let linger a little longer than normal, on his cheek before stepping up to the microphone.

"Thank you so very much for this award. I would like to thank my staff and coworkers at Motherland Advertising. To my family and friends, thank you all for your love and support. I couldn't have gotten this far without you. God bless you." Braylin ended her short speech and made her way back down the stairs to her table.

It was David, not Donovan, who stood to pull out her chair and make sure that Braylin was seated comfortably before taking his seat.

"Good job, girl. I guess all those long nights paid off for something." Donovan was an ignorant SOB and everyone knew it.

Visibly annoyed, Braylin refused to let Donovan ruin her moment. "Anyway, friends and family, I have an announcement to make." Everyone turned toward her, but before she could get a word in edgewise, Bronx's phone started ringing.

The emcee was announcing the closing of the ceremony, and Bronx finally answered her cell phone. "What?"

Braylin couldn't believe that Bronx really just answered her phone as loudly as she did. She shook her head in disgust.

As everyone stood to leave, Braylin told Nayla that she'd be calling her soon. "Again, thank you so much for coming."

"Thank you for having me, love," Nayla said.

"I ain't had yo' fine ass yet, ma," Donovan said.

Completely turned off, Nayla bid everyone else a good night and called for her car.

"Really, Donovan?" Braylin was furious and wanted to do something she'd never done before—punch him in his face. But that wasn't even her style. What she did know was that she was fed up with Donovan. She knew that she couldn't justify carrying around a dead weight like him—Bronx, too, if she was honest with herself.

In an attempt to defuse the situation, David walked over to where Braylin was standing, "Congratulations, Ms. Smith. Your limo is waiting." David put his arm out to escort the young woman who he wished was his out of the building.

While they all walked to the limo, David never let go of Braylin's arm, and she didn't want him to. She wished that she had met him first.

The driver opened the door, and David assisted Braylin in, hopped in, and almost closed the door, forgetting that the others were waiting to get in. In his heart of hearts, he knew that if given the chance, he could love her in a way that Donovan never would.

During the ride, they kept looking each other in the eyes, and Braylin's parents noticed. Not that either one of them minded; both of them longed for someone to take their daughter's focus off of Donovan.

"Young man, this is our stop." Victoria looked at her husband and grabbed his hand, and they bolted out of the limousine.

"This is the office, honey. What are we doing here?" Victoria leaned over, kissed her husband on his ear, and he knew everything he needed to know. Everyone inside the limo chuckled as they pulled off.

"Yo, man, drop me off up here at my homie's crib," Donovan demanded.

"And where might that be?" The driver snapped.

"The apartments down there. Why? Just do your job."

That was it. The driver had had it with Donovan. "Look, I'ma pull the hell over, and you can just get out right here."

"Sir, do you want us all to get out now?" Braylin only said that because she didn't want Donovan to know how happy she was that he was being put out.

"No, Miss. Just this thuggin' fool. If you don't mind me saying, you would be so much better off without this slimy sucker. Get out my car, man."

"Yo, I got your slimy sucker. I'll see you again, dude, and when I do, it's gonna be me and you."

"Son, don't do anything stupid. Just go on up to Bobby's apartment and we'll see you later." David was the calm in the midst of this storm.

"A'ight, Pop. Later, Bray, Bronx." After listening to his dad, Donovan calmed down some and simply got out of the car.

The driver breathed a sigh of relief. "Okay, who's next?"

Bronx spoke up first. "Can you take me to my job around the corner?"

"Yes, ma'am." The driver shook his head as he realized where they were headed.

Braylin couldn't believe that Bronx was going straight to work without going home and bathing first. She simply hung her head in shame.

David noticed the sadness in Braylin's eyes. It was one of the things that Donovan never would have picked up on, or if he did, he wouldn't have acted like he cared at all. He patted her hand as if to let her know that whatever was wrong, it would get better, one way or another.

They pulled up at The Pretty Kitty, and Bronx happily jumped out of the car and leaned back in the window and said, "Y'all don't do nothing that I wouldn't do! Bye." That left it wide open for them to do almost anything.

"Bye, Bronx," they said in unison.

"Where to next, Miss?"

David looked at Braylin, and she stared back into his eyes and knew that if Donovan didn't want to do right by her, then there was someone who did, and that someone was David.

"My place," Braylin said. Even though they both knew what they were about to do was wrong, it felt so right.

Ten minutes later, they were at Braylin's apartment, and David was putting the Ojays' "We Cried Together" on the home entertainment system. He was about to sit down on the couch while Braylin changed clothes, but he heard her sobbing loudly in her room. He wandered around until he found her bedroom and knocked on the door. "Braylin, are you okay?"

"I'm fine." She was clearly trying to stifle her sobs. She really wasn't fine; there was so much that wasn't right that she wasn't sure where to even begin.

"Umm, can I come in, Braylin?" By the time David realized what he had said, it was too late, because Braylin was opening the door, standing there in her bra and matching G-string, wiping the tears from her eyes and looking at David, not as Donovan's father, but as the man that should be kissing her tears away and stroking her between her thighs until all her stress melted away.

Stretching out her arms, reaching for David, Braylin simply said, "Please, come in."

She was tempted to reach down and rub her vagina until it became moist with anticipation. David stepped over the threshold of no return and passionately kissed Braylin on her lips. The kiss defined the moment when they crossed the point of no return.

He guided her backward while never breaking their kiss. His tongue slipped out slowly as if it were asking for permission from Braylin's mouth to be allowed to go further. Her only reply was to moan and pull him closer to her.

"David?"

"Yes, Braylin?"

"Make love to me . . . please, just make love to me."

In his heart of hearts, as much as he wanted her, he knew that what he was about to do was wrong. Then he thought about his son still messing around with at least one of his grandkids' mothers, not to mention a slew of other women.

He bent down and lifted Braylin up slowly while caressing her thighs and flicking his tongue across her diamond-hard nipples through her bra, easing her panties off her body while never removing his mouth from some part of her body. His touch alone made Braylin shudder in sheer pleasure.

So this is what I've been missing messing with Donovan all this time.

"Aahhh, yes!" David hadn't even touched her pulsating core yet, and she was already moaning in pure ecstasy.

Her entire body was pulsating with excitement as he slowly began kissing his way down to her thighs. The pace that he was using to discover her was maddening yet toe-curling in a way that she forgot even existed. His sexy and skillful lips finally found her swollen pearl and began to kiss it passionately, while effortlessly penetrating her with his tongue. David sucked and licked her pussy. She was relishing in the fact that she was drowning him with her juices and he was determined to drink as much as possible.

He could tell she was beginning to black out from having multiple orgasms. He placed a supportive arm behind her back and kept going, taking Braylin deep into the throes of passion, bringing her back and taking her there again with each stroke of his tongue.

He wrapped his arms around her and planted a huge, wet kiss on her full lips. She tried to pull away from David, but the feeling of his body against hers, his lips on hers, and the taste of his tongue inside of her mouth was too much for her to resist. She melted into him, wrapped her thick arms around his neck, and returned his passionate kisses.

David slid his left hand up and massaged her breast. A deep-throated moan escaped her lips, and her slick walls contracted. *Fuck me, baby.* She wanted David so badly that she was weak in the knees. How long had it been since she'd genuinely been made love to? *Too damn long,* she reasoned as David's kisses moved south, stopping at her neck, leaving love bites before suckling her full breasts. He then licked her stomach, pausing only to plant butterfly kisses on her navel before sliding his tongue in between her thick thighs again.

"David, no," she moaned. "No, David," she moaned again.

Just as he approached her honey well, David stopped, looked up at Braylin, and asked, "Do you really want me to stop?" Her thighs quivered as honey began to drip from her well.

David didn't hear her response. He buried his head between her thighs, and the only audible sound in the room was the slurpy-splashy sound of his tongue snaking in and out of her deep, wet abyss.

Damn, her pussy is like honey, sweet and sticky.

"No, David, please don't stop," she finally managed to answer. "Oh, David!" she cried as he plunged his thick, long tongue deeper and deeper in her heated opening. She couldn't help but buck against his face as he continued to make love to her with his mouth. "Yes, yes, yes, oh, yeah!" She wrapped her thighs tighter around his head, leaned back, and completely let go. She released her love juices all over his face and neck, and watched it drip slowly down his shoulders.

Shuddering with pleasure, Braylin leaned down and drew his face to hers and kissed him passionately on his lips, savoring the taste of her own release.

"I never knew that I would enjoy making love to anyone with my mouth this much," David gushed as he slowly rose up, still holding on to Braylin's thick and luscious hips. His heart was racing in excess of 100 beats per minute. Noticing her heavy breathing and the satisfied look on her angelic face pleased David, and a huge grin adorned his ruggedly handsome face.

Braylin returned his smile, but as soon as she looked past him, a look of horror replaced her smile. "David, look!" she shrieked as she covered her face with her hands.

"Baby, what is it?" David asked as he turned toward the door. They had an audience.

Neither he nor Braylin had taken the time to close the blinds before entering their own world of pleasure, and sure enough, there was an older man standing outside the window, looking in at them, grinning. He was enjoying the show so much that he'd removed his shriveled penis from his pants and was stroking it right there in plain sight of anyone passing by.

"Hey, buddy! What is your problem?" David quickly questioned the man before shutting the blinds. He didn't want to witness the old man's ejaculation, because he'd no doubt release a cloud of dust from his old balls.

Turning to Braylin, David stretched his arms out and said, "Come here, beautiful."

"David, I'm so embarrassed. I can't." She kept her eyes closed and her face covered. She was so ashamed. How could she have been so careless? And poor Mr. Akins. She couldn't be angry at him for watching them. The man suffered from Alzheimer's and was always wandering outside. Mrs. Akins had her hands full trying to keep up with him.

"I promise you have nothing to be embarrassed about. You are gorgeous, Braylin." David lay down on the floor and pulled her down on top of him. She was apprehensive until David slid down, coming face-to-face with her dripping wet pussy. That was all it took to ease her nerves. David's powerful tongue became reacquainted with her dripping wet love tunnel, and they were instantly taken back to heaven again. Thoughts of Mr. Akins were completely forgotten.

"Mmm . . . David, you are . . . mmm . . ." David had her feeling so good that she couldn't even form complete sentences. "David, oh, David . . . mmm . . . damn!" She grabbed his head and a handful of his short hair. David simply moaned and continued his quest to please the woman who was finally his.

He felt his manhood swell as she leaned back and locked her legs tighter around his neck and began to buck wildly against his face. It was then that he knew that she was coming. "I'm comin', baby. Oh my . . . oh, I'm . . . oh, yes, I'm comin'!" She spread her legs and squirted her sweet release all over his face.

Braylin was in pure awe after that, as she had never experienced an orgasm quite that powerful before. She looked down at David and smiled while stroking his smooth, close cut fade as he caressed her body.

Braylin had never felt anything like that before, and she was determined that she wasn't going back to mediocre loving after that night. By the time David entered her with his long, thick manhood again, all it took was a few slow strokes before she was thrown completely over the edge of eroticism with the most intense orgasm she had ever experienced.

Leaning forward, he huskily whispered in her ear, "I love this thickness on you, beautiful."

"I love the way you love this thickness, baby." He made her feel like a sexual goddess, like she was on top of the world and nothing or no one could ever stand in her way.

The way David was loving her body told her that she could have anything she wanted, whenever she wanted it. What Braylin wanted at that very moment was to go down south and let his delicious-looking dick get acquainted with her luscious mouth. He was kissing her nipples as Braylin started on a path down his body. Just as she was about to take him into her warm mouth, he positioned them in the perfect meal for two, a sixty-nine.

"Tell me what you want, baby. Kiss and lick on me, everywhere you want me to do the same to you."

"Kiss me here." She kissed his broad chest. "Mmm, kiss me here, baby." Following directions to the tee, he kissed her belly button. "Oh, David, kiss me here," she moaned, spreading her lips further apart and massaging her clit against his nose as she took him deep into her wet throat.

"Say no more." Braylin's perfect lover went downtown like she was his last meal and he intended to get every single drop. He wasn't like her ex, Savon. That man used to always lap at her pussy like it was a doggy dish and he was a malnourished bulldog. And he certainly wasn't like Donovan's no-foreplay self.

After being under David's hypnotic spell, Braylin couldn't imagine anyone ever being a better lover than him.

He entered her again, and she lost herself in their own special rhythm.

"Oh, shit! David!" She clawed his back as she came all over his latex-covered manhood, and loved it. "Oh, David, I'm sorry, baby. I hope I didn't hurt you."

He stared directly in her eyes and spoke softly. "It's okay, baby. That's what my back is here for, for you to claw at. I wanted to give you an orgasm like you've never experienced before, baby. You were bound to react some type of way."

Smiling, she looked down and noticed that he was still rock hard. All she could think was, *Dayum . . . as hung as he is, and he's still hard as a rock. Oh my God, I'm falling in lust.*

After making love again, they climaxed together and drifted off into a peaceful sleep.

As the rising sun began peeking through the curtains, Braylin rolled over, looked at David, and smiled, feeling in her heart that he could very well be the one—the one to love her like an old school love song. This was the love she'd always wanted, needed, desired, and dreamed of. Marsha Ambrious's "Your Hands" began to softly play on the iPod dock in the background, and she stroked David's head, feeling blessed to be sharing this special moment with him, knowing that she never wanted to let go.

Meanwhile, Donovan and his "homeboy" Bobby were kissing and feeling each other up in his apartment when Bobby got the bright idea to invite Bronx over for a threesome.

"You think she'll suck my dick while you bang me out from the back?" Bobby stood up and shook his ass in Donovan's face.

"Man, get that freaky bitch high enough and she'll do any-damn-thing. You still got that bag of X?" Donovan pulled down Bobby's pants and slapped him on the ass before sticking his tongue inside the fat man's anus.

Palmer

As promised, Palmer got up early Saturday morning and took Jason and Poopy to the park. His plan was to spend the entire day with the two of them, playing and trying to forget about his worries. Then Sunday, he would spend his day with Nayla. Finally.

He looked up from running around with Jason and Poopy to see Amanda, one of his coworkers. She immediately noticed him and ran over.

"Hi, Palmer! Who is this cutie?" the office whore asked while pretending to be interested in his son.

"Amanda, this is Jason." Palmer turned to his son and said, "Jason, tell Ms. Amanda hi."

"Hi, Ms. Amanda! This is my dog, Poopy!" Jason grinned, barling his missing front teeth. He was so adorable. "Come on, Poopy, let's go play!" Off they went. Poopy was fast on Jason's heels.

"Don't go too far, Jay," Palmer called after his son before turning to Amanda and asking, "What brings you here so early on a Saturday morning?" He had never seen her there before.

"Oh, just trying to get in a li'l exercise. I wanna keep my body sexy and tight." The whore batted her fake eyelashes at Palmer while showcasing her fake boobs.

"Is there something wrong with your eyes?" Palmer asked her with a puzzled look on his face.

Feeling embarrassed, she replied, "No. My eyes are fine." She couldn't help but to roll her eyes at Palmer. He was fine, but he had to be slow if he didn't know she wanted to take him home and fuck his brains out.

Just then, Jason ran up to them. Amanda bent down and kissed him on the forehead. Quickly, Jason wiped off the kiss. When she noticed Palmer checking out a nicely-dressed fat woman, she reached up to hug his neck, pressing her firm body into his. Her behavior was very inappropriate in front of his son and the other people in the park. Palmer gently nudged her away. It was then that he noticed that Nayla had witnessed the whole scene. If the look she returned to him could kill, Palmer would have died right there. Without saying so much as a hello, Nayla walked off.

Palmer turned to Jason and told him, "You and Poopy sit right here and wait for Daddy. Understand?"

"Yes, Daddy." Jason stroked Poopy's silky coat.

"May I stay here and keep him company?" Amanda asked. She was quite satisfied with herself when she saw that heifer run off. Why would Palmer want someone that huge when he could have her, a perfect size six?

"Sure." Palmer wanted her gone, to be honest, but it was best that he not leave his son unattended in the busy park. "Thanks."

"Nayla! Nayla! Please wait!"

She turned around with a look of pure disappointment on her face. He saw the tears in her eyes, even though she was trying to hide them.

"What do you want, Palmer?" Her once sexy tone of voice was replaced with one of anger. "Don't you have to get back to your young, skinny, white wife?" Before he could even offer an explanation, she said, "Don't bother calling me, Palmer." And with that, she turned and walked away.

Nayla

Judea and Nayla sat in Nayla's office having one of their heart-to-heart conversations. It was almost lunchtime. Their girl talk had become the norm when it was slow in the office. Judea and Nayla had become fast friends. Nayla was so thankful that she had hired Judea despite her lack of experience.

"Judea, we've got to get the adjacent office prepared for Braylin to move into."

"I thought she had decided that she'd mostly work from home? But I know that ain't what's botherin' you. So what's-a-matter with you?"

"Judea, I had taken your advice and asked Palmer out. I was very excited over our upcoming date."

"So what went wrong? Why you sound so sad if y'all going out?" Judea thought they were making the situation a lot harder than it had to be. They should have just stopped beating around the bush, like Judea and Lamar had done from day one. When you like somebody, you don't play games, because life is way too short.

"We're not going." Nayla was so very disappointed. "I saw him with his wife and kid at the park. He was trying to play me."

"His wife? He told me his wife had died." Judea was confused. There had to be some kind of mistake.

"Wife, girlfriend, it's all the same. I saw him with another woman in the park. And of course she just had to be a skinny white woman." Nayla was so frustrated. It was so hard to find a good black man, especially if you weren't a skinny model-type with dead brain cells. She wasn't prejudiced, but seeing Palmer with that white woman made her so mad. Or maybe it wasn't because the woman was white—maybe it was because Nayla had mustered the courage to ask him out only to have her heart broken no sooner than she let down her guard.

"Maybe you need to talk to Palmer and find out just what's goin' on, Nayla. Thangs ain't always what they seem," Judea advised.

"I'm still not ready to speak to him. I don't even want to talk about him anymore." Nayla could be really stubborn sometimes. "Anyway, tell me what's been up with you and Lamar," Nayla asked, trying to change the subject.

"Well, we've been seein' each other er' day since my first day here." Judea beamed. At just the mention of Lamar, she got a certain glow about her. Judea proceeded to tell funny stories about her and Lamar's lunch dates. The two of them were perfect for each other.

She seems so happy, Nayla thought. She was happy for Judea. She wanted her own happiness as well. Truth be told, she had feelings for Palmer. That's why it hurt so much to think that he could be just another married or attached lowlife pursuing her.

"Ms. Judea, you can take a longer lunch today. I've got a long business luncheon to attend," Nayla told Judea.

"Okay, Nayla. And er'thang will work out soon." Judea encouraged her before leaving Nayla's office.

Nayla left for her meeting, hoping and praying that Judea was right.

Judea

Judea called Lamar on his work phone and told him that she was able to take a long lunch.

"Baby, I's packed us a lunch basket. How 'bout we have a li'l picnic right at your desk?" Lamar was so in love and wasn't afraid to show it.

"I'd really like that, boo. I'll see you in a few minutes." She hung up the phone, smiling as wide as the sun was bright that day.

Just then, Palmer walked in. He knew that Nayla took her lunch around this time, and he thought that it would be better to deliver the package while she was not there.

"Hi, Judea." Palmer tried to paste on his best smile.

Judea noticed that he wasn't his usual self. He was just as miserable as Nayla. They were going to drive Judea crazy if they didn't get their acts together soon.

"Hi there, Palmer. How you doin'? You seem real sad. What's a matta?" Judea asked.

"Nayla saw me and my son at the park Saturday. One of my coworkers had just joined us. I had no idea that she would be there. Nayla saw us together and assumed that we were together because Amanda, my coworker, unexpectedly hugged me. I tried explaining myself to Nayla, but she wouldn't listen to me," Palmer said with a look of despair on his face.

"So the woman Nayla saw you wit' wasn't your wife or girlfrien'?"

"When I told you my wife was dead, I wasn't kidding. That girl, Amanda, is far from my type. I don't mean to disrespect women, but she's the office whore. I would never jeopardize my life or my son's life like that. I'm sure that she likes me, but I'm only interested in Nayla. I even wrote her a poem." He reached inside his shirt pocket and removed a piece of folded paper. "I was wondering if you would please put it on her desk." Palmer thought the poem might be his last hope of winning Nayla over.

"Sure. And don't you worry none. I'll talk to Nayla fo' you." *I been doing a lot of reassuring today.*

"Have a good day, Judea. And thank you so much."

"You too, Palmer." Judea bid him good day. She then set the box of fabric samples in Nayla's office and placed the poem on her desk. She was in such a hurry to get ready for her lunch date with Lamar that she completely forgot to leave a sticky note saying the poem was from Palmer.

Lamar was always so prompt, and she didn't want to be late. She ran into the private restroom that Nayla had reserved for her and freshened up. She finished off with a reapplication of her lip-gloss. She thought about buying lipstick, but had no idea what color would go with her skin. In Altoona, everybody just wore fire hydrant red lipstick if they wore any at all. Judea opted to be natural and just wear lip-gloss or wrap her Vaseline in aluminum foil so she could stick it in her purse.

She heard Lamar outside in the office calling for her. "Judea, baby!"

"I'm in here, baby." She blushed at their affection for each other. "Be out in a minute." *I gotta look good fo' my baby.*

Lamar had gone from being Lamar to her baby. And she wouldn't have it any other way. Her heart did a flip-flop. She was in love and it felt so good.

Braylin

Braylin had made it her business from the night that she and David first made love to always have "late business meetings" at least three nights a week. She no longer even desired Donovan, and she really wanted nothing more than to kick him out of her place and her life. It was months before Donovan even realized that Braylin had stopped chastising him for everything, and that it didn't even seem to faze her if they had gone an extended period without sex.

"Braylin, what's good, baby?" Donovan was sitting in the living room, candles lit and soft music playing.

"Hey, Donovan, what's all of this?" *This jackass hasn't done this since we first got together*, Braylin thought.

"It's just a special evening for my special lady."

"Your special lady? Am I being punked? Where are the cameras?" She laughed. He didn't.

"Why you joking around? I'm trying to be here for you and show your fat ass that I love you."

"You love me? You don't love me. You know why you don't love me? It's because you don't love yourself."

"You know, Braylin, I should have known a spoiled, fat bitch like yourself wouldn't know how to appreciate having a man like me at home with yo' ass," he sneered.

"Excuse me?" Braylin was ready to slap fire from his face.

"Oh, you heard me. It's stupid heifers like you who make black men go out and marry white women. Then you sit on your fat asses, crying with your girlfriends over ice cream and cake about how all the good black men are switching out."

Braylin raised her hand, drew back, and slapped spit from his mouth. When he opened his mouth to speak again, she back-handed him with the same hand. If Braylin had a gun, she probably would have shot Donovon in cold blood and spit on his corpse. How dare he disrespect her in her own home?

"Call Jenny Craig and see if she can recommend a diet for fat and stupid chicks."

Braylin balled up her fist to punch him square in his nose, but instead of hitting him, she laughed. It was almost sadistic how calm she was.

"You know, Donovan, if you want to go spend some time with one of your whores, you didn't have to pick a fight. You are more than welcome to go, permanently."

"Aw shit, girl, you know I ain't really going no-damn-where."

Don't do me any favors, Braylin thought as she walked off. If she wasn't about to spend some time with David or hang with Nayla and Judea, she'd rather be alone.

Months had passed since David and Braylin had made their initial connection. "Oh, David," Braylin moaned as her lover took her higher into ecstasy. He was so gentle and in tune with her needs. He was definitely the best lover she had ever had. Not only was he making love to her body, but he sent her mind into another world. Together they made the most beautiful music.

As soft music played in the background, she began to cry tears of joy as he went down and began to lick all the stress and drama of the day away from her sweet flesh. "Oh, David, nobody does it like you. Nobody!"

The seductive smell of jasmine-scented candles filled the air as their bodies intertwined on the floor next to the fireplace. Their passions burned hotter than the logs in the radiant fire as strokes from his tongue brought her near orgasm.

Suddenly and without warning, the front door opened. Standing in its entry was Braylin's live-in situation, Donovan. "What the *fuck*?" he screamed, not wanting to believe the scene before him. His woman was with another man in their home.

The outburst startled David and Braylin. They broke their embrace and sat on the floor, buck naked.

Donovan's face iced over with pure pain as tears began to run down his cheeks. Even though he knew he had done Braylin wrong more times than he could count, he never thought that Karma would come back so strong. "Pops?" He was even more in shock that his girlfriend's dick-on-the-side was his own father.

"Why you in my house with my woman, Pops?" Donovan asked the man he had looked up to his whole life.

David felt wrong about hurting his son. At that moment, it didn't matter that Donovan never deserved Braylin. "Son, I'm sorry." He felt low for messing with the only woman that his son had ever claimed to love. "Son, I am so very sorry." David gathered his clothing. He had to get out of their home. The pain on his son's face was more than he could stand to see.

"I'm sorry, Donovan, but I need attention too," Braylin said. She thought being caught was what she wanted. After being hurt so many times by Donovan, Braylin was angry, but seeing the look of pain on Donovan's face made her feel so guilty. Maybe he deserved it, but she wasn't evil and didn't believe in revenge. She felt awful and embarrassed. What complicated the situation even more was the fact that she felt something real for David. He wasn't some ploy to get even with Donovan. She knew it in her heart of hearts that she wanted to be with David.

Just as Braylin was beginning to feel completely horrible about the situation and hurting Donovan, in walked Bronx and some other woman who looked like she was part Asian. "Donovan, is it cool? I wanna suck some—Oh, shit. Braylin. Hey, Bray . . . what you doing here?" Bronx's dumb ass had to be high. It was Braylin's house. What did she mean, what was *she* doing there?

Braylin blew a gasket. "Bitch don't 'Bray' me. You been fucking with him all along, haven't you?"

"Look at you messing around with his daddy," Bronx shot back.

The other girl just shook her head. That's when Braylin noticed that other girl's shirt said "Chyna Wuz Here."

"And you're the other trick that's been in my house, writing on my damn bathroom mirror with lipstick." Braylin stood, as naked as the day she was born, and slapped both Bronx and "Chyna."

"Bronx, I never want to speak to your trifling ass again, and take Donovan and this other fucking slut with you. Everybody get out!" Braylin screamed at the top of her lungs.

"Bray, you don't mean that." Donovan tried to smooth talk Braylin.

"Donovan, I'm sorry, son," David said.

"Yo, man, don't say shit to me!" Donovan snapped back.

"Ay, Dee, I'm pregnant," Chyna said with a smirk on her face.

"Oh, word? Me too, bitch!" Bronx and Chyna high-fived each other.

"Get the fuck out!"

"Braylin, you don't mean that." Donovan stared at Braylin with tears in his eyes. He wanted to hate her as much as he hated his father in that moment. He tried to hate her, but he couldn't. Then, and only then, did he realize how wrong he had done her and how much he had taken her for granted. She was the only woman he had ever loved. If only he could have held on to her.

"Baby, we can work it out. I'm sorry. I never knew Karma could come back this strong." He was pleading. He fell to his knees with grief so strong it was as is if he'd lost his mother all over again. "I know I did you wrong, Bray, but my pops?"

"Yes, I do mean it. Donovan, get out of my house. I'm tired of being hurt by you repeatedly. I never meant to fall in love with your dad, but he held me when you were out being a trick."

"Fine. If that's what you want, I'll leave. But it doesn't mean I don't love you," Donovan whimpered.

"It's too late for that, Donovan. Just get out."

Donovan got up off his knees. "Let's go, you stupid tricks," he said to Chyna and Bronx.

"Whateva, fool. You betta get ready to take care of your babies growing in our bellies," Bronx said. Chyna and Bronx walked out, arm in arm, as Donovan followed with his head hanging.

David turned to Braylin. "Braylin, do you really mean what you just said? You're in love with me?"

"Yes, David, I'm in love with you. You've shown me what it means to be truly cared about, and I really want to see where we can take this."

David simply walked to her, took her by the hand, and kissed her gently. "I never meant to fall in love with you either, but I did."

Nayla

Nayla had just gotten back from a brunch meeting with Braylin. She sat at her desk reading a poem that she thought that Judea had left for her. Nayla was stumped. She really didn't know how to tell her in a nice way that she was strictly dickly. The poem was about making love. That was not going to happen between the two of them. It had been a while, but not so long that Nayla would settle for a clit instead of a dick.

To Make Love

To make love to my mind is to
make love to my soul. To make
love to my soul is the equivalent
to making the most beautiful love to my
body.
So, you see, to make love to me is to
make love
to all three.

To make love to all three is to truly love me.

After reading and re-reading it, Nayla finally called Judea into her office.

"Judea, can I see you in here for a moment please?" she asked over the intercom.

"Sure, Nayla, jus' a minute." Judea always responded so quickly. Professionally, she had come a long way in a short time.

Judea walked into Nayla's office, looking wide-eyed with curiosity. "Did I forget to type something or copy something fo' you?"

"No, Judea, that's not it. Have a seat."

She took the seat across from her boss and friend. "I found this poem on my desk, and I was wondering if it was you who left it for me."

Judea opened her mouth to explain, but Nayla was on a roll. "Because if it was you, then sweetheart, friends we will always be, but that's all we will ever be. I don't mess with women." *Anymore.* Judea was cute and sexy in a country 'Bama way, but she didn't have that hard dick Nayla's body was craving.

Judea could not stop laughing.

"Judea, what is so funny?"

She was now standing in front of Nayla, slapping her thighs laughing like she was a clown at a circus. "Even though I ain't had no man physically don't mean I want the same thang I got!" Judea exclaimed adamantly. Tears were rolling down her face from all the laughing.

"Oh, Judea, I apologize. Please forgive me." Nayla felt so stupid. She hoped like hell that she hadn't offended her. She was a wonderful friend.

"Don't worry 'bout it none. I guess I fo'got to say it was from Palmer."

"From Palmer?" Nayla balled it up and prepared to throw it in the garbage.

"Wait, don't do that!" Judea exclaimed. "Palmer ain't married, and he ain't got no girlfrien' either. Palmer's wife died a few years back with the cancer. That woman you saw with them in the park was a coworker. Palmer said she really get 'round the town, if you know what I mean. She want him, but he don't want nobody but you."

Judea had to pause long enough to take a breath. The laughing and now the long speech had no doubt left her feeling winded. She pointed her finger at Nayla. "And quit actin' like you don't want him. You know you want dat fine man jus' as much as he want you."

"The child is his son, right?" Nayla asked nervously. She had always been nervous about family life. She longed for a family but knew that she wouldn't have the amount of time needed to dedicate to a child. "I'm not ready for kids, Judea. Sure, I'm sick of being lonely, but I'm still not ready for any kids."

"Nayla, I love you, but quit making excuses. Get to know Palmer and his son. Let yo'self be happy. Let God be yo' guide." For Judea to be so young, she was so wise.

"Nayla, please think 'bout what I done said. I'm goin' on a coffee break. Can I get you any-thang befo' I go?"

"No, I'm fine. Thanks, Judea. For everything."

Judea left Nayla with a whole lot of thinking to do. It shouldn't have mattered that Palmer had a son. He obviously took very good care of him and made an effort to spend quality time with his son. *Judea is right, I need to pray about the situation. It's been a while since I prayed sincerely about anything. It's high time I started.*

"Dear Lord, if this is the man for me, please let me know. I'm not asking for a huge sign or nothing, just a knowing or feeling in my heart. I also want to thank you for all of your blessings. In Jesus' name, Amen."

Nayla felt so much better after she prayed. She went into her bathroom and took a long, hot, luxurious bubble bath. That was one of the benefits of being the boss. Everything was at her disposal. After her bath, she didn't put clothes back on but remained in a silk robe. She felt so relaxed and rejuvenated. God had set it in Nayla's heart that Palmer was her blessing, and it was time that she accepted it.

"Judea, whenever Palmer comes in with today's last delivery, please be sure and let him know that I want to see him in my office."

Judea answered affirmatively, and Nayla could imagine her with a smile on her face.

"Thank you. You can go ahead and take the rest of the day off when Palmer comes." Nayla smiled to herself as she turned off the intercom.

She tried to work the rest of the day, but naughty thoughts entered her mind as time ticked on.

Finally, Nayla heard Palmer's sexy-ass voice outside. "Are you sure, Judea?"

"I'm sho. She gave me direct orders to tell you to come into her office when you got here."

After Judea bid Palmer a good evening, she got on the elevator. Then, Nayla heard a knock at the door.

"Come in," she said seductively.

As he entered, Nayla opened her arms and beckoned him to come to her. No more playing hard to get. No more doubts. She was about to truly relax, relate, and release!

Palmer looked confused. "Hi, Nayla. I'm surprised that you wanted to even see me, much less hold me."

"Palmer, I'm tired of beating around the bush. I want to hold you, learn to love you, and make love to you." Nayla eased her legs open. She was ready to open her heart and her legs to Palmer, and there was no turning back now.

Palmer finally went to Nayla and kissed her more passionately than she could have ever fantasized. She grabbed him and kissed him back with the same passion. Then, she took his hand and gently pushed him down on the chaise lounge.

Standing over him, she instructed him to take off his shirt. He did. His dark chest was so wide and beautiful. She reached to rub it before pulling at his belt buckle to help remove his pants. His dick, even bigger than Nayla had imagined, jumped out at her. She had to stop and stare for a moment at that beautifully huge manhood standing straight up out of his boxers. His dick looked so good, and she couldn't wait to taste it.

Palmer reached up and opened Nayla's silk robe only to see that there was absolutely nothing on underneath. "Baby, were you really waiting for me?"

"Yes, Palmer. I was waiting to give myself to you. If you want me." Nayla stared at him with pure desire in her eyes.

"*If* I want you?" Palmer looked at her as if she had lost her mind. "Woman, there is nothing I want more."

He took her large breast into his hands and eased his mouth around her pert nipples. The more he sucked, the more Nayla felt like silk. She eased herself down onto his lap and watched him devour her hard flesh as if it was the best meal he had ever tasted.

If you like that, baby, just wait 'til you taste this wet pussy. Then she eased off him and began kissing his shoulders and his chest. *Mmm . . . he tastes so good. He's so clean, and his cologne smells so erotic.*

Nayla ripped his boxers off with one hand and grabbed his long, erect dick with the other. Eagerly, she took his swollen manhood into her mouth, and his moans of pleasure were all the ammunition she needed to suck him feverishly, as if it would be the last time she would ever be able to taste him. She stroked and massaged his nut sack with her pinky finger while making passionate love to him with her mouth, until he shook uncontrollably, releasing all of his love juices. Nayla happily swallowed every drop.

He came up behind her and spread her legs and pussy lips farther apart, penetrating her with his tongue. Nayla knew that their love had just begun.

Judea

Tonight's my big date with Lamar, and he said it's gonna be real special like. Judea got ready for work. *I don't have nothin' special to wear. Lamar done seen all my clothes.* Judea put on what even she hoped would be her last sailor dress. *Nayla will know how to help me!*

Judea was so excited about asking for Nayla's help that she only took the time to kiss Lamar good morning before dashing onto the elevator. "I'll see you when I takes my coffee break, baby." She waved to him as the elevator doors closed.

"Nayla! I needs yo' help!" Judea screamed, thanking God that Nayla had come in early that morning. Lord always knows what you need and when you need it.

"Judea, what in the world is the matter?" The way Judea was screaming, Nayla would have thought that someone was after her. She was waiting for someone to step off the elevator any moment, shooting up the place.

"Tonight's my big special date wit' Lamar, and I's sick of wearing these doggone sailor dresses. I ain't got nothin' special-like to wear. Help me, please."

Nyla looked down at Judea's outfit and smiled. She thanked God that Judea had finally seen the light and come to her for help. She had wanted to approach her but didn't want to offend her.

"Judea, I'll tell you what. Why don't we go to the spa today? I don't have any meetings scheduled, and Braylin's away at a conference. We can shut the office down and spend the entire day at the spa."

"The spa? I always wanted to go to the spa." Judea's bright eyes grew wide, and a huge smile formed across her lips.

"Yes, girl, but first, let's go down to the warehouse and get you some clothes." Nayla knew just what would flatter Judea's face and frame. "And let me call Palmer. Instead of having lunch together, we can have dinner."

Judea couldn't help but smile. She was so glad those two had finally gotten together. She would never tell Nayla that she had come back to retrieve her purse that day Nayla sent her home early. Judea didn't want her boss to know that she had heard the two of them getting busy. It sounded like they were working on making twins.

"What about the packages?" Judea asked. Palmer was there every afternoon with a delivery.

"Thanks, Judea," Nayla said before turning her attention back to the phone. "And Palmer, will you please leave today's delivery with the lobby secretary? Thanks. Can't wait to see you either. Sure. I don't mind if Jason joins us. Okay. Bye for now."

Judea knew it was rude to listen in on other people's conversations, but she couldn't help it. "I's so glad that you finally lettin' yo'self be happy, Nayla."

"So am I." They boarded the elevator. "So am I."

Nayla took Judea down to the ground floor of the building to Ample Delights' clothing warehouse. There were beautiful dresses, pantsuits, and lingerie everywhere.

Judea felt like a kid at a toy store. "I like this one," she said, pointing to a gown with shiny beads on it. It was beautiful.

"Yeah, Judea, but this is a special occasion gown, and you aren't going to a formal event," Nayla explained to a very confused Judea.

"So . . . this too prom-like?"

"Yes." Nayla shook her head. She knew she had her hands full with Judea's makeover.

"What about this one?" Judea held up a cute denim jacket dress.

"That's a cute piece, but not for tonight." Nayla took the dress off its padded hanger and handed it to Judea. "But it will be good to wear to work tomorrow. Go ahead and get it. I designed it so it could also be worn as a jacket too."

Judea hesitated. She couldn't pay for more than one dress.

"It's on the house, Judea."

Nayla was getting a kick out of seeing Judea so excited over the stylish clothes. Nayla spotted the perfect dress for that night's date.

"Judy," Nayla said, using the nickname she sometimes called Judea, "this is the dress for you for tonight." She held up a sleek black satin knee-length, form-fitting dress with a little flare at the hem. When she held up the dress, she knew Judea loved it.

"I ain't never seen nothing like that except on the television set," Judea marveled.

"Well, tonight you can feel like the star you are. This one's a fourteen. Go and try it on."

The dress fit Judea perfectly. Nayla could hardly believe that her beautiful secretary was transforming into a sexy diva. She couldn't wait until they arrived at the spa.

Judea looked in the mirror. She couldn't believe her body had been hiding under those dang blasted sailor dresses. "Maybe I shouldn't. I likes it, but maybe it showing too much." Judea turned from side to side, admiring her own shapely hips.

"Baby, if you got it, flaunt it. And just because you're advertising doesn't mean you're selling." Both women laughed. "You look beautiful, and you deserve nothing less, Judea."

Judea's large eyes expanded like a balloon when she walked into the spa. "Nayla," she whispered as she nudged her boss. "Why is these women half naked?" Almost every woman she saw had a towel wrapped around her body. A towel and nothing else was all that covered their private areas. Judea immediately covered her eyes with her hands.

Nayla laughed. Judea's innocence and inexperience was too cute. She pulled Judea's hand from her eyes. Still, Judea squeezed her eyes tight. "It's okay, Judea. Women come here to relax. That's why they only have on towels. Besides, we've got to got the works. So, we don't need any clothes in the way as we get in the sauna, get massages, facials, and all that good stuff."

"Massages?" Judea's eyes popped open. "I always wanted me a massage and a facial. But what we gon' do 'bout this thick hair of mine? Lord knows I's tired of that hot comb every mornin'."

Judea had beautiful hair. She just didn't know how to style it. Luckily, Nayla had everything under control. She gave Judea a sisterly hug and said, "Relax. I got this."

And she didn't lie. Judea felt so relaxed after sitting in the sauna and getting her massage. Nayla sure knew how to pamper herself. Judea left the spa looking and feeling like a new person. Her long hair was now layered and feathered. Her beautiful skin tingled. She even got her first ever professional manicure and pedicure. She felt like a true diva. No one would look at her and guess that she was from a small town called Altoona.

"You look beautiful." Nayla had gone back to Judea's apartment to help her dress for her date.

"How can I ever repay you, Nayla? I know all this wasn't free." Judea couldn't help smiling at her own reflection. She really did look and feel beautiful.

"You don't owe me anything, Judy. If anything, I owe you even more for bringing Palmer and me together."

They hugged again until the doorbell rang. It was Lamar.

When Judea opened the door, Lamar's jaw fell to the floor. "Girl, I'd drink your bathwater," he said to Judea and followed up the statement with a long whistle. "You sho' look even mo' beautiful than usual."

"Thank you," she blushed. "I owe it all to Nayla."

"No. You owe it all to your mother," Nayla said. Judea gave her a confused look. "I didn't give you that beautiful smile and that junk you got in your trunk."

"Stop it." Judea playfully slapped Nayla on the arm. "And get on out of here so you won't be late for yo' date with Palmer."

"I sho' is glad you got all prettied up. This gon' be a special night," Lamar told Judea as they walked downstairs. "We taking a cab tonight."

Judea didn't know what Lamar had up his sleeve. She felt like Cinderella.

Nayla

Nayla was so nervous; she was getting ready to meet her boo's son for the very first time. Yes, Palmer had gone from being just Palmer to her boo. Nayla had never referred to anyone as her boo before. She had seen pictures of Jason, and he was absolutely adorable. She could only hope that she would have a kid just as cute and smart one day. But first things first. She had to meet the kid Palmer already had first.

As she was stepping out of the shower, her phone rang. Nayla was reluctant to answer the phone, but she did anyway, without checking her caller ID. "Hello?"

"Hey, sexy gal," her ex sang into the phone. It was as if she could see him grinning through the phone. "Can I come see you?"

He has some damn nerve! The last time Nayla wanted some from him he tried to bring his bitch with him. *I know damn well he doesn't think for one hot minute that I'm going to let him crawl up between my thick thighs tonight, or any other damn night.*

"Hell no, Randy! I don't need or want to see you anymore. Good-bye." And with that said, Nayla slammed down the phone. He had lost his chance.

Nayla had to sit down on the window seat and take a deep breath to calm down after she hung up the phone. Randy was the one person who could alter her mood without saying much of anything. As much as he infuriated her, she still found herself smiling. It felt good to let him know that she was doing just fine without him.

After a minute or two, Nayla was back to normal—she just had to simply relax, relate and release. She walked into her closet and tried to decide what to wear. Nayla wanted to look nice for Palmer, but she didn't want to overdress for the occasion. After all, they were taking Jason to UNOs for pizza and then to the aquarium. She needed something simple and conservative, yet slightly sexy. She chose a pair of jeans, a black shirt, and black boots.

Nayla had told Palmer that she would pick them up around seven. Not wanting to be late, she applied her favorite scented lotion all over her body. The pear fragrance tickled her nose and brought a smile to her face. Instead of full makeup, she decided on lip-gloss and just a touch of mascara. After slipping into her outfit, she grabbed her purse and keys and rushed to the car.

"Say hi to Ms. Nayla," Palmer instructed the handsome little boy who stood shyly at his father's side. They lived in a beautiful building. Their apartment was nice, too. Simple—a bachelor's taste, but nice.

"Hi, Ms. Nayla." Jason ran up and gave her a big hug. It surprised her, but it was a nice surprise.

"Hey, gorgeous." Palmer looked at Nayla, and she was ready to melt. She knew that she needed to keep it together, being that they were not alone.

"Hey, yourself." The minute she said it, he started laughing at her. *Did he know what I was thinking?*

They stood there for a long time just staring at each other before his son brought them back to reality. "Daddy, I'm hungry," Jason whined. He tugged at his daddy's shirtsleeve.

"Of course. Let's go."

Nayla took Jason's hand. It was nice holding a little hand. She looked at his handsome father and asked, "Ready?"

"Yeah, baby. Just let me grab my jacket." And out the door they went.

"Ms. Nayla, I can count to fortry," Jason announced. He was so cute.

"You mean *forty,* son," Palmer corrected, trying his best not to laugh.

"Yes, Daddy, that too." Jason was a hoot. Flashing his toothless smile at Nayla, he asked her, "The way I say it sound better, don't it, Ms. Nayla?"

"Well, Jason," she answered, trying not to laugh, "the way your father told you is the right way. Don't you want to grow up to be just as smart as your daddy?"

"I guess. I just don't like saying stuff perfect all the time," Jason rationalized, more to himself than anyone.

They all sat in the booth at the restaurant, Nayla and Palmer discreetly holding hands under the table. "Did you enjoy your pizza, Jason?" Palmer asked his son.

Nayla loved watching the two of them interact. She could picture herself being a part of their world for the rest of her life.

"Yes, Daddy. Can we go see the fish, now?" Jason asked with wide eyes and a huge smile.

"We have to let Ms. Nayla finish her pizza." The two of them had finished their meals, and there she sat, so wrapped up in their interaction that she had barely touched her food.

"Actually, guys, if you're ready, I can take this to go. It's really not a problem," Nayla reassured them, which made Jason a very happy little boy. She was falling in love with him. He was bright, respectful, upfront, and friendly—all the decent qualities that he would need to make it in the real world as an adult.

Jason was telling her all about the different things he liked to do in school before they were rudely interrupted by a familiar face. The same skinny ho who had been pushing up on Palmer the last time Nayla saw him at the park ran right up to him and kissed him on his cheek. The nerve of her. Acting as if Nayla's big ass was not even there. Nayla knew the trick couldn't have missed all of her assets.

"How are you, papí?" she asked Nayla's man.

I have her papí all right, Nayla thought. But before she could even say anything, Palmer let her have it.

"Amanda, first off, I have no interest in you whatsoever. Second of all, this kind of behavior is not appropriate in front of my son. And last, but most definitely not least, this is my girlfriend, and you have no right to disrespect her like that." Palmer had a look of fury on his face that not even that slut could mistake for any other emotion.

Palmer took Jason by the hand and slipped his other arm around Nayla's waist. Amanda was left standing with an ugly scowl on her face as the three of them walked away.

"Palmer, I had a beautiful time tonight." They had just tucked Jason into bed. Watching him drift off to sleep as Palmer read to him made her heart do flips.

"Baby, I loved having the two most important people in my life finally meet." Palmer looked into Nayla's eyes, and she knew that he was serious. Her heart began beating fast. At that moment, she wanted Palmer and Jason to be a part of her life. Her once lonely life was over. In her mind, she heard Etta James singing "At Last."

Judea

Lamar and Judea had just been seated at their table. Lamar had made reservations at Olive Garden. Judea was so impressed. She had never been to a restaurant where the wait staff got all dressed up. Lamar even asked for a bucket of ice. The server looked at him strangely, but she obliged the confident Lamar.

Once the server returned, Lamar reached into his pocket and said, "Here you go. Thank you." He had given her a dollar.

"Umm . . . thank you, sir." The server couldn't help but chuckle to herself as she turned and walked away.

Lamar pulled out a bottle of pink Champale from his pocket. He placed it in the bucket of ice while smiling at his lovely date. He had a night full of surprises for Judea.

"Oh, Lamar!" Judea squealed while batting her eyelids flirtatiously. She felt so special in her beautiful dress. All eyes were on her, and she couldn't thank Nayla enough for the makeover.

"Baby, I done tol' ya how special you is to me." It was as if he could read her thoughts. "And you just so fine tonight, Judea." He winked his approval, causing her to blush.

A little later on in the dinner, he asked her, "You likes teddy bears, don't ya?" When she nodded yes, he handed her a bear with a box in its hand. "Open dat dere box, baby."

She was expecting it to be a pretty locket or something, but never did she think her eyes would see what they saw. It was a beautiful three-quarter carat diamond engagement ring.

"Oh, Lamar. Oh. Oh, my . . . Lamar . . ." It was beautiful. "I ain't never had nothin' this pretty befo'. This what I thank it is, baby?"

"It ain't no cubic zirconia. It's the real thang," Lamar boasted. He was proud of himself. He had saved up enough money to buy her that ring from WalMart. It had been special ordered, too.

"That ain't what I meant, Lamar West." Judea wanted to make sure it was an engagement ring before she overreacted.

He began to laugh. "Yes, baby." He got out of his chair and down on one knee. "Judea Divine Hamilton, I love you with all my heart. Will you marry me?"

"You serious?" Judea asked, obviously in shock.

"Yes, baby. I'm ser'ous. Please say somethin'," Lamar begged, praying that she wouldn't say no.

"I, uh, oh, Lamar . . . Yes!" Judea screamed, with joy in her eyes and in her heart. She started running around to every table, showing off her brand new engagement ring, screaming, "I's gettin' married now!" The people all nodded and smiled at her. They gave her a round of applause as joyful laughter filled the dining room.

Lamar was happy that she was happy, but he wished that she would rejoin him at their table so that he could kiss his fiancée. Finally, he stood up and said, "Baby, c'mere." His new bride-to-be rushed to his side, happy as could be.

"Yes, my love." She felt warm all over. She looked at him with seductive eyes, and he grabbed her and gave her the most passionate kiss ever. After she finally came up for air, Judea beckoned the server. "Check please, ma'am." Then she whispered to her soon-to-be husband, "I've always wanted to say that," and giggled.

Judea could hardly wait to return to Altoona and exchange vows with Lamar. Her family would be tickled pink when they saw her diamond ring.

Nayla

After several months of steady dating, Palmer and Nayla seemed quite happy. Nayla and Jason got along well and had become the best of friends, but Palmer knew that something still wasn't right.

Palmer prayed that God would send Karmen's spirit to him just once more. He had to let his late wife go. He wanted to give his heart fully to Nayla, but he first had to release Karmen. She would always be his first love, but Palmer was ready to build a life with Nayla in Karmen's absence.

Karmen finally came to him while he was napping. "Hello, my love," she whispered in his ear.

Palmer shot upright in bed when he heard her voice. "Karmen?" Tears filled his eyes as he took in her beauty. She stood before him as if she had never left him.

"I felt you, Palmer," Karmen explained as she clutched her hand over her chest. "I could hear you calling out to me. What's wrong?"

Palmer didn't know how to put his thoughts into words. "Karmen, I met someone, and I like her a lot. She's great with Jason. No one will ever take your place, but—"

Before he could finish, she responded, "You need someone who can love you in a way that I no longer can, Palmer. I had God send her to you. Nayla will be good for you and for Jason. You have my blessing. Make her yours and love her completely."

Palmer reached out to hug Karmen, but she blew him a kiss and faded away before he could embrace her. In the midst of his tears, his lips drew upward into a smile. Finally, his heart felt free. He could finally give Nayla his all.

Palmer knew that meant only one thing: he was ready to propose to Nayla and ask her to be his wife. Before he could ask Nayla for her hand in marriage, however, Palmer wanted to talk to his son.

The next morning, Palmer called Jason out of his room. "Come here, son."

"Am I in trouble?" Jason asked. "Daddy, I didn't mean to roll off all the toilet paper. I just wanted some, but the smell-good roll gave me all of it."

Palmer couldn't help but burst out laughing. "Jason, I wish you had told me instead of letting me find clean toilet paper all over the floor. But that's not why I called you. I want to talk to you about something else."

Jason breathed a huge sigh of relief. Of course mimicking what he had seen adults do, he over-exaggerated this act by wiping his brow and then putting his hand to his chest and saying, "Whew, that was so close." Jason was such a ham.

"Jay, how do you feel about Ms. Nayla?" Palmer asked his comedic son.

"I love Ms. Nayla. She's pretty like Mommy, and she's really nice to me," Jason told his father as he jumped up and down for no apparent reason. Palmer was in awe at his son's energy. The boy seemed to never be still.

Palmer tried to explain why he was asking Jason about Nayla as clearly as possible. "Jay, son, the reason I'm asking you this is because . . . I would like to make Ms. Nayla a part of our family."

"You mean she would be my new mommy? Now I'll have a mommy here with me and my angel mommy?" Palmer nodded affirmatively. "Yay! I'm gonna have a mommy here with me!" Jason screamed.

Palmer was relieved to see Jason happy with the thought of Nayla being a part of their family. Now Palmer really prayed that she wouldn't turn him down. He prayed that she would say yes.

"Nayla, does this fit right on me?" an excited Judea asked as she tried on her wedding undergarments. She was putting the garter around her neck.

"Yes, Judy, except that garter goes on your thigh, not around your neck." She tried her best not to laugh out loud. *My friend is so very funny. So innocent.* Nayla loved that about her.

Her wedding was just two months away, and Nayla was so happy for her. Nayla would be lying if she didn't say that she had begun thinking about weddings and marriage herself. She could easily see herself being Palmer's wife and a mother to Jason.

"These some awful big er'rangs."

Nayla had to turn around to see what Judea was talking about. When Nayla saw that she was talking about the charms that were supposed to go on her shoes, she couldn't help but laugh so hard that she almost fell out of her chair.

"Judea, those are shoe adornments." Nayla shook her head. "Don't worry about those. They just came with the set. You don't need them on your shoes."

"Oh, okay, 'cause I was thankin' them some mighty big ear bobs."

"Judea, what the hell are ear bobs?" Nayla asked with a smile.

"You know . . . er'rangs."

Laughing, Nayla said, "Come on and change so we can go to lunch with Braylin."

When they got back from lunch and the three of them were sitting in her office, Palmer knocked on the door. When Judea opened the door, he was dressed in a tuxedo and was holding a bouquet of red roses and a small black box.

"Palmer . . ." Nayla lost her voice to shock and surprise.

"Come here, sweetheart." He asked her to sit down near where he was standing. Nayla kissed him, and he handed her the most beautiful roses she'd ever seen. "Nayla Monique Anderson, you have impacted my life in ways that I will never be able to express with words. I would like to show you my gratitude and my love for the rest of my days." He dropped down to one knee. "Will you be my wife?" He opened the black box, revealing a beautiful three-carat, heart-shaped solitaire diamond set in a platinum band.

For the first time in her life, Nayla was speech-less. Judea and Braylin both started screaming, "Say yes! Say yes!"

It took Nayla a second to compose herself. "Palmer, I can't think of anything I'd rather be doing with my life than spending it with you. Yes, I will marry you."

He slipped the beautiful ring on her finger. When they kissed, she knew without a doubt that they would be together forever.

Braylin kissed and hugged them both, tears streaming down her face. Judea ran up to them, looked at Nayla and said, "We's gon' both be marr'ed ladies now!"

Palmer and Nayla had a whirlwind engage-ment. They hired Atlanta's fiercest wedding planner, her high school friend, Sunshine Royal. She chose gold, ivory, and burgundy as her wedding colors. She loved designing her own gown, as well as the gowns for the bridal party. Their wedding took place October twenty-fifth, on Nayla's mother's birthday. Their day was so special it had to have been touched by God.

What made their beautiful moment in time complete was when Palmer and Nayla made love for the first time as husband and wife.

She thought their lovemaking had been amazing before they got married, but it was nothing compared to the way it was after they exchanged vows.

That night, as she emerged from the bathroom of their honeymoon suite, Palmer looked at her with pure desire in his eyes and said, "You have never looked more beautiful than you look right now. Come to me, my caramel vixen." Palmer took her into his arms and said, "I love the way you look, the way you feel, the way your curl hangs slightly over your eye. You just look and feel so sexy."

Her new husband took her hand and placed it on his thick, long, massive and pulsating manhood. The next move she made surprised Palmer. Nayla pushed Palmer on the edge of the heart-shaped bed and ripped his black silk boxers, unleashing his manhood. She dropped to her knees and took her husband's full length into her warm and eager mouth. Palmer's carnal moan of pleasure only excited her to go further. She stroked and licked him until pre-cum oozed from his shaft.

She had been using a tiny clitoral stimulator while sucking on him, and Nayla was already wet and eager for him to penetrate her throbbing pussy. She discreetly removed the stimulator and mounted Palmer with her thick and luscious thighs. She placed his strong hands on her ample and curvy hips, leaned forward, and kissed him with the wonderful taste of him on her lips. Nayla opened her legs wider and invited his alluring dick into her awaiting pussy. She ground her hips in rotation with his, and they made their connection as man and wife.

Finally, Nayla understood that a woman can have it all: a successful company and love. And it surely didn't hurt to learn that her husband, the delivery guy, was born into wealth. But above all, Nayla had a family to come home to.

Braylin

One year later. . . .

Braylin was in pain as she tried to push their little girl into the world. "David, I love you, but we can't ever do it again."

He grinned at his fiancée and said, "We can't do *what* ever again?"

"You know what we can't do—agh—do again!"

David was laughing at Braylin. He couldn't imagine loving anyone as much as he loved her, and he couldn't wait to hold their baby girl in his arms.

"Braylin, I love you, girl."

"I love you too." She pushed again with as much energy as she could muster through the pain.

She still couldn't believe how their love story all began, but she was grateful for it all, even the pain and heartache that she had gone through with Donovan. Once upon a time, she would have sworn that he was the one, but David was her chocolate Prince Charming.

She thought back to the night that David proposed to her, the night she believed that they had conceived their daughter. That night, as she emerged from the bathroom, David had looked at her with pure desire in his eyes and said, "Braye, I love everything about you. You ooze sexiness to me. You are the most beautiful woman I have ever known."

Braylin was brought out of her reverie as she felt her daughter thrust forward.

"Braylin, push!" the nurse yelled.

"That's it Braye, baby. One more push and she'll be here." David was stroking her hair with one hand and gripping the bedrail with the other.

"Aaargh!" With the last push, their little one came into the world, making her presence known and letting her voice be heard.

"Baby, she has a head full of hair and she looks just like you." David smiled through tears.

"Really?" Braylin beamed with pride before falling back on her pillow in total exhaustion.

"Sweetheart, what should we name her?" David looked at his bride-to-be with love.

"After you, Nathanial David Jones."

"How, babe?"

"Easy. Natalia Daveeda Jones."

"Natalia Daveeda Jones. I love it."

Nayla

"Baby, I got a letter from Judea today." She smiled at Palmer as he sipped his morning coffee. He looked so sexy even this early in the morning.

"Oh, cool, babe. What does it say?" The three couples were best friends.

> Dear Nayla and Palmer,
> How y'all doin'? I hope y'all and my li'l Jay are all right. I miss y'all! Y'all gon' have to come visit soon. I bet Jay growin' like a bunch of weeds. Please send us a picture of him.
> Guess what? Me and Lamar havin' a baby! I'm three months with chile, and Lamar done already named the baby John-John. Mama and Daddy are thrilled. Daddy has already gotten to work building the baby a crib and all.
> We wanted to ask y'all to please be the baby's godparents.

I love y'all and I miss y'all. Call me soon.
With Love,
Judea—or, as you says, Judy

"It was so nice hearing from her, baby. You know I would love for us to be the godparents to little John-John. I just hope that they will be the godparents to our little one."

Wow, it must really be in the water. Braylin just had a baby, and now Judea's pregnant too. Nayla smiled to herself.

With a confused look on his face, Palmer said, "Baby, what are you talking about? Judea and Lamar are already Jason's godparents."

"I know, Palmer." Nayla looked at him and rubbed her belly, hoping he would catch on.

Palmer suddenly got a wide-eyed look on his face, as if he had finally caught on to what his wife was trying to say. "Are you saying what I think you're saying? We're having a baby?"

"Well, I would rather it be you, but I guess I'll do you the honors." Nayla couldn't stop smiling and laughing as Palmer wrapped his arms around her. "Yes, baby, I'm having your baby." She looked at her husband and fell in love all over again. Nayla loved him so much, and now, she was blessed with the ability to give him the ultimate gift of love, a baby.

They laughed and cried tears of joy, knowing that their new baby would be just as special and just as loved as their precious Jason.

Epilogue

One year later. . . .

"Palmer, baby, I can't believe I'm actually excited to be going to Judea's family reunion. I just hate that Braylin and David can't make it."

"Well, baby, she's on bedrest with baby number two. Besides, I think that maybe you're just excited about seeing our friends and seeing our godson, just as much as you know Judea and Lamar are pumped up to see our little baby girl."

"True, I am. I can't even front," Nayla said, grinning from ear to ear.

"Mommy! Daddy!" Jason was standing outside their bedroom screaming at the top of his lungs. "Can I come get in bed with y'all?"

"Come on, son," Palmer replied.

Nayla wouldn't have it any other way. Her life was complete. She had the best husband on the planet and two beautiful children who she absolutely adored.

***

"Judy!" Nayla screamed as she laid eyes on her best friend.

"Nay!" Judea screeched back at her as they ran into an embrace. "I's so happy to see you!"

"Girl, you know I'm happy as hell to see you." Nayla grinned. "Look at you, Ms. Divine Diva."

"Lamar, bring the baby here!" Judea screamed, not even realizing that her husband was right behind her.

"Palmer, baby, come here. Bring the kids with you." Taking the baby from Palmer's arms, Nayla proudly announced, "Judea, Lamar, this is your goddaughter, Judea Monique Jackson."

"She is absolutely precious," Judea cooed as she took the baby girl from Nayla's arms. "And this y'all's godson, Jonathan Lamar Palmer West."

"Well, hello, handsome!" Nayla immediately fell in love with her godson, as Judea did with her goddaughter.

"Daddy, Uncle Lamar, what are Mommy and Auntie Judea so happy about?" Jason had a puzzled look on his face. "Babies don't do anything but eat, sleep, and cry."

Roaring with laughter, they scooped Jason up and filed into the house.